THE LAST MISSION

Robert Tecklenburg

International Standard Book Number 13: 978-1-60452-182-5
International Standard Book Number 10: 1-60452-182-1
Library of Congress Control Number: 2022930529

BluewaterPress LLC
2922 Bella Flore Ter
New Smyrna Beach FL 32168

This book may be purchased online at -
https://www.bluewaterpress.com

FOR LARRY AND MIKE
SEMPER FI

Soldiers may accept the need to be the first
To die in a war, but there is often
An unseemly scramble to avoid becoming the last.
--Max Hastings from RETRIBUTION

Prologue

Sergeant Joe Catledge down shifted the black Peugeot 601 sedan as smoothly as Barney Oldfield and aimed it onto a straight, open stretch of street. He hoped to reach the safety of the American position in Hotel Intercontinental at the heart of the Saigon's old city area. Still, he could not outrun bullets. The ping of lead striking the side and rear panels echoed through the interior of the old car.

"Faster, Sergeant, faster," Lieutenant Colonel Rolly Dixon urged from the back seat.

"Yes, sir," Joe responded automatically, shifting again. He pushed his foot to the floor. The transmission screamed, and the entire vehicle vibrated from the increased strain. "That's as fast as she'll go." The rear tires spun out on the wet pavement, causing the Peugeot to fishtail. But Joe had her under control, quickly adjusting the steering to compensate. "I got it," he said, but Colonel Dixon seemed too preoccupied to notice.

Dixon, commander of the American Embankment Team in Saigon, had just returned from business to the north and seemed anxious to reach headquarters. Up to their ears in Annamese gunfire, Joe was anxious too.

A bullet smashed through the back window, passed between them, and struck the windshield, lodging in the front glass. The back window shattered, raining glass over Dixon. Cracks ran in all directions in the windshield from the point of impact. Visibility instantly became problematic as Joe attempted to peer through a giant spider web.

Bullets pummeled both sides of the street, striking off the sides of buildings. Up ahead, a mortar explosion threw pieces of brick and steel in all directions. Looking out the side window, Joe saw two Gurkhas move across a side street, both firing light machine guns as they moved forward. As the car raced by, he heard several more explosions. *Grenades*, he decided.

"We're caught in something ... something real bad, sergeant. But they can't be shooting at us," Dixon said evenly, trying to sound convincing. "The United States negotiated neutrality here. Keep moving."

"Yes, sir, don't have to worry about that," Joe replied, glancing quickly in the rearview mirror to see his commanding officer tightly clutching the pouch. *What does he have in that diplomatic pouch that's so valuable?*

Two more bullets hit the left rear panel.

"You okay, Colonel?" Joe asked, glancing in the rearview mirror again.

"Can't the bastards read? 'US Army' is painted all over the damn car!" Lieutenant Colonel Dixon slid further down in the seat. He held the diplomatic pouch with his left hand while holding an Army .45 pistol with his right, ready to fire. "Damn Brits," he growled, beads of perspiration dotting his forehead. He peered out the side window, looking for a target. "They insisted we paint on something says were Americans to let everyone know we're neutrals here. Now I wonder if that was such a good idea."

Thick dark smoke spilled from hastily boarded windows, blackening the wood. The heavy smoke funneled downward along the narrow street, mixing with mist from an earlier cloudburst. The low-hanging smog bank distorted visibility and cast everything and everyone in gray shadowy shapes. Joe stared straight ahead, trying desperately to ignore the rapidly spreading inferno beginning to engulf them. Tongues of yellow flame shot skyward from gaping holes in the roof tiles, licking and dancing along the tops of the brick buildings.

"Brits, Frogs, Yanks – I guess we're all the same to the Annamese, sir," Joe said. His stomach ached from fear.

"Yeah, but that's not what Thach promised me." His commander rose up in the seat and looked quickly behind them.

Joe saw the street was empty. "They're firin' from the Arroyo La Valanche," he said, as deep explosions rumbled off to the left. "Sounds to me like the main battle's goin' on over there."

In the distance, toward the east, explosions mixed with small arms fire. The smell of cordite and burning wood drifted in through the side windows and hung in the hot stale air inside the sedan as Joe urged it forward. "Look! There! Is that another Gurkha?" Joe asked, keeping both hands tight on the steering wheel. They watched a small man dressed in a British uniform dart across a street. He carried an Enfield strapped across his back with a fixed bayonet cutting the air.

"Looks like they're fighting the Annamese for control of the La Valanche Bridge," Dixon said.

Joe concentrated on the street directly ahead, still gripping the wheel tightly. "We gotta be getting close to the Saigon River," he said, trying to sound hopeful.

"How far now?"

"'Bout a half mile yet, Colonel," Joe replied, guessing. "Looks like the whole damn city is on fire." Smoke rose from tops of buildings on both sides of the street.

"Maybe we can make it to the Jap positions along the river," Dixon urged.

"Maybe, but that's another mile or so, ain't it?"

"Yeah, but it's straight down this street. No turning or crossing open ground."

Two more bullets penetrated the rear side window, lodging harmlessly in the opposite door panel. "Sounded like 25 caliber, sir," Joe said. Perspiration soaked his fatigue jacket. He loosened his sweaty right hand from the steering wheel and quickly wiped it on his trousers.

"Where in hell they get a Jap rifle? Probably helping them, eh?" The remaining glass shards in the back window had fallen, leaving it completely open. "I'll have to have a talk with Colonel Imano again."

"Yes, sir," Joe replied. His complete attention at that moment was on another bridge approaching rapidly. "Hold on, sir. We gotta make it over." He downshifted into first to squeeze more torque from the 2100 cc six-cylinder engine, then floored the gas pedal. The front tires shot straight into the air at a near forty-five-degree angle as the car flew up and over the top of the short, high bridge built mostly for pedestrian traffic. It crashed back down on the brick with an angry thud. Both of them hit the roof. "You okay, sir?"

"Yeah, yeah. Keep going."

Joe floored it again, and the old sedan bounced along the narrow street just as a volley of bullets struck the concrete embankment on the far side.

Finally, there it was. Not more than a hundred yards to the right of them across the smoke-darkened field, Joe could make out the Hotel Intercontinental, headquarters for the American Embankment Team. It was nestled in the old French quarter next to the opera house at the head of *Rue de la Liberté*. The old sedan raced down the brick street.

"What's that?" Dixon yelled, pointing to a collection of large pieces of wood, twisted metal auto frames, and barrels blocking the street as they made a final turn for the hotel. Stacks of rubber tires placed in front burned furiously, belching black smoke and partially concealing the small figures scurrying around the barricade. Straining to see through the smoggy twilight, Joe focused on the Vietnamese fighters that appeared like tiny apparitions on top of the metal auto skeletons. The entire scene took on an apocalyptic air.

Joe caught Dixon looking down again at the leather pouch. It was the way Dixon looked at it that bothered him. *Do the contents of the pouch have something to do with the Vietnamese? Is it why they openly violated our neutrality?*

"It's an ambush!" Dixon shouted, trying to peer through the inferno. "I see Annamese on top! With rifles!"

Joe saw that Colonel Dixon was now sitting upright, stiff as an arrow, his eyes large from fear and adrenaline. Joe spied two figures quickly moving a machine gun in place atop a fire-darkened bus, pointing it down the street toward their oncoming car, aiming directly at them.

"Stop!" Dixon ordered.

Joe simultaneously hit the brake pedal and punched the clutch, throwing the shift forward almost into the dash and then downward to slow the vehicle. The old gears screamed in anger, but the sedan slid to a sudden stop about thirty meters from the barricade. He stared out the cracked windshield at a man standing atop the debris waving a flag over his head. When a slight breeze unfurled it, he saw a yellow star against a deep red background.

"Catledge, get out and tell 'em who we are, damn it," Dixon ordered.

Joe gave his commanding officer a hard look but obeyed. He pulled on the emergency brake, threw open the door, and jumped out, waving his hands above his head. "American! American!" he yelled. "No shoot!"

The machine gun immediately opened fire. A shower of bullets whizzed overhead. "American!" Joe yelled one more time, then turned and dived for cover behind the sedan.

The little figures responded immediately with another burst from the gun. The bullets riddled the front of the car, striking the radiator and dissolving the windshield into a heap of glass shards. Joe looked back, couldn't see Dixon, and hoped he was hugging the floor. Following the burst, the car's back door creaked open, and Dixon slid out onto the brick street, crawling until he came up beside Joe.

"You okay, Colonel?" Joe rasped.

"Yeah. Get ready to run for that field."

Joe looked over to his left, then at the barricade. "I'll cover you," he yelled. "Go!" He opened fire with his automatic.

Dixon fired off three quick rounds, then ran. Gunfire exploded from the entire width of the barricade. Bullets struck him across the back and side, throwing him forward onto the damp street just feet from the field. Joe, seeing the colonel fall, quickly moved to the side of the sedan behind the opened door. Steam rising from the punctured radiator partially concealed his movements. In a crawl-run low to the ground, he headed straight for his commanding officer. "Colonel? Colonel!" he demanded, hitting the brick flat on his stomach behind the prone figure. Bullets tore at the street around him, sending up pieces of brick and dust. The air above his head filled with lead pellets. Seeing a growing pool of red around Dixon's motionless body and his blood-stained uniform, Joe knew immediately that he was dead, yet he still gripped the pouch tightly in his left hand.

Joe fired his .45, throwing the remainder of the magazine rounds into the black smoke, ejected the emptied magazine, and reached into his belt for another. He scanned the street in front and the sidewalk alongside, firing rapidly at anything that moved.

I gotta get outta here, he thought, now acting on adrenaline alone. The field, with its short, interlacing hedgerows, stood between him and the hotel. He knew he had no choice but to take that route.

Now! But wait. He remembered the leather diplomatic pouch still in Dixon's hand and reached across the growing pool of blood to wrest the pouch from the dead man's fingers. Quickly he shoved it inside his shirt.

Crack! Crack! Crack! He fired three rounds from the his pistol, then released the empty magazine. He slid in a fully loaded one, his last. Then he was gone. His heart pounding, he raced to a hedgerow, running the full length of the field. Small arms fire pursued him. He heard the distinct sound of bullets whizzing above his head and dived for cover behind a hedge.

Two Annamese left their barricade to chase him across the field. At short intervals, they stopped to fire their bolt-action rifles. They were clearly determined to kill him. Pieces of leaves fell around him, and small branches snapped directly above his head as bullets passed close by.

Poking his head above the hedge, Joe fired off three quick rounds at the two figures now approaching him at a dead run. He saw one go down. The other disappeared behind a hedgerow running parallel to his. That was his chance. He jumped up and ran toward the hotel.

Chapter 1

Captain Charles Stanek strolled across Memorial Bridge. He stopped for a minute to watch the Potomac slowly flow under him. Since he had time to kill before his meeting with his former commanding officer, General William Donovan, and because it was such a balmy fall day in Washington, he decided to walk. He removed his garrison cover and stared into the placid water. A light southerly wind blowing gently up the Potomac messed with his neatly combed, sandy brown hair. It felt good.

Charlie considered the upcoming meeting with the general. *Maybe he just wants to say his goodbyes,* he thought. But, deep down, he knew better. Donovan was not the type for sentimentality.

Since the end of the war in Europe, Charlie had been working in the Pentagon, shuffling papers and waiting for his discharge. He was bored. *But work in the Pentagon still beats sleeping on the ground in the damp forests of Eastern Europe, trying to stay alive,* he constantly told himself. He often thought of Jan, Lieutenant Jan Novotny, who had been killed by the Germans. Jan had served with Charlie in Eastern Europe, and they had grown close. *I wonder what he would have said about my job as a paper-pusher,* Charlie thought, watching a small sailboat tack against the soft breeze. He remembered that Jan had loved the army.

Charlie had been a perfect choice for the Operational Groups that would train, supply, and lead guerrilla forces in occupied Eastern Europe. With his background in Eastern European languages and history, Charlie seemed like a natural for the OSS and was given a special assignment. Donovan had Charlie accompany him when he traveled to Moscow in December of 1943, following the Tehran Conference. Their objective was to get the Russians' assistance in setting up a clandestine operation in occupied Eastern Europe to rescue downed American and British pilots.

The general persuaded the Russians that the pilots could be smuggled through German lines into liberated Russian territory. From there, they could be quickly returned to Italy. It took several weeks of hard negotiations, but the Russians, always pathologically suspicious of foreigners, reluctantly consented.

Charlie and Jan dropped into the mountains a week later. Charlie was constantly reminded of those long months in Eastern Europe where he remained until he had been extracted on January 15, 1945, only days before Warsaw fell to the Russians under Marshal Zhukov's command. His work was at an end and General Donovan prudently got him out, rather than have him become a 'guest' of the Red Army. Charlie agreed wholeheartedly, believing with good reason that his life was seriously at risk if their secret police got hold of him.

Twenty minutes later Charlie was standing in front of the desk of General William Donovan. He had aged, but Charlie saw that he still had that air of proud defiance. The star on his uniform sparkled.

The last time they were together, it was a wintry day in February. Charlie had just returned from a two-week furlough. The general had informed him that he would be detailed to the Pentagon until his discharge came through.

Donovan greeted him with a steaming cup of coffee in a china mug. "Take it, Captain," he said. "You might need it."

Charlie was caught off-guard by the comment but did as he was ordered. He was a damn good soldier, but now wanted nothing more than civilian life.

"Good to see you," the general said, clasping his hand. "Well, the world has certainly changed since last we talked. How are things with you?"

"Fine, sir."

"Sit down. Sit down," the general said, and they both sat conversationally in front of the desk. "How do you like your assignment at the new Pentagon building, with all that brass? That's the military's future over there."

"Can't complain, sir," Charlie replied, massaging a small crescent scar above his right eye with his forefinger, a nervous habit. The scar was the result of a fistfight he'd had as a teenager. The other boy, a full head taller, had fared far worse and learned the hard way that Charles Stanek never gave up. Head slightly cocked, Charlie looked silently at the general.

"You may like the backslapping and brown-nosing so much that you'll be reenlisting. You thinking about that, Captain?"

"I'm getting out. Going back to Wisconsin. I figure the discharge will be coming through any day now."

"I see," the general said with a frown. He leaned forward, intent. "Stanek, your country still needs you. You're one of the best field agents we have, and with all the drawdown, the only one I can completely trust with this mission."

Another damn mission, he thought, his stomach already twisting into a knot. The war was over. He didn't care anymore.

"Thanks, but no thanks." He set the coffee cup aside on the general's desk and stood up, anxious to leave.

The general glared up at him. "Stanek, you understand what I'm saying?"

"I've had it, General. One year on the run from the Germans and the NKVD, blowing up bridges, hiding in caves, all the killing... That's enough excitement for a lifetime. I'm through."

"What would you do back in Wisconsin? Be a farmer? Milk cows?"

"I'm tired of war and frankly, sir, I'm sick of the Army," Charlie replied. "Three years will be enough for me. I might find someplace quiet and peaceful where people leave each other alone, so I can think and figure things out."

"We all want that, Captain, but it's just a dream we hold onto. It helps us stay sane," General Donovan replied. "And we have work to do."

Charlie massaged his eyes, studying, considering.

"You can't ever go back to recapture some lost innocence, and it's foolish to ever think you can, Captain," Donovan said softly. "Remember that."

"It's time to move on then," Charlie grumbled.

"Hell, you're damn good at soldiering," the general said, sounding sincere. "You're a survivor. One of the best."

"That won't mean much as a civilian."

"Sit down. Hear me out, Captain. That's all I ask."

"Yes, sir," Charlie mumbled. Reluctantly he took a seat facing the general again.

"We have a problem. We lost our most experienced Asia hand in September. Did you know Lieutenant Colonel Roland Dixon?"

"No, sir. Never heard of him," Charlie said. His tall, lanky frame slid down slightly in the hard wooden chair as his resolve weakened. *I'm not going to get out of this without a fight.*

"He was head of the general's intelligence section for much of the war. Or rather, he briefed them on Jap movements, troop concentrations. MacArthur trusted him ... hell, even stole him away from OSS to run his operation. The son of a bitch. No mutual admiration there, Captain, between Mac and me."

"What happened to Dixon?"

"Killed in an ambush in Saigon about four days ago. It was done by local Annamese insurgents. Mac insisted that Dixon be appointed to head up the embankment team there, so I relented. I didn't have much choice. But anyway, his mission was to work with the Brits to establish some type of post-war settlement. You know the routine. Disarm the Japs and set up an arrangement for a new government." General Donovan scowled. "Dixon getting killed should not have happened. We're neutral there. Even had an agreement with the Vietnamese."

"I would have thought there were better assignments than heading up the embankment team in a backwater like Saigon, especially for someone with good credentials."

"He insisted on going. Pressured Mac to give him the job. Said he wanted to work with the Brits. With General Gracey's staff, he said."

"Hmm," was all Charlie said. After a moment, he added, "So, somehow he got caught up in the fighting. Is that it?"

"We suspect he was murdered."

"Murdered? You don't think he was just in the wrong place at the wrong time?"

"Maybe, maybe not," the general said. He got up and paced in front of his desk. "We had an agreement with Pham Ngoc Thach, the Viet Minh representative in southern Vietnam. We negotiated it when we arrived. American neutrality would be respected by all the Vietnamese groups. And it had been respected, up till then. Curious."

"What's curious?"

"The timing of the ambush," Donovan said slowly, "and something else."

"What's the something else?"

"Where did I put it?" He searched through the files on his desk. "Here it is. I want to read this to you, Captain. It's Dixon's last message sent through Kandy, Supreme Allied Command for Southeast Asia. It's an appeal from the Viet Minh leader, Ho Chi Minh, addressed to President Truman." He read the communiqué aloud:

Executive Committee of Southern Vietnam's Republic brought to power by huge manifestation of Annamese people occurred on August 25, 1945, Saigon, and all provinces of Cochin-China. Annamese people expressed unanimous will to live free and independent under democratic policy. Hoping sincerely giant American Republic having fought to defend liberty of the world will support Indo-China in independence movement. Annamese people firmly rely on sympathy on the part of American proponents of justice and liberty. Peaceful salutations, Ho Chi Minh.

General Donovan set the paper aside and looked at Charlie. "This was given to Dixon two days before he was killed. The Vietnamese insisted that it be delivered directly to the President."

Charlie fidgeted, growing impatient to get out of Donovan's office.

"That sounds pretty damn friendly, doesn't it, Captain?"

"Yes, sir, it sure does."

"We don't know why the insurgents would want to kill Dixon. It just doesn't make any sense."

"People die unnecessarily in war, General. We all know that."

"I always suspect the communists," General Donovan continued. "We learned in Europe, didn't we? When there's backstabbing going on, they're usually behind it."

"Usually," Charlie replied, looking at Donovan indifferently.

"Yet, if the communists killed Dixon, what's their motive? From that letter, it seems clear they're seeking our support for their cause."

"Seems like it," Charlie said. "Why are you telling me all this?"

"I want to count on you, Captain. You're the man for the job," the general said cheerfully, looking into Charlie's eyes.

"I haven't agreed to anything," Charlie replied, taken aback. "I don't even know what you've got going out there, General. And I don't want to know."

"Stanek, I need you," he replied softly. "The United States has a situation over there that must be handled ... handled by someone with your background and experience."

"I speak Russian and Czech. My knowledge is of European history," he replied, frustrated. "I don't know anything about the region. And General, how many times must I tell you? I'm about to become a civilian again."

"You know more than you think," Donovan said, pressing on. "Let me give you a rundown on the players. We have the Chinese, who still have not withdrawn from the north, then the Jap Army that has yet to be disarmed, and the *Indochine*se, dominated by the communists, and of course the French, who want their empire back. In the middle of all this are us and the Brits. Oh yes, one additional player. Stalin has recently sent a Russian delegation to Hanoi to meet with the Control Commission. Their reasons are unknown to us. And you probably know as much about those boys as anybody."

"Find yourself another man," Charlie said flatly.

At first, General Donovan said nothing, just looked hard at Charlie. "You still haven't told me. What happened to you, Captain? For four days you just disappeared. OSS in Bari sent radio messages to your team. Lieutenant Black's team searched for you, even with the Germans closing in."

"You knew where I was."

"Yes, Captain, I'm afraid I do. But your job was to get all four of those teams out of Slovakia, and you wasted valuable time. Those four days were critical to their escape."

Charlie said nothing, but his face flushed.

The general's voice hardened. "Houseboat and Day missions could have succeeded. Those men didn't have to die."

"General, there was nothing I could do for them," Charlie said, unwilling to give an inch. "You should never have left thirty men on the ground there, when it was already too late. The Germans had defeated Svoboda. By then, the Czechs and Slovaks were running for their lives." He shifted in his chair. "At Tri Duby, I got the POWs, the pilots, hell, even those New Zealanders out."

"You could have – should have – found a way, before the Germans got to them. They were your top priority."

"Black took it upon himself to hire a civilian guide, a Slovak who wasn't cleared by the partisans. He turned out to be a collaborator who betrayed those two teams to a German security patrol. That's why those men were lost."

"No, Captain, you lost it."

"General, I was grieving but I never lost my focus," he answered with as much composure as he could muster. "They killed her. The Nazis took her away and probably murdered her. Still, I did all I could to get those teams to Russian lines."

"You were distracted from your mission. You delayed them so that you could rescue the woman."

"One week earlier, and I could have found her. I know it."

"She was a dedicated patriot who knew her duty," the general said. "She would have found a way to carry on if it had been you who was killed." He sighed and scratched a bald spot. "You committed the worst sin in my book."

"Which was?" Charlie was steaming, struggling to hold his anger in check. He couldn't fathom why Donovan was pursuing this.

"You fell in love, and then jeopardized our entire operation because of it."

Charlie finally lost control. He came straight up out of the chair. The general reacted quickly and stood up, too. Charlie caught himself glaring at him eye to eye. "You're smiling. Why the hell are you smiling?"

"Believe it or not, I understand your anger, Captain. None of us are born to be soldiers, to risk death, and to kill other men. We have to learn it, and I think you've learned well. That's why you're so damn good. Sit down, sit down. I'm sorry that I offended you," he said in a soft voice. "No hard feelings."

Charlie took a deep breath and sat down again, but he was still seething underneath.

"All I meant was that in war there's no room for love when you have a duty to perform, when others' lives depend on it. That's why you failed, Captain." Donovan eyed him sternly, then added in a lighter tone, "But you have a chance here to make things right, to reset the scales."

Charlie scowled. Donovan was hitting him with everything in his arsenal, trying to get him to accept this mission. He sighed and sat back in his chair. "You want me to stay in the Army. Is that it?"

"For this mission. After..." The general shrugged. "The war is over. It's a different game out there."

"Sir?"

"Politics, Captain. There's international politics involved in this assignment, and I need someone I can trust completely."

"The assignment?"

"An easy one for you. Find out what happened to Lieutenant Colonel Dixon. Why he was killed, and by whom. Simple enough?"

"That sounds too simple."

"I need you. The President of the United States needs you," the general said.

"Sir, the OSS is folding. What are you talking about?"

"You're right. Our agency is closing down, but there is still one last mission to complete."

Charlie shook his head. "You close down, and I'm on my own."

"Never, Captain," the general reassured. "This is high priority. I will brief the President daily on its progress."

Charlie stared in surprise.

"Yes, the President has contracted with me to run this op. The bastard hates me, but even a Missourian can see that you and I are the best men for the job. You come highly recommended, and General Marshall signed off on you. The President approved. How does that make you feel, eh?"

"I don't like the sound of any of it," Charlie said, again rubbing the scar above his eye.

"It has high visibility, but the mission is not complicated at all."

"The war is over, and I've done my duty," Charlie said slowly, but there was no denying Donovan had convinced him. Silence reigned in the room. Shadows grew longer, inching across the oak floor. Finally Charlie said, "You got me where you want me, General. Damn it, I guess I have to go."

"Good. Our whole foreign policy structure between India and China hinges on establishing stable relations with the peoples in that part of the world. We have to find out what happened to Lieutenant Colonel Dixon and ensure that our agreements with the *Indochine*se peoples will hold up during all the turmoil I expect over the next few years there. Our presence is currently limited to OSS teams on the ground in Saigon, and in a place I haven't even heard of – Laos."

Charlie listened quietly.

"You will travel as an army officer on a diplomatic mission for the President of the United States. That should impress the locals," he said with a quick smile. "Don't hide the fact that you're an officer in the US Army – just don't broadcast it. Your diplomatic status is very important to this mission. You will tell only your team members that you hold the rank of major."

"Major?"

"Yes, I've promoted you, effective immediately. Congratulations."

"Thank you," Charlie said. But he didn't feel grateful.

"Oh, and one more thing." General Donovan stood and walked over to his desk, reaching over to grab a large manila envelope. He opened the envelope and poured its contents onto the desk.

Charlie watched as large sparkling crystals rolled across the dark mahogany. "Some big rocks ya got there, sir," he said with a whistle.

"Diamonds, Captain ... uh, sorry, Major. Uncut diamonds. Not of exceptional quality, but they still have a value of around seventy-five thousand."

"What do they have to do with this mission?"

"Dixon was carrying them when he was killed. He was coming back from an area identified as the Central Highlands."

"You think the diamonds might have something to do with his death?"

"That's possible. I need you to find out."

"Where'd they come from? Anyone know?"

"We suspect they were mined in Indochina."

"They have diamonds in that part of the world?"

"I don't know, but they tell me the French have been mining coal there for years. One real question is: Who else knew about the diamonds?"

"I see your point, sir. They could add to the intrigue, what with all those armies still there trying to stake out a claim."

"Remember, Major, don't get involved in the political mess there. And don't let anyone distract you from your mission," the general said, leaning against the desk.

"Not a problem, sir."

"And something else. Effective immediately, we'll be absorbed somewhere into the War Department," Donovan said, almost as an aside. "But that will not affect your mission. I've taken all precautions to ensure that you're covered. You'll be traveling on a diplomatic passport with a letter of introduction from the President. You are Major Charles Stanek, special envoy of President Truman to the Allied Control Commission in Indochina. And I'll be your only contact for this mission. Here are your orders." Donovan handed him a manila envelope. "This will be my final command operation, and I'm counting on you to make it a success."

"Yes, sir." Charlie removed the documents from the envelope and quickly reviewed them. "My name is already typed on the orders."

The general didn't respond, but escorted Charlie to the door. "I need you in Saigon before the middle of October. There'll be a plane waiting at Andrews tomorrow at 0800. Goodbye and good luck, Major."

Chapter 2

Colonel Andre Pavlov cast a short muscular reflection in the narrow and only window in his fourth-floor office in the Lubyanka Square complex. He frowned, reminding himself that Lubyanka was now called Dzerzhinsky, in honor of 'Blood Felix,' who first headed Cheka.

Now too, Cheka, the Soviet State Security forces, have been renamed as the State Political Administration – GPU. He smiled. *The names may change, but everything remains much the same. The secret police still go about their business as we chose.*

The day was gray and sunless. He noticed a chill in the early morning air. "Fall already," he mumbled, lighting a cigarette. It had been a short summer and winter was coming. He tried to remember the last winter the guns were silent in Moscow and the rest of the country. *More than four years ago*, he guessed. He blew out a stream of smoke against the window and admired the Kremlin on the far side of Red Square, marveling at how the majestic old building had sustained only limited damage from German bombing and artillery.

Inhaling again, he stared idly at the cigarette he held between his right thumb and forefinger. Years of heavy smoking had turned the skin yellow from tobacco stains, but he refused to quit. Even the pain in his chest wouldn't deter him from this one simple pleasure. And these were American cigarettes, a rare luxury in war-ravaged Mother Russia. "Cam-els," he said slowly, reading from the pack. Effortlessly, the smoke tumbled from his lips into the cool, damp room.

Again he drew deeply from his cigarette, thinking back over his years in service of the motherland in the NKVD. Since the old days, those years following the Revolution, when espionage was handled by Cheka, he had performed his duty, much of it unspeakable in mixed company. In '43, he was transferred to the Smersh Detachment at Premier Stalin's personal request, to catch collaborators and traitors to the motherland in German-occupied territories. He frowned again. *Now I search for spies within our own ranks.*

He considered his upcoming meeting with Major Gregor Zerenowsky, who had said it was of immediate importance, a matter of national security. Andre was suspicious. Zerenowsky was one of Beria's men, mostly concerned with internal affairs – not state security, which was his job. Turf was paramount to Andre Palov.

Zerenowsky was also Ukrainian. Andre smiled. *As far as I'm concerned, all Ukrainians are suspect.* The Germans had made his job much easier. If Ukrainians who had survived the occupation were not starving, they were collaborators, traitors to the motherland. He had already sent thousands to labor camps in Siberia, and he fully intended to ship out thousands more. But in July, he was given a new assignment – locate and destroy the notorious espionage ring headed by the elusive spy known as Rasputin.

He heard a knock at his door and returned to sit at his desk. "Come in, Major. I've been expecting you."

Major Zerenowsky entered. A large man and somewhat younger than Andre at thirty-five, he was not fat, but had grown flabby from desk duty in Moscow. Andre had checked Zerenowsky's background and knew of his great knowledge of the terrain of South Russia and the Ukraine, especially near Stalingrad. He also knew Stalin had considered him an invaluable asset during the war and that he had been elevated to major by Comrade Khrushchev after the surrender of the Germans at Stalingrad in February of 1943. Zerenowsky was now assigned to the staff of Lavrenty Beria, chief of The Peoples Commissariat for Internal Affairs – NKVD. Andre considered Beria a dangerous adversary.

With just a few steps, Major Zerenowsky stood at the desk and saluted. "Good of you to see me on such short notice, Comrade Colonel Pavlov." He had removed his green barracks hat to reveal thick, bushy dark hair with flecks of gray. His Red Army uniform was immaculate with freshly pressed creases.

"Sit down, please," Andre said, returning the salute. "Cigarette?"

"No, Colonel." Zerenowsky looked briefly around at the drab office.

Andre took another deep drag from his cigarette. "Now, tell me, what is it that's so important?"

Zerenowsky leaned forward in his chair. "Colonel, we suspect that there is a traitor on Marshal Malinovsky's staff."

"I see." Andre sat back in his chair and blew smoke in the air. "Explain."

"I have learned through my contacts in Washington that a Russian has been turned."

"Is the spy here in Moscow?"

"In Manchuria, Colonel, at Malinovsky's headquarters," Zerenowsky said, sounding confident. "We must find him quickly before the Americans and British receive valuable intelligence that could jeopardize our strategic position. It's a very delicate situation."

"Who is he? You must tell me now who this traitor is," Andre pressed. He coughed sharply from deep in his lungs, and the Camel trembled in his fingers. "Is this about Rasputin?"

"We have not discovered who he is, Colonel. My contact only reported that General Donovan expects valuable information and is sending a special agent from Washington. That is all he knew. Comrade Stalin suspects Rasputin."

Andre slammed his palm on the desktop. "We have been after Rasputin for months! Who knows how long the traitor and his ring have been supplying the Americans and the English with our military secrets?" Andre ground the burning stub of his cigarette in a nearby ashtray.

"Sir," Zerenowsky prodded, "if he is indeed in Manchuria, you may finally have your chance to destroy the notorious spy."

"We have been close to catching Rasputin several times, but he has always slipped through our fingers. Like air." He coughed harshly again. "What information has the bastard stolen now?"

"We don't know, sir, but possibly he is aware that our Far East defenses are vulnerable. And perhaps the British and the Americans have an interest in our transport of captured Japanese infrastructure."

Andre hacked and gasped for breath, then spit into a small brass spittoon beside his desk. "Why are you informing me of this situation?" he finally asked.

"May I speak frankly, Colonel?"

"Of course."

"As you probably know, I am Ukrainian," Zerenowsky began. "But I have put the motherland – the *Russian* motherland – above all else and have dedicated my career to Comrade Stalin. Now, I am suspicious of Comrade Beria's intentions toward me. It seems he no longer feels he can trust me because I am Ukrainian." He paused. "I want to work for you, Colonel.

Permanently. And I have important assets that can be invaluable to a colonel who could soon become a general."

"I think I understand you, Major," Andre said, watching and listening carefully. "Assets, you say. For example?"

"Yes." He nodded, appearing confident. "My work with General Donovan's Office of Strategic Services has, shall we say, enabled me to make friends in the West. They are influential people, eh? They could be invaluable contacts."

Andre was not interested in his so-called assets. "From your work with Comrade Beria, you must know him well. Tell me something interesting. Just between you and me. A few ... personal secrets, eh?"

"Personal secrets, sir?" Zerenowsky asked, immediately on guard. He stared at Andre, looking confused.

"Yes, personal," Andre said, watching the Ukrainian carefully. "We have heard rumors about your boss's sexual intrigues, his proclivities. I would like to hear what you know."

"Colonel, I know nothing, nothing at all about such things."

"I see." Andre looked down and pretended interest in some papers lying on his desk. "We will have your concerns investigated immediately," he said curtly. "No need for you to get involved, Major. I will consider your request for transfer."

"I understand."

"If there's nothing else you can tell me..." Andre looked up expectantly at Zerenowsky.

"Ah, Colonel, it is not as simple as that," the major said. "However, we do believe this man we are looking for may be a member of the military delegation sent to Hanoi to meet with the Allied Control Commission and with the Vietnamese. Did you know the Vietnamese are already fighting against the French for their independence?"

"No, I didn't," Andre replied, impatient to get rid of the Ukrainian.

"We must assist them, but ... but we must be careful. We do not want to anger our allies unnecessarily. The forces against our Vietnamese brothers are considerable, so their struggle may be short lived."

Andre nodded. "Of course." He shook loose another Camel from his pack, tapped the cigarette on the desk, and lit up.

"Have you been briefed on the situation there?" Zerenowsky asked.

"Yes, I'm familiar with the mission. To observe the military situation and establish a liaison with the Vietnamese." But he cared little about it. The Ukrainians and the Cossacks, not the Vietnamese, were his problems. He was quickly losing interest in the discussion.

"That sums it up, Colonel," Zerenowsky confirmed. "But according to our sources, the traitor will make contact with the American somewhere in Indochina."

"Yes, we've already discussed that, Major. Is there anything else? Perhaps, you have more information on Rasputin?"

"There is something else..." Zerenowsky said, his voice trailing off.

Andre looked up, vaguely interested. "What?"

"The security on our atomic project has been breached."

Andre sat forward, puffing quickly on his cigarette. "What does that mean?"

"It means, Colonel, that someone has been able to access important information on the status of the project. We do not know what information, if any, has been stolen, only that security has been compromised."

"Do you suspect Rasputin of this as well?" Andre asked. He recognized immediately the language of intrigue and knew Major Zerenowsky was adept at the game. That was how one survived in Stalin's Soviet Russia. Not unlike a strategy in war, the best protection was to get your opponent before he could expose you and destroy you.

"The methods appear to be the same. He is very clever and always works from the inside. He has plenty of cash – dollars and pounds – and knows who to buy off. We can't take any chances. Do you understand, Colonel?"

"Yes, of course. That is serious, very serious. How reliable is your source?"

"He has been our most dependable agent in Washington throughout the war. He is a high-level officer for the Americans' OSS. We call him Attila. There, we have fooled even General Donovan, eh, comrade?" Zerenowsky smiled. "Attila sends us valuable information."

"Can Attila help us find Rasputin?" Andre asked. "Has he given you any information on who Rasputin is?"

"No, Colonel. Rasputin is General Donovan's best kept secret inside the Kremlin."

"Do you have any information at all on who this traitor will contact in Indochina?"

Zerenowsky smiled. "The Americans now have OSS men on the ground in Saigon. So we must rely on our new Vietnamese allies to help us discover the identity of the American before he makes contact with Rasputin."

"And the British? Are they involved?"

According to Attila, MI-5 has not been briefed. General Donovan evidently runs this operation himself, receiving information from Rasputin directly, with no outside interference. But, of course, they always know what their American cousins are doing, eh?"

"So it would seem," Andre said, taking a deep drag on his cigarette to buy time to consider and think things through. He was still suspicious of the Ukrainian's motives, but he knew taking action on locating the spy Rasputin would please Stalin, and that was most important. *I can always blame Major Zerenowsky and have him shot if we fail to get the spy,* he decided, looking up at the major. "I must act quickly."

"Of course, sir," Zerenowsky said. "I have a plan that may snare two rabbits in one trap."

"A plan, eh? Let's here it."

"First, Colonel, my transfer."

"I will consider it, Major," Andre replied, but he had already decided to allow it.

Zerenowsky nodded. "I understand that your detachment is directed to hunt for spies and traitors to the motherland. But I thought I could assist you on this very important case. Here are my orders." He pulled a neatly folded letter from his inside tunic pocket and handed it to Andre.

Andre saw Stalin's seal immediately. He opened and read the letter quickly, finding their leader's signature at the bottom of the single page.

"As you can see, it is signed by Comrade Stalin," Zerenowsky stated.

"Yes. It appears you have already been assigned to me." Andre looked up at Zerenowsky and squinted. *Beria's men are not professionals like my branch*, he thought. *Just brutish thugs. They are expendable.*

"Colonel, we are both working to serve Mother Russia, are we not?"

"Major, I am a NKVD commander, assigned to the Smersh Detachment by Stalin himself. And you?"

"What about me, comrade?"

"You are Ukrainian ... yes, Ukrainian. Not good for you, Major, not good at all."

"Are you questioning my loyalty?"

"Your family, Zerenowsky, son of Ivan... What about them?" Andre asked, his voice like the hiss of a snake about to strike. *Can any of you be trusted? I sincerely doubt it.* He gave the major a hard look.

"Colonel Pavlov, if this mission is successful, your career will be helped immensely. I can guarantee that. And Stalin has already approved, eh?"

"Yes, it must not fail, Major Zerenowsky, or you will surely be spending the new year in Siberia with your relatives ... or worse, eh?"

"It will succeed, Comrade Colonel."

"Good. Then we will catch the spy and persuade him to tell us about others. With luck, we'll smash Rasputin's network for good. *Smert Shpronam!*" He raised his fist and struck it hard against the desk.

"Death to spies," Major Gregor Zerenowsky repeated, sounding no less enthusiastic.

Chapter 3

Charlie's landing at Tan Son Nhut Airfield on the outskirts of Saigon was rough. Thinking about the war again in a fitful sleep, he got a surprising jolt when the DC-3 hit the rock airstrip with a bounce. *Hell of a way to wake up*, he thought, rubbing his stomach where the seat belt tightened and held him against the bulkhead. A few minutes later, he stepped off the plane. The heavy humid air struck his face like a hot washcloth. He was the only passenger on the regular run from Manila.

Looking around for his ride into town, Charlie sought out the terminal. He saw the one-story yellow stucco building on the east side of the airstrip, surrounded by palm trees with sandbagged machine gun positions well placed between them. He noticed the Union Jack flying proudly from the flagpole. Then he saw a large man wearing khakis leaning against the only jeep at the edge of the runway. He was relieved he didn't have to wait to be picked up.

The man waved. "Charles Stanek?" he called, walking over to greet him. "The name's Catledge, Sergeant Joe Catledge." He stuck out his well-tanned hand. "I'm taking you into town. Just throw your gear in back."

Charlie laid his one piece of luggage, a heavy corduroy shoulder bag with leather straps, in the back of the jeep and jumped in. "Glad to meet you, Sergeant Catledge," he said, looking him over closely. "Play any football?"

Sergeant Catledge took off his hat to swipe his hand through thinning blond hair. He shook off the perspiration that quickly collected, then scratched his thick shaggy mustache. "Yup," he replied. "A little in college before the war."

"That the uniform of the day around here, Sergeant?" Charlie asked, looking at Joe's sleeves rolled above his elbow and shirt out of his trousers.

"Yeah?" he replied.

"You look like you've adapted well, and in such a short period of time."

"Had to, sir," the sergeant replied simply. "Where's your weapon?" he asked, noticing Charlie was not armed. "You need to get yourself a weapon. Never know. Friend or enemy – you can't tell one from the other around here."

They roared through the gates, passing the Gurkha sentries in a rush of dust. For the next several miles, no one spoke. Adjusting to the alien ground, Charlie closely observed the throngs of people they passed. Most walked or pedaled bicycles, while some rode in rickshaws pulled by other humans or pushed by young men on bicycles. The only vehicles he saw were military. Tea shops lined both sides of the road. In the distance he saw rice paddies. It made for quite a contrast – the large transports landing and taking off over paddies where men and women toiled with hand tools. A water buffalo plodded along through the brown paddy muck, pulling an ancient wood plow, followed by a man in a conical straw hat and shorts, ankle deep in mud. The man occasionally waved a strip of bamboo at the long-horned animal to guide and encourage him.

Sergeant Catledge slowed to turn the corner, downshifting. The gears ground and clattered as he forced the shifter upward. "New jeep?" Charlie asked, suddenly looking at the driver.

"Yup," Catledge answered, keeping his eyes on the road. "Got it in the mail a couple of days ago. From Manila. Just haven't got the hang of it yet." He shifted again and floored it. The jeep jumped forward.

"Who are those soldiers? They sure as hell aren't dressed like Gurkhas," Charlie said, pointing to four soldiers in light brown uniforms, their rifles slung across their backs.

"Japanese. The British allow them to continue operating as police here," Catledge replied casually. "You'd think they'd allow the Annamese to police themselves. Guess the Brits are afraid of the natives."

The Japanese stared at the jeep as it passed them. One of them pointed and said something to the man next to him. They both nodded.

"How long will that continue?" Charlie asked, thinking about how little he really knew about the situation here.

"Damn good question," the sergeant answered. "I suppose until the French are strong enough to take over."

"Status quo, antebellum?"

Catledge squinted at him, then replied, "Yeah, like before the war."

"I guess that's why the natives here are rebelling. Do I have that right?"

"You got it, Major."

They had entered the city of Saigon and were traveling down a narrow, dusty street. Charlie pulled a map from his bag and unfolded it. After studying it for a minute, he said, "Sergeant, you met Colonel Dixon at Bien Hoa. Uh, that's north of here, according to my map. You didn't know where exactly he was coming from, but he had arranged for you to pick him up at a designated time. Do I have that correct?"

"Yeah, that's right. He went up north on a mission. Something about meeting with the Jap garrison commander in Dalat. Jus' told us he'd received information from the Japs and was going to follow up a lead. He wouldn't tell Major Blankston, our new CO, more than that."

"Anything else?"

Catledge scanned both sides of the road while he drove. Charlie imagined he was still on guard after the gauntlet he'd run, trying to get Dixon back to safety. "He said he had two reliable contacts he was going to meet up with," Catledge said. "In a place called Xuan Loc, jus' north of Saigon. That's where I left him. On our return from Bien Hoa everything seemed pretty routine till we hit the outskirts of Saigon. That's when we drove right into the middle of some goddamned battle. Annamese rebels were fighting to take control of the city, and the British were trying to stop 'em, I learned later. There had already been fighting in and around the city. You know, sniping, roadblocks, that sort of thing. But Jesus, the whole damn city erupted that day."

Charlie nodded. "September 22, the day Dixon was killed by rebels," he said softly to himself. *What was he doing so far from Saigon alone without his team? Curious.* Charlie was trying to consider every angle.

"Anyone at Clark brief you on the military situation here in Saigon?" he asked.

"Just before we boarded the plane to fly here, they told us that it was a damn mess. One of MacArthur's boys said to contact the Brits after we arrive." Catledge shrugged. "Be careful and trust no one," was the way he put it. He said the American mission in Indochina is to establish a presence as part of the Allied Control Commission, and to work out agreements with the Annamese that would protect American diplomatic and economic interests. The British gave Dixon a good briefing on the military situation around Saigon when we first arrived, but no one said anything about the possibility of open insurrection." Catledge glanced over to Charlie and added, "Hey, I'm just a sergeant here. Ask Major Blankston. He's in charge now."

"He's in charge now."

"Do you work closely with the British?" Charlie asked, trying to get as much information as quickly as he could. He still felt unprepared for the situation he would confront.

"We operate independently of the Brits and keep our distance from their activities."

"Then what went wrong when you and Dixon got into Saigon?"

"Up till then, the locals had left us alone to carry out our mission. They knew who we were," he said, looking at Charlie. "But that day it didn't matter. They opened up on us anyway."

Charlie saw that the sergeant was very alert to his surroundings, even while talking and driving. He watched Catledge as his eyes closely followed civilians walking along the road.

"Before the twenty-second, no problems of any kind?"

"No problems between us and the natives, anyway. Sure, the city's been a powder keg since the end of the war, what with the Vietnamese demanding their independence from the French, but we were viewed by the native factions as liberators, not conquerors."

Charlie knew he had to size the sergeant up as a soldier, and quickly. His life might very well depend on it. *I've known NCOs like him. Tough and cynical as hell,* he thought. *And they have no time for officers, especially those they have no respect for.* According to his record file, he was combat-experienced and spoke Chinese. University of California. Served with Stillwell in the China Theater and was handpicked by Donovan for this mission. *Not a handsome man, but he looks big and strong as an ox. I think he's a man I can trust.* "Married, Catledge? Any family?" he asked.

"No, no family. No one," Joe Catledge replied without taking his eyes off the road. "Ya think I'd be in this business if I was married and had kids?"

Charlie smiled. *That's how they pick us.* He knew by his own experience.

"I'm their perfect recruit," the sergeant said with a grin. "No family. My parents were killed in a car accident in 1934. I was raised by a grandparent. She died the year I graduated from high school. No other surviving relatives – that I know about, anyway." He shrugged. "I went to college on a full-ride football scholarship. Didn't graduate, though. The war, you know."

"You picked an interesting line of work."

They both laughed.

"What'd you do in China?" Charlie asked.

The sergeant shot him a how-do-you know my business kind of glance.

Charlie explained, "I got to read your file, Sergeant. Standard procedure. You know that."

Catledge eyed the road. "I spent most of the war in ChunKing, in Chiang Kai-shek's headquarters. I was part of Stillwell's liaison with the Chinese government."

"Bet that was interesting," Charlie said, but he was distracted by the sights and sounds of Saigon. The smell of fish sauce and decay hung in the air, mixed with smoke from small cooking fires. "What's that they're roasting?" he asked, smelling the air.

"Could be monkey, dog. Hell, I don't know, an' I'm never gonna eat it, anyway."

Holding up a pineapple, a vendor yelled at them as they passed his fruit stall. Charlie saw that every inch of usable space was being used. The streets and sidewalks became increasingly congested as they neared the heart of old Saigon. Catledge slowed the jeep to a crawl.

"I bet it was interesting working with the Chinese."

"Not really," Joe said with a shrug. "As a military advisor, I had to watch their army get mauled by the Japs. Almost got captured once myself."

"It sounds like you're a real Asia hand."

"If I lived in East Asia my entire life, I still wouldn't be able to figure 'em out," he said, pointing to Vietnamese walking along the street. "They jus' see the world differently." The big man wiped sweat from his face with his forearm and downshifted to maneuver around an old man dragging a sow along by a rope, followed closely by two piglets.

"And you know how difficult it is working with the regular Army boys. Competition in Stillwell's headquarters over intelligence assessments was just as bad as in MacArthur's command – from what Colonel Dixon told me, anyway."

"Yeah? I wouldn't know. I worked alone. In Eastern Europe."

"With the Russians?"

"And others," Charlie said.

"Were the Ruskies as bad as Chiang Kai-shek's boys to work with?"

"Worse, probably," Charlie replied.

They neared the Saigon River, the heart and soul of French Indochina. "Tell me about Rolly Dixon, Sergeant," Charlie finally asked. "How long did you know him?"

"Less than a month. We first met at Clark Field just before we arrived here. That was on September fourth. He was a career soldier. West Point, the whole works." Catledge pulled the jeep over and parked on the narrow brick street. Vietnamese passing by stared at them. Both men got out of the vehicle, and immediately a crowd began to form around them. "This is where I stopped the car. The barricade was over there, about forty, fifty yards," the sergeant said, pointing up the street. The debris had already been cleared.

"What can you tell me about his personal life? Anything that might shed light on his work here?" Charlie asked, anxious to get the basic information-gathering out of the way. He needed to get some sleep. The long plane ride was finally catching up to him. Not used to the tropical heat and humidity, he took out a green handkerchief and wiped his face. "Hotter'n hell, ain't it?"

"Always is, when it's not raining," Catledge replied. "I know Dixon was married and had a bunch of kids – five or six – I think he told me once." They both eyed a poorly dressed man who touched the jeep. "He'd been in the army for at least twenty years. Came in during the twenties. No touch!" Catledge yelled. The man quickly pulled his hand away, bowed, and walked off down the street.

"All that was in his file," Charlie said. "What else can you tell me about him?"

The sergeant thought a moment. "He was a loner. Never spoke much with any of us. One thing I thought was strange."

"What?"

"He brought a lot of gear with him. Not just the usual. He had a footlocker full of files, maps, that sort of thing."

"Why? You think he was planning to stay a while?"

"When I asked, he said it was documents, references to American companies for negotiating agreements here. Allied Control Commission papers on Japs wanted for war crimes. He had his own agenda, I think."

"You didn't know what it was?"

"He never confided in me. Why should he?"

"You found that unusual?"

"We're not diplomats, Major. We're just here to show the flag. I didn't think there were that many American documents about this place."

"Your mission?"

"The British are here, so we're here. It's their fleet that will protect our interests, not anything we do. That's all I know."

"Was that Colonel Dixon's opinion?"

"Hell, I don't know. Like I said, he didn't talk to the rest of us much. He was real focused, though. I got to say that for him."

"What do you mean?"

"We had just set up shop in the Intercontinental when he was already trying to meet with the British and even the Japs. Blankston told me later he was checking Jap troop rosters with his list of suspected war criminals."

Charlie frowned. "War criminals? Was that part of the mission?"

"Nowadays, it's part of everyone's mission. And it was something he knew a lot about. From his work on MacArthur's staff."

"I see. How many men on the team?"

Catledge shrugged. "There were nine of us who landed. We lost Dixon – and Corporal Smith, best damn radioman there was. He was wounded at the hotel the same day. Hit by a damn sniper when he walked across the lobby. Well, they haven't sent any replacements. They haven't sent anyone ... just you, Major, to investigate."

Charlie thought he sounded angry or tired maybe.

"Now Harry Blankston's in charge."

"Major Blankston, yes," Charlie repeated his name for clarity.

"For the time being, anyway. We all got a lot of points, Major Stanek. We're all ready to go home."

"I hear you," Charlie said, forcing a smile. "Tell me. Do you think Dixon was targeted?"

"Bastards tried to wipe us all out. I got back inside the hotel just in time. They surrounded the place, had us under fire. If it weren't for the Gurkhas, we'd all be dead. They lifted the siege and evacuated us." Catledge paused briefly, and Charlie waited patiently for him to resume. "The Annamese knew exactly who we were, Major. Those shooters at the barricade didn't mistake Dixon for no Frenchman or anyone else. I'm sure of it."

Charlie watched him as he looked at the ground, kicking at the dirt. *The man's ready to go home*, he decided. "That sounds like a planned, well-coordinated ambush then."

"That's what I thought," the sergeant said, nodding. "We still haven't found his body. Did you know that?"

"I was told."

"Look out there," Catledge said, pointing at the field. "At the hedgerows. They chased me through that field all the way back to the hotel. See over there?" He pointed at the far side of the field, indicating a four-story tan building with a red tiled roof. "That's the Hotel Intercontinental." The building blended into the area well, surrounded by brown, red-roofed colonial structures, including a very ornate two-story building immediately across from it. "All those buildings over there were built by the French."

Charlie noticed the few palm trees lining the street around the hotel were broken and charred. He also noticed blackened scorched areas under many of the hotel windows. "The French built most of this city, I understand," Charlie commented, looking in the direction Joe pointed. "You said *they* chased you? Who were they?"

"They. The goddamned Annamese," Catledge growled, looking hard at Charlie. "Major, you need to understand the military situation here in Cochin China."

"Tell me." Charlie knew he had touched a nerve. And it's *Mister* Stanek, remember? I'm traveling as a diplomat. That's my cover, so don't forget."

"Right ... Mr. Stanek. The *Indochine*se can agree on one thing. They all want to be independent from the French. Among the Vietnamese, the strongest faction seems to be the Viet Minh, a collection of leftists and nationalists dominated by the communists. They are strongest up north around Hanoi, but they are trying real hard to gain control down here before more of the French Army returns. Right now, the strongest military force here are the Japs. They're still garrisoned everywhere – Phnom Penh, Dalat, Cam Ranh Bay. An' now they're sympathetic to the locals. You know, 'Asia for the Asians.'"

"I've heard that before," Charlie replied. "What about the British?"

"The Brits are here to receive the Japanese surrender, repatriate them, and to keep order, but the Brits have only a small force here in Saigon. General Gracy told Dixon they will mediate between the Annamese and French to establish a viable form of government acceptable to both sides until a more permanent arrangement can be implemented. The Annamese don't believe him and neither do I."

"What do you mean?"

Catledge looked at him with sarcasm. "The British and French want their colonies back. The Annamese don't believe the British will stand in the way when the French are strong enough to assert themselves and assume full control of Indochina."

"What's our position on that?' Charlie asked.

"I think we support free and open elections, not a return to the old ways, but hell, I don't know. You need to ask Major Blankston."

"Good point," Charlie said, observing the people surrounding the vehicle in a new light. "You're saying that the natives don't want to see the French return at all."

"You got it," Catledge replied. "The trouble really started a couple of weeks after we arrived. The British released all the French Legionnaires from Saigon Prison. That's where the Japs had 'em."

"What kind of trouble?"

"The buggers went on a rampage," he said. "Found their weapons and turned into vigilantes, summarily executing Annamese an' anybody else that got in their way," the sergeant explained.

They got back into the jeep, and Catledge started the engine. "Come on, I'll show you where the barricade was set up."

"Americans my friends. France bad ... very bad," a young Vietnamese man, dressed simply in shorts and a collarless cotton shirt, called out as he pedaled by, staring at them.

Before they could move their vehicle, they had to disperse the curious bystanders, vendors, and children who had gathered to stare at the foreigners. Farmers carrying their produce to market on their backs stopped when they saw the much larger Americans. "Move! Get outta the way!" Catledge growled as the jeep began to move forward. Slowly he drove through the crowd and back into the middle of the street.

"Right about here," he said after driving about fifty yards. He braked the vehicle, shifted into neutral, then stood up to point at an area of the street in front of them. "This street was blocked off with burned-out cars, tires, wood, anything they could find. They had set up a machine gun over there," he said, still pointing. "I think it was a Jap gun. It sure sounded like one."

"Are the Japs supplying the natives, then?"

"The Vietnamese get their weapons wherever they can," Catledge answered. "Even some American weapons are showing up. They took 'em off the French. And I can assure you that French soldiers carryin' American weapons is a picture not lost on the local population here. They can add two and two an' come up with four."

"Hmm..." Charlie said. "I have to get out and take a look." He walked over, studying the site and trying to picture the ambush. Debris still littered the side of the street, but he saw no shell casings. That wasn't surprising. Metal, any kind of metal, was probably very valuable. He felt eyes watching them from the shadows.

"You, American?" someone yelled out from the darkness of one of the buildings.

"Come here," Charlie said, motioning with his hand.

A brown-skinned man wearing a black cotton shirt and pants stepped from the shadows. He was barefooted.

"You speak English?" Charlie asked.

"A little," the young man said, hesitating. "I learn from priests."

"Did you see a battle here sixteen days ago?"

The man looked around carefully. "I see him." He pointed at Sergeant Catledge.

"What else?"

"I see soldiers in the street shooting. They wait for cars to come, then shoot."

"What soldiers?"

"Soldiers who drink tea here. Some with the yellow star on their hats. Wait," the young man said and disappeared momentarily into the darkness. When he returned, he carried a faded green hat. He handed it to Charlie.

"That's Rolly Dixon's hat," Sergeant Catledge called to Charlie from the jeep. He got out and quickly walked over to them. "Where'd you get that?" he asked the man in a threatening voice.

"I find on street. Here," he said, pointing at the brick.

"Thank you," Charlie said. "What else did you see?"

"Nothing," he said. "Bullets everywhere. I hide."

"I see." Charlie bowed politely, and both he and the sergeant returned to the jeep. "Let's get out of here, Sergeant. I've seen enough for one day, and I'm beat. I need to get some sleep."

"Right." Catledge shifted the jeep into first gear, and they slowly inched their way up the crowded street again.

"What's here that's so important? I mean besides rice, rubber, and French pride?" Charlie asked when they turned the corner for the hotel.

The sergeant looked at Charlie for a long second before replying. "Indochina is a valuable prize because there's gonna be big money made here when business gets back to normal. Agriculture, sure. But more importantly, oil. Dixon negotiated an agreement with the Viet Minh to safeguard Texaco and Standard Oil. Both companies already have people here working to get their operations up and running. They're staying at our hotel."

"What about the diamonds?" Charlie asked, suddenly dropping the question in the sergeant's lap. He figured the enlisted man was well-informed and should have an opinion. "The diamonds that Dixon was carrying ... did you know about them?" Charlie turned his head slightly to watch Catledge's reaction.

"As I've already written in my report, I didn't know what was in the pouch until later when Major Blankston opened it."

"And no one knows who gave the diamonds to Dixon?"

"I don't."

"I need to speak with his contacts. The ones you mentioned earlier."

"I think I can locate at least one of 'em for you. A French colonial by the name of Bocquât. Rene Bocquât. I've met him. The colonel and I worked with him a couple times. He's got a rubber plantation just north of Saigon, along the highway. He found us a good man for the colonel's trip north."

"I'd appreciate talking to him, Sergeant."

Chapter 4

Early the next morning, Charlie left his room on the second floor of the Intercontinental and went to the Embankment commander's room at the end of the hall. He rapped hard on the door.

"Yeah, who is it?" a voice called from inside.

"Charles Stanek. I believe you're expecting me."

"Come in, come in."

Charlie opened the door and entered. Major Harry Blankston's office was a cramped room that also served as his sleeping quarters. The furnishings were sparse – a single bed, a three-drawer dresser with a small electric lamp on top. A clay pot filled with water sat on top of a nightstand. His clothing was stacked in one corner, and weapons in another. French windows opened to a narrow balcony. Charlie saw that the windows were closed. *Protection*, he decided. Beer bottles littered the floor. *This room smells like a Milwaukee tavern at closing time,* he thought, but tried not to show his disgust.

"Major Stanek, good to finally meet you," Major Blankston said, rising from a wooden chair and extending his hand. "I had hoped we would have met yesterday."

"Yes, I apologize for not waiting," Charlie said, not really sorry at all. "But you weren't around. I needed to get some sleep."

"Of course. You probably have your own way of doing things. I can understand that," Blankston said. "So, how can I be of assistance?"

Blankston motioned to a second chair, but Charlie shook his head. "Major, my investigation shouldn't take long or take up too much of your time. If everyone cooperates."

"You have my full support, Major."

I bet, Charlie thought, but nodded and forged ahead. "To begin, I would like to interview team members. Everyone here during the fighting that night," he said. "Also, I must see any reports, summaries, that sort of thing. I know you completed your own investigation, and I may not have everything on it."

"I've already sent off everything I had, and you probably already saw it. But I have copies here," Major Blankston said, pointing to a stack of papers on the floor beside his bed.

Charlie frowned. *The son of a bitch is going to be difficult to work with. I'm on his turf, and he doesn't like it. He's one of those 'I've been around, and you can't tell me anything' kind of soldiers.* Charlie resisted the urge to sneer as he said, "I gather you're wondering why Washington sent me to conduct the investigation, aren't you, Major?"

Blankston gave him a poker face stare. "I received General Donovan's message notifying me of your arrival, but I'm still a bit confused, Major Stanek. Hell, just a few months ago, Americans were dying by the thousands all over the Pacific, and nobody seemed to give a damn about the loss of one man."

"I understand your concerns. All I can say is that this part of the world has taken on more importance. Dixon was tasked with a large role out here, and his death not only complicates things but raises a number of red flags." *I'm trying to placate the major while not really telling him anything. Damn impossible,* Charlie thought. "Any word? Have you found the body yet?"

"Talk with Major Hiroaka. He's in charge of finding Dixon's body."

"The Japanese are looking for one of our soldiers?"

"They are claiming jurisdiction, and it was authorized by the British," Major Blankston replied. "The Japs haven't found him, but Hiroaka assures me they have troops out looking. They have the manpower and knowledge of the city. They also have many more contacts among the natives here. I suggest you take it up with him."

"I'll schedule a meeting with Major Hiroaka first thing," Charlie said. "How do I find him?"

Blankston turned away, as if dismissing Charlie, and reached for his cigarettes on the bedside table. "I've assigned Sergeant Catledge to give you whatever assistance you require in your investigation. He'll escort you to the British and Japanese camps."

"Thank you," Charlie said. "Major, one more thing. What can you tell me about the diamonds that Dixon was carrying?"

Blankston stopped in the middle of lighting a cigarette and stared at Charlie. "The diamonds? I was wondering when we'd get around to that. I know very little, only that he had been carrying them when he was killed. We assume he picked them up somewhere north of here. Dalat, perhaps."

"Why do you think he was carrying them? For what purpose?"

"I've reviewed all our correspondence, talked with the British, and I've discovered nothing," Blankston said with a shrug. "Not a clue, not a reason." He lit his cigarette and took a long puff.

"If you don't mind, I need to look over all of Dixon's papers. Anything that might shed some light on what he was doing in Dalat, and how he came to possess those diamonds."

"That can be arranged."

On Blankston's suggestion, Charlie decided to interview the Japanese policeman first. Stepping out of the jeep, he followed Sergeant Catledge across a crowded street to a three-story concrete building. Out of the corner of his eye, he saw a high barbed-wire fence attached to the side of the building. Vietnamese milled around inside the enclosure or squatted silently on the ground. Others, mostly women and children, stood outside the fence, talking to some of those inside.

"Japanese justice, eh?" he said, nodding to the fenced enclosure.

"Yeah, justice," Catledge replied with contempt.

Charlie eyed two guards standing at attention on each side of the double door. The two guards saluted. Inside, the building seemed cavernous – long dark hallways with high ceilings and mahogany-trimmed doorways, all closed. Charlie and Joe saw soldiers everywhere.

"They took the building over from the Colonial gendarmes. Cells are in the basement with the overflow out back," the sergeant whispered. "Hiroaka's office is over here."

They knocked on the door and stepped inside. A Japanese officer in a neatly pressed uniform left the desk and approached them. A sword hung on the wall behind him.

"Major Hiroaka, my name is Charles Stanek, and I've been sent by President Truman to investigate the death of Lieutenant Colonel Rolly Dixon." Charlie extended his hand and introduced the sergeant. "Sergeant Joe Catledge, my aide."

"Good to meet you, Mr. Stanek," the major said and bowed proudly. "Welcome to Saigon, now that we are no longer at war. The sergeant and I have already met." They shook hands. "Please sit down."

They sat in chairs in front of the major's desk.

Everything about Hiroaka snapped with precision. *He doesn't act like a soldier of a defeated nation,* Charlie observed. "Major Hiroaka, you speak very good English."

"Ah, yes, Mr. Stanek. UCLA, Class of 1938," he said with a smile. "Engineering."

"I'm impressed," Charlie answered. He didn't quite know what to think. *Officially, this man remains a prisoner of war until repatriated.* "Major, what's the status of your investigation into Lieutenant Colonel Dixon's death?"

"It is very bad to kill an American now," Major Hiroaka replied. He shuffled several papers on his otherwise immaculately clean desk. "I have five hundred men out now looking for his body," he said, looking down. "But we still have not found it. The natives? I don't know." He shrugged.

Charlie and Catledge looked at each other.

"Is someone hiding a dead man, Major?" the sergeant asked, confused and a bit surprised. "Who benefits from that?"

"Sergeant," Charlie cautioned. "What could have happened to him, Major?" he asked. "Was he mixed up with others killed during the fighting, perhaps?"

"Don't you think we looked into that?" Major Hiroaka said, looking directly at Charlie with piercing brown eyes. Charlie recognized them as the eyes of a cop, and the man wasn't going to take any guff from an American. Sitting there, back straight, arms on the desk directly in front of him, hands palms down, the major betrayed no outward feelings to Charlie. "But we don't give up," he added. "I think maybe the natives threw him in the river. That is not unusual. As with the gangsters in your Chicago, yes?" Major Hiroaka looked hard at Charlie.

Charlie could see that the Japanese major was trying to figure out just who he was and what he was doing on this side of the world. "You have come a long way to investigate the death of one man, sir," Major Hiroaka said.

"Is there anything else you can tell us, Major? About his death, I mean?" Charlie asked, ignoring the major's probing.

"When we find more, I will tell you," Major Hiroaka said. He stood abruptly and bowed. "Good day."

"Oh, one more thing, Major," Charlie said, remaining seated as Sergeant Catledge rose to leave.

"Yes?" the Japanese officer replied. He seemed surprised.

"As you probably know, having spoken already with Colonel Dixon and the British, locating Japanese soldiers wanted for war crimes is a high priority. I must know what you and Colonel Dixon talked about concerning this issue."

"Talked about, Mr. Stanek?"

"Come now, Major, surely he requested assistance and information from you. I must know what it was."

Hiroaka sat back down again, ran his hand through his short black hair, and closed his eyes just for a second. "Sit down, Sergeant, please."

Catledge sat again as ordered.

"He did not ask me for assistance in his search, but he did request information," Major Hiroaka said.

"What was that information?"

"Colonel Dixon searched for one of our soldiers who he seemed to know much about."

"Who was that?"

"Captain Isoruki Suzuki."

"You knew this man?"

"Yes, for most of the war, he served here at the Saigon jail. He transferred to a prison in the Central Highlands sometime early last year."

"Why do you think he was looking for just him? There must be many others who are wanted for one reason or another."

"He did not say, Mr. Stanek. But I gave him the information he wanted and I never saw him again."

"Surely you must have some idea, Major?"

Major Hiroaka hesitated, then spoke. "I think because Captain Suzuki had a very bad reputation as a block supervisor here and later at the Plei Toan camp up north. That's why he was transferred. It seems that the Vietnamese search for him also."

"Anything else that you can tell me?"

"No, Mr. Stanek."

"Thank you, Major." They rose to leave. "Oh, Major."

"Yes?"

"What do you know about diamonds?"

"Diamonds, Mr. Stanek? Is that the real reason your president sent you to Saigon?" he asked.

"Answer the question, please, Major."

"I know very little about diamonds."

"Tell me about the little that you do know."

"Mr. Stanek," he said, obviously irritated, "earlier this year, diamonds belonging to the French were stolen from one of their banks here in Saigon. The four gunmen were dressed like local peasants wearing masks, but witnesses at the scene, Vietnamese employees and bystanders, have stated that the men were not Vietnamese. That they did not look like Vietnamese."

"Did they speak?"

"Evidently not. No one heard any distinguishable words, Mr. Stanek."

"What about weapons, vehicles?"

"Ah yes, very good questions. They carried American pistols – .45 automatics. But, according to witnesses, they left in a French automobile, a Citroen. Two bank employees were shot and killed."

"How did they know about the diamonds?"

"I cannot answer that question."

"Any suspects?"

"We suspect Japanese soldiers only because of the eyewitness accounts describing them. To Americans, we Asian people all look alike. But here, the differences between us and the Annamese are quite glaring. And there was a cohesiveness and discipline among the thieves that was characteristic of Japanese soldiers," he said, looking down at his desk. "That is all I know."

"Any leads?"

"We have ruled out most soldiers from Saigon and I have investigated them thoroughly. My informants say no one here has seen or heard any mention of the diamonds. I think it was ... how do you Americans say it? An inside job."

"Because?"

"Because the crystals were hidden in the bank vault since before the war, few people knew of their existence."

"Are you still investigating the heist?"

"Heist. Yes, that's the American word. No, Mr. Stanek, my command has ordered me to drop it. They say I now have more important duties."

"Like finding Colonel Dixon?"

"Yes," Hiroaka said, avoiding eye contact. "It shames me to have to tell you about this disgraceful incident."

"We appreciate your assistance and your candor," Charlie said with a growing appreciation for the Japanese policeman. They rose to depart.

"Mr. Stanek, I must warn you," Major Hiroaka said quickly. "Be watchful while you are here in Indochina. Things are not always what they seem." He stood again, turned, and walked out the back door of the office.

"What the hell does that mean?" Charlie asked, looking at Sergeant Catledge.

The sergeant shrugged. "Hell if I know."

"He certainly seems to have a handle on his job. Very competent, I'd say. You'd think he was still in charge out here. Instead of the British."

Catledge smiled and shook his head. "Maybe he is," he muttered. "Who knows?"

"You think he was holding back?" Charlie asked as they walked back across the street to the jeep.

"I think, if he could have, he would already have found Dixon's body, sir," Catledge said, climbing into the vehicle. "Just so we wouldn't get involved. It's a matter of honor for him."

"He's a good cop, you think, eh?" Charlie asked. "You think he knows more about the diamonds?"

"Maybe holding back something. Remember, he's still a Jap officer."

Back at the Intercontinental, Charlie sat with Sergeant Catledge near a window in the lobby, surrounded by Vietnamese marble and ornately carved wood columns and cornices done in the late Empire style. They casually watched the locals pass on the sidewalk in front of them between the hotel and the opera house. Their simple loose-fitting cotton shirts reminded Charlie of Ukrainian peasants. It was already getting dark, and a British-imposed curfew was in effect, but it didn't seem to be cause for concern. Earlier that day, workers had replaced the glass windowpanes that were destroyed by small arms and mortar fire during the riots. Charlie didn't see soldiers or military vehicles around. Only the Gurkha guards who had been assigned to protect the hotel were visible. They stood behind sandbagged positions just outside the lobby door. A British light machine gun pointed out and across the square in front of the still majestic opera house with its boarded windows.

Charlie and the sergeant sipped whiskey from glass tumblers. It was good American bourbon that Charlie brought from the States. He figured it would come in handy to loosen up the mood if necessary. They drank it straight up. There wasn't any ice to be had anywhere in Saigon, according to Sergeant Catledge.

"So, Dixon was returning alone from a three-day trip north when you picked him up?" Charlie said softly.

"That's right," Catledge replied, gulping down his drink. "You gonna offer me another?"

"Help yourself," Charlie said, watching impatiently as the sergeant filled his glass from the bottle.

"Thanks," Catledge said. "I haven't drunk good bourbon since early forty-four." He belched. "Listen, Major, maybe you need to make contact with the Annamese leaders here in the south." He belched again. "Good stuff." He laughed at himself. "Makin' me homesick."

"You mean talk with the men who may have ordered Dixon's death?"

"We're all friends now. That's the official word, anyway," he said with a short laugh as if he were clearing his throat. "I'll get you in to see the main commie. His name is Tran Van Giau, and he heads the Southern Committee of the Viet Minh. Who knows? They may even help you find the body. I've already seen crazier things goin' on around here since we landed."

"Then as soon as we can, we meet this Tran Van Giau."

They sat in silence for a couple minutes. Catledge lit a cigarette and held his full glass in his other hand. He seemed more relaxed – of course, bourbon could easily do that. "One more question," he said.

"I'm listening," Charlie answered, thinking about how he would deal with the Vietnamese when he met them. "What's on your mind?"

"Stan-eck," Joe said slowly. "What kinda name is that?"

"Stan-yak. It's Stan-yak," Charlie said patiently, looking over at the sergeant. "It's Czech."

"Eastern Europe somewhere, right?" he said, obviously a little high from the bourbon. "Hitler took it, didn't he?"

"That's right. Hitler had it, but now it's liberated."

"You born there?" he asked good-naturedly.

"I'm an American, just like you, Sergeant," Charlie answered, beginning to lose patience.

"Right off the boat, eh?"

"My father was." That was enough for Charlie. "I think you've had enough, Sergeant." He grabbed the bottle, corked it, and set it on the floor between his feet.

"You're not a talker, are you, Mr. Stan-yak?" the sergeant said, a look of disappointment on his face. "Not that I want to talk politics or anything. I just like a little chatter with my whiskey."

"Waste of goddamned time," Charlie growled. He stared into his empty glass.

"You see a lot of fighting in Europe?" the sergeant asked.

"More than I expected," Charlie finally replied. "There were too many enemies to deal with. I mean beside the Nazis."

"Like who?"

"Like the damn Russians. I never knew from day to day what they might do."

"What about the people you worked with?"

"The Czechs. I made some good friends ... and enemies too."

"What were the women like?"

Charlie didn't reply but stared at the marble floor, at his shoes. His mind wandered...

Brown, but nothing adequately describes the rich color of her hair...

"I must go, Charles. They're retreating. Don't you see? This is our chance to drive the Germans out of Czechoslovakia for good."

"What about us?"

"Oh, Charles! The freedom of Czechoslovakia is much more important."

Charlie shook his head to dislodge the memory.

"Hey, Major ... I mean Mr. Stan-yak. Are you okay?" Sergeant Catledge asked. "Where'd you go?"

"Just thinking," he replied softly.

"I see that. I didn't offend you, did I? I have a big mouth, so don't get upset."

"No," Charlie said, quickly refocusing on the man sitting beside him. "So, Sergeant..." He looked hard at the other man. "What did the war take from you?" He knew he was directing his residual anger toward him, but didn't much care. "How many friends did you lose?"

"Friends? I don't have any friends," the sergeant said flatly. "It's better that way."

"What about Dixon? Did seeing him shot down there in the street bother you?"

"I did all I could for him. There wasn't anything else I could do but get the hell outta there." The sergeant scowled. "I didn't betray my commanding officer by leavin' him to die in the street, if that's what you're gettin' at."

"I didn't mean to insinuate that you did," Charlie said. "What did his life mean to you?"

"Not a damn thing, because I didn't know anything about him," Catledge replied evenly. "I did my duty to Dixon and for my country. Now it's time to go home. To watch UCLA win the Rose Bowl."

"If they get that far, Sergeant," Charlie said, trying to smile. "Good night. We'll talk in the morning." He got up and dragged himself out of the lobby, feeling exhausted. He still held the empty glass.

"Hey Stan-yak," Catledge called after him, "good taste in booze." He held up the half-empty bottle Charlie had left behind.

Charlie turned and forced a smile. "Hey, Joe," he said impulsively, "have another – on me."

Joe uncorked it and poured a short one. "To the bloody lifers."

Charlie turned away and continued up the wide staircase.

Chapter 5

Charlie and Joe, following a two-hour drive over rough, almost impassable roads, entered the coastal resort town of Vung Tau. Charlie heard the surf from the South China Sea pounding against the beach just beyond the village.

They approached the worn two-story brick and stucco villa compound the Vietnamese were using for their Southern Command Headquarters. Charlie studied the old colonial mansion, impressed by its simple elegance. He also noticed the bomb craters that dotted the grounds, and the pockmarks in the walls from small arms fire.

They were instantly surrounded by khaki-clad soldiers who stared at them in silence. He noticed the hodgepodge of weapons they carried – older French, mostly, and some Japanese. But here and there he saw an M-1 or a Browning automatic rifle.

A young Vietnamese woman came out of the double mahogany doors to greet them. Also dressed in khaki, she walked slowly toward them, erect and proud. But unlike the male soldiers they had seen, her skin was not sun darkened but light, almost white – the texture of rare porcelain. She was the first woman Charlie had seen not dressed in what he had been told was the traditional *ao dai*. Her long black hair was tied into a bun held with a simple comb.

"Welcome, Americans," she said in very good English. She bowed gracefully. "I am Nguyen Phuc Truin, but you may address me as Comrade Truin. I will be your interpreter while you speak with Tran Van Giau, our commander."

"I am Charles Stanek, American representative to the Allied Control Commission," he said, fixated on her beauty. Her brown eyes were so deep they seemed to hold the world. He felt like a deer caught in the headlights of a car. "And Sergeant Joe Catledge, of the American Embankment team," he added, almost as an afterthought. Charlie and Joe both shook her hand. To Charlie, it felt soft and cool to the touch.

"Please come." She turned and led them back into the mansion and up a curving wooden staircase. Charlie was enchanted by her simple, elegant charm. "Then you are an American diplomat," she said. "We have been waiting for the Americans. Commander Giau is anxious to speak with you ... on behalf of our leader, Ho Chi Minh."

As Charlie and Joe followed her, Charlie noticed how well she filled out the khaki trousers with smooth rounded muscles. It had been a long while. The military garb did nothing to detract from her beauty.

Greeting another soldier at the door, Comrade Truin led them into a large, well-lit room. She bowed to an older man, then turned to face them. "Mr. Stanek from President Tru-Man and Sergeant Cat-ledge, I present to you Comrade Giau, our leader here in Cochin."

She spoke to the man only in Vietnamese. Comrade Giau bowed politely and waved his hand to two chairs positioned in front of the large mahogany desk he sat behind.

"Please sit, gentlemen," she said, mimicking his gesture. "You may ask your questions." The tropical sun flooded through the open French doors, highlighting the ornate wood paneling in the room. The desk and chairs were the only furnishings. The desk was strewn with papers and maps, some of them turned upside down.

Charlie stared at the maps. *Battle maps?* he wondered.

Watching him, the old man smiled softly. "Do you know Vietnam?" he asked in Vietnamese, looking at Charlie. Comrade Truin translated.

"No, sir, this is my first trip," Charlie replied.

"How do you like our country, Mr. Stanek?" Gau asked through Truin.

"Very beautiful," he said, smiling at her. She blushed.

Comrade Giau watched the exchange. "I see, Mr. Stanek, that you are not dressed like a soldier. Are you a diplomat representing your country, or a soldier?" Comrade Truin translated his question slowly.

"I am an American soldier on a diplomatic mission, sir. And I am investigating the death of an American Army officer killed during the disturbances last month."

Giau nodded that he understood. "We were hoping you brought more from your President Tru-man. We understand your interest in learning how he died ... yet, my country needs more from your president. To prevent a war." The young woman translated his words slowly so that they would grasp the old man's meaning and have no doubts.

"I am not prepared to discuss relations between our countries, sir," Charlie said. "My mission is to discover who killed an American soldier in your country."

"How can I assist you with this?" Comrade Truin spoke for Giau.

"Mr. Giau, do you know anything about how Lieutenant Colonel Dixon died?" Charlie observed the old man while he spoke with the young woman. He easily saw that the old man was very gaunt and wondered if it was from hard work or just age. His skin was pale, almost pallid. Even here in the heat, he wore a long-sleeve shirt and tie. A pair of rimless spectacles lay on the stack of papers.

Listening to the translation, but never taking his eyes off Charlie, Comrade Giau replied without hesitating. "I understand he died during a battle to control Saigon, Mr. Stanek. A battle between us and the Europeans. The French," he said, speaking slowly so that Comrade Truin didn't miss one vowel. "Your soldiers were mistaken for Frenchmen. I am very sorry. In battle, mistakes sometimes happen, as you must know."

"Your troops didn't see the markings on the vehicle, sir?" Charlie asked. He fully expected a direct answer.

"You must understand that our soldiers are workers and peasants. What do they know of your special markings? And, it was a French vehicle," he said. "Tell your president that Americans are our friends, and we are soliciting his support for our cause. You are, in fact, our example. '...all men are created equal, that they are endowed by their Creator with certain unalienable rights...' he cited from the Declaration of Independence in clear English. He nodded and smiled when he had finished.

Surprised and impressed, Charlie stared at the old man. "I see," he finally said. "You're saying Dixon's death was a simple case of mistaken identity." He looked to Comrade Truin.

"We didn't know," she replied.

"Then you are saying that this incident does not signal a change in your policy. You recognize American neutrality, and our agreement is still in effect?" He wanted to get the conversation back on track.

"Yes, Mr. Stanek," Giau said.

Charlie glanced at Joe.

"We respect the rights of all foreign interests," Giau continued.

"Why is the American government supplying the French Army with arms, Mr. Stanek?" Truin asked him. "Do you know that they are using those weapons against the Vietnamese people?"

Charlie saw that the young woman was genuinely concerned. "I am not knowledgeable on our military policy toward France. I suggest you put your concerns in writing, and I will see that they are forwarded." He did not want that issue to distract them from the reason for his visit. "Sir, I am requesting your assistance in recovering Colonel Dixon's body," he said slowly but with growing impatience.

Comrade Giau watched them. He tugged at the long wiry whiskers on his chin, and then spoke slowly to Comrade Truin. "You must realize that supplying our enemy is an act of war against the Vietnamese people," she translated.

"The death of Lieutenant Colonel Dixon is my highest priority. But I will notify Washington of your concerns, Mr. Giau, Madame Truin," Charlie stated again, and noticed her surprise when he said her name. He stood up. *Hell, this meeting is over. What a waste of time.* "I hope we can work together to recover his body." He tried to mask his disappointment but knew they could see through the attempt.

Joe also stood. They bowed and extended their arms to shake the other man's hand. He reciprocated, then suddenly turned and spoke at length to the young woman.

"Comrade Giau wishes you both wealth and much happiness," she said as the Vietnamese man suddenly disappeared from the room. "Also, he says I will accompany you in your investigation so that you can speak with others who may know of your colonel's unfortunate death. I am to help you find the body. Is that acceptable to you, Mr. Stanek?"

"I appreciate the offer. Sergeant?"

"Sure," Joe agreed. "We'll meet you at the Hotel Intercontinental in the morning. Is that okay, Miss Truin?"

After escorting them to their vehicle, Truin bowed politely. "In the morning then. Goodbye, Sergeant Cat-ledge. Mr.

Stanek," she said, looking directly at Charlie before heading back to the old mansion.

"You know the old man is sending her along just to keep an eye on us," Joe said.

"Of course, but we could have a worse escort. And she may be useful," Charlie added as an afterthought. Something about the young woman intrigued him. The way she held her head, the light in her dark eyes.

They drove slowly through the village, the ocean only meters away on their left. It was monsoon season, and the vegetation along the road was deep green with dazzling arrays of flowers. Clouds rolling in from the ocean hung heavy to the ground. Vung Tau, except for the Viet Minh compound, seemed like a sleepy village. On the beach, fishermen had pulled their small, long wood boats up on the sand to sell their catch to local women. Charlie observed a crowd of mostly women and children. Everyone was on the beach to barter and chat.

It began to rain on the beach, but the villagers didn't seem to notice the curtain of rain sweeping toward them. Joe stopped the jeep. "Here it comes," he said. "Let's get the top up!" They quickly got out, pulled up the canvas top, and fixed it in place.

The ride back to Saigon took longer. They ran into several roadblocks – the first two erected by French soldiers and the last a British ID check. Charlie could appreciate the Brits. They were determined to restore order, regardless of whose toes they stepped on. He thought about their meeting with the Vietnamese. *Not much accomplished. At least I now know something about who leads the Vietnamese here.*

"What'd you think of the communists?" Joe asked after clearing the last roadblock. "Can't trust 'em. They say one thing an' do another. That's what I think."

"Who *do* you trust around here?" Charlie asked. "The Japs? Or the French?"

"I just watch 'em all and not trust anyone. Safer that way."

Chapter 6

*S*he stood across the empty room, the moonlight reflecting off her naked body, her creamy white skin glistening. But shadows crept toward her, strangling the light.

"Marie!"

She didn't move.

"Marie!"

"No! No, no, no!" Charlie awoke shaking and covered in perspiration. But the small room was empty, quiet. A light breeze blew in through the open window. He'd had been dreaming again. There was no Marie, and he was on the far side of the world.

He heard a knock at the door.

"Mr. Stanek?" a woman's voice called softly through the door.

Yes, Saigon, he reminded himself, slowly getting his bearings. Raising himself up on his elbows, he looked around in the early morning light, then carefully and quietly rolled from his bed. "Who's there?" he whispered, now standing behind the door, back against the wall, with his weapon in hand.

"Mr. Stanek are you awake?" the female voice repeated. She knocked again. "It is Comrade Truin. From Vung Tau. I've been sent by Comrade Giau."

"Truin?" he said slowly. "Yes, Miss—or rather, Comrade Truin."

"I've come to take you. We have an important meeting," she said.

What's she talking about? His mind raced. Abruptly, he swung the door open. "What meeting? I was never briefed by your people on a meeting," he said, standing in the doorway, clad only in boxer shorts.

She looked him up and down quickly, then looked down politely, as was custom. "I am sorry, but it's very important for us. You come right now, please," she said and bowed graciously. She continued looking at the floor, her face red from embarrassment.

"Okay. Give me five minutes to shave and clean up, and I'll be ready," he said, and then noticed that he wore only his shorts. "Oh, sorry," he said with a laugh and partially closed the door.

"Mr. Stanek, I will wait for you downstairs in the lobby," Comrade Truin said hurriedly and turned to leave.

"Yes, thank you. I'll be down shortly." He closed the door.

Shaved and dressed in a newly pressed white shirt, Charlie quickly covered the flight of stairs. He found the young woman standing in the middle of the expansive lobby. Her beauty did not escape him, even at this early hour.

She bowed when she saw him. "*Chao anh,*" she said as a greeting in her language. "We have much to see today. But I think it is important that we go alone."

"Alone? Why the secrecy?" he asked, concerned. *What is she up to?*

"Too many foreigners will arouse suspicion, and my people still believe your country supports us, Mr. Stanek," she said as if reading his mind.

"Tea?" a young Vietnamese man asked, holding out a small tray with a porcelain teapot and two cups. The man was dressed in western clothes except for his sandals.

Charlie saw that Comrade Truin was going to accept. "Ah, yeah, that's good. Thanks," he said, accepting the cup of green tea.

"My cousin, Khanh – Nguyen Dinh Khanh," she said as an introduction. "He will serve you while you stay in the Hotel Intercontinental."

The tea tasted bitter. "Tastes like Russian tea," he commented without thinking.

"Oh?" she asked with a smile. "The Russians ...your allies, yes?"

"They *were* our allies. Now? Charlie shrugged. "So, will we find the men who shot the American today?" He smiled politely. "Just you and I?" *Where is she taking me? I would be a fool to trust her,* he thought.

"First we must meet with Comrade Dinh, Mr. Stanek."

"Please call me Charlie. It's easier that way," he said.

"And you may call me Truin," she replied. Our names are very confusing to foreigners, especially Europeans, I think. You see, we place our family names first. My family name is Nguyen, but we generally do not address each other in that way. Too formal, and there are many families in my country with the name Nguyen. We have a middle name and a given name, which is how we refer to each other. I am called Truin."

"That clears things up a bit," he said, smiling. "Now, who is Comrade Dinh?"

"Pham Truong Dinh, Mr. Stanek, Charlie. He is Comrade Giau's assistant. Comrade Giau has ordered him to meet with you."

"Comrade Dinh?"

"Yes," she said, hearing his concern. "Don't worry. You have questions that he can answer. Questions about Colonel Dixon's negotiations with the Vietnamese people. Then we will find how he died."

"Very well, Truin. It sounds like you have my itinerary already planned for me." *What else does she have planned for me?* He wondered.

"It is not an order, Charlie," Truin said politely.

"We'll meet with this man, but I'll decide where we go next." *If I make things too easy for her, she'll consider me weak.*

"As you wish."

They rode together in an ancient French Citroen driven by Truin's friend she called Khanh to a small house near the sprawling outdoor market that served the city of Saigon. "Why drive a French car?" Charlie asked, curious. "I take it the French aren't your favorite people right now."

"Not many cars available, Charlie," Truin said. "We use what we can find."

On the sidewalk in front of the house, several food vendors sold noodle soups, tea, and coffee. Truin led Charlie inside through an area where Vietnamese sat around small tables, smoking and talking, then they walked up a narrow flight of stairs to the second story. Two armed men stood outside a closed door.

Truin spoke to them in Vietnamese. One of the soldiers opened the door and motioned for them to follow. They entered and were greeted by a thin man wearing a neatly pressed brown shirt and khaki trousers. He wore a Japanese Nambu automatic pistol strapped to his waist. He stood, bowed, and uttered a simple greeting in Vietnamese.

"He is Comrade Dinh, Charlie. Please sit." Charlie looked around the small room that contained only a few chairs and a simple table. The balcony doors were wide open to the street below. Charlie decided it was a temporary meeting place only.

"Comrade Dinh says welcome to Saigon."

"Thank you, Comrade Dinh." Charlie extended his hand.

Dinh turned to Truin and handed her four sheets of paper with neatly scripted writing. "He has brought our notes of the meeting Lieutenant Colonel Dixon had with Comrade Giau. I will read them to you."

They all sat down. Charlie listened carefully while Truin read. He interrupted only once for clarification. On the long trip from Washington, he had read and reread copies of the radio messages Dixon had sent that explained the agreements he was negotiating with the French, but little mention was made of contacts with the Vietnamese.

"Did Dixon discuss any agreements with Giau?"

After considerable dialogue, Truin replied, "Yes."

"But?" Charlie asked, sensing more.

"As you know, Charlie, Ho Chi Minh has declared our independence from the French and we expect that they will fight to preserve their colony."

"What is it you want from me?" Charlie asked, knowing he had nothing to offer them.

"Weapons," she said. "We wish to buy arms from the United States. It is urgent, Charlie. Please, you represent the President of the United States. Surely you have surplus from the war."

"I have no authority in this matter," he said. "I can only relay your request to Washington."

"You cannot make a decision on this matter?" Truin asked. She seemed surprised.

"No."

The two Vietnamese again engaged in a protracted discussion. "Why are you here in our country, Comrade Dinh asks."

"As I have already said, to investigate Lieutenant Colonel Dixon's death and ensure that our agreements are still in effect."

Truin and Charlie listened quietly while Dinh ranted in his native tongue. Charlie understood not a word but got his meaning.

"Comrade Dinh does not believe that you came all this way for only that reason, Charlie, or that you even represent the President of your country," she said. "He suspects that you are here for another reason."

"Tell Comrade Dinh that I have told him the truth," Charlie replied with growing frustration. "I think this meeting is over." He got up, bowed to the man, then waited for Truin to stand.

She spoke briefly with Dinh. They bowed to each other gracefully, and then she turned to Charlie. "You must have patience," she said to him.

They left the building quickly. *That meeting was a complete waste of time*, Charlie thought.

Chapter 7

They rode in the Citroen to the outskirts of the city. Neither spoke of the meeting with Dinh. The meeting had left Charlie with a bad feeling.

In an older section of the city where mostly damaged homes were hastily patched with bamboo, wood, and metal debris, Truin parked the car. They walked the rest of the way, almost half a mile. He followed her through narrow alleys, past teashops, and into markets teeming with Vietnamese.

Again, Charlie felt very much alone in a world he knew nothing about. He was acutely aware that the young woman was in control. He felt for his .45, stuck in the small of his back. It was an unconscious action. He was glad Joe had insisted on him carrying a personal sidearm for protection when he had first arrived.

People watched him without any expression of emotion, yet Charlie could still feel their anger and deep suspicion. *They have learned to trust no one*, he thought. *Even the children keep their distance. They think I'm French.*

Truin stood in a doorway, waiting for him to catch up. "Don't worry, Charlie. No one here will harm you," she said in a reassuring tone. "You are with me."

"I have very little choice, do I?" he said, but she did not appear to hear.

"We know about you, Charles Stanek," she said, and resumed walking.

Charlie followed but remained on the alert.

"The Russians say you worked with them during the war against the Nazis. Is that true?"

"Yes, I fought the Germans during the war," he said, trying not to sound surprised. "And the Russians were our allies, as you probably know."

"I know many things about you, Charlie," she said with a smile. "That you have no wife, for instance." She looked down at his ring finger.

"That's an easy one," he said, "Who told you that I served with the Russians during the war?" He rubbed the small scar above his eye, feeling more nervous by the minute.

"Our friends, the Russians in Hanoi, Charlie," she said. "They ask us why you are in Vietnam. Why are you here?"

"I've told you my reasons, Truin," he answered. "If the Russians ask more questions about me, tell them ... tell them to go to hell." The thought of Russians sent chills down his back.

"I will tell them you said it," Truin answered. "I admire your courage, Charlie." They walked on in silence. "You will now meet the commander of the soldiers who fired on your Lieutenant Colonel Dixon and Sergeant Catledge," she said.

Skirting the narrow, dirt-packed streets, they navigated their way through more vegetable stalls, small mechanic shops, and teahouses. The smells assaulted his senses – the stench of animal and human waste was powerful. His eyes watered. He recognized the smell of humanity packed together, struggling to survive. Leading the way, Truin covered her mouth and nose with a silk handkerchief. She stopped when he coughed. He pulled a handkerchief from his pocket to cover his mouth and nose. She watched him quietly as he surveyed the scene. They both resumed their trek in silence.

A short distance later, they came to an older home heavily damaged by indirect fire from mortars. The tile roof looked as if it had been punched open. Rays from the early morning sun streamed in. Shrapnel had torn gaping holes in the wooden walls, and the shutters were splintered.

An old woman greeted them and led them into the home's single room. She offered hot tea to her visitors.

Charlie politely accepted it. Truin thanked the woman. They both sat on chairs provided. He suspected they were the only chairs in the house.

Silently sipping his tea, he looked about the room, curious. He saw no one else but heard noises out back. He positioned his chair so that he could more easily watch the back door. He saw that Truin never took her eyes from him. "Where are your soldiers?" he asked her.

She smiled. "They are all around us, Charlie. Many of those men you saw when we came here are our soldiers."

After a few minutes, a short thin man entered from the back. He limped. Truin stood and bowed. The man reciprocated and looked immediately at Charlie, who did not bow. She spoke to the man in Vietnamese.

Charlie finally held out his hand. After hesitating, the man shook it briefly. Charlie saw immediately that he was armed with a revolver. *British Webley,* he knew from his experiences working with British airmen. *Good choice if he can find ammunition for it,* he thought. "Greetings from the President of the United States," he said, hoping to impress the man with the importance of his mission. He looked to Truin to translate.

She looked at him, amused, but translated. "He says, 'Welcome, American. I am Captain Nguyen Phuc.' He says, 'Ask me a question.' He will tell you the truth, Charlie."

Will he? Charlie wondered. "Tell him I am here to discover why the American Dixon died, and where his body is so that I can take it home to America for proper burial." He paused for her to translate. When he saw Captain Nguyen nod, he continued. "Did you recognize the car as driven by an American when your men opened fire?"

The man shook his head. "He said he was ordered to shoot all foreign soldiers," Truin said.

"Who gave him the order?" Charlie asked.

The two Vietnamese went back and forth. Charlie detected the emotion in their voices. Finally she said, "There was so much confusion that day. On the barricade, his men were ordered to stop all cars. 'No one must pass' the captain says."

"I see," Charlie said, thinking for a moment. "Did the Americans try to surrender?"

Positioning herself between the two men, she translated quickly and softly.

The man frowned. He spoke to Truin slowly and cautiously. "We did not know their intentions," she said. "We thought they were French soldiers, foreigners in our land."

"Was the car clearly marked?" Charlie asked, knowing the answer.

"He says he did not understand the marking, nor did his soldiers."

"Didn't one of the soldiers get out of the car and yell 'American'?"

Charlie saw the blank look when she translated the question. "He saw only his enemies," Truin said, translating when Captain Nguyen finally answered.

"Did the captain know that the Americans carried something of great value?"

When Truin translated, the captain looked down and nodded. "He knew," she told Charlie. "He says he was told on the radio that the tall man carried a national treasure."

"And then?"

"He says we are all friends again. He believes the matter is settled," she said. "That is all he knows."

"But now? We are his allies?" *If alliances change that quickly, it's a damn dangerous place,* Charlie thought.

"Americans, Vietnamese, friends," the soldier said and extended his hand to Charlie.

Charlie hesitated at first, then accepted it. The man bowed deeply.

"What did you tell him about me?"

"I told him that you support our cause."

"Why do you think that?" he asked, surprised.

"American people also fought a war to become free from the English," she said, looking at him. "And you fought beside Russian patriots in the Great World War. Our cause is like yours. It is just."

"Can he find the American's body? Please ask him," he urged. The other subject could wait.

"He said he knows about the dead after the battle," Truin replied directly without asking the soldier. "After the fighting, he ordered his men to bring all the dead to the street – both his soldiers and the enemy."

"Was Dixon among the dead? Can he remember?"

Another discussion ensued between the two Vietnamese. Following their exchange, the man got up and walked to a small dresser in a corner of the room. He retrieved something, then returned and handed the object to Charlie.

Truin translated. "He said that he remembers the dead American. He took this from him." She handed Charlie a single metal dog tag.

Examining it, Charlie saw Rolly Dixon's name etched on the metal.

"He said he knew that someone would come for it one day," she said. "He is very sad, Charlie.

"What happened to his body? I must find it."

"If they were not claimed, they were given to an old ferryman on the river, Old Man Quoc, to dispose of." She spoke quickly to the Viet Minh soldier, and he answered her. "He has given me the address of this man. We will go there."

"Let's go," he said. They left the house with one of Captain Nguyen's soldiers escorting them to their car, but before they reached it, two Japanese military vehicles boxed them in. Five soldiers with rifles jumped from the back of the trucks and surrounded them. Two of his soldiers stepped between Charlie and the two Vietnamese. One pointed his rifle at him while the second disarmed him. Another pushed Truin, forcing her back with the Vietnamese soldier, whose hands were immediately secured behind his back. With precise movements one of the Japanese searched the young woman, his hands roaming her body from neck to ankle.

With growing anger, Charlie saw that the soldier was obviously enjoying his work.

Truin hissed at him as he fondled her breasts.

The soldier laughed, then ran both hands slowly down her thighs and legs.

She stood there without flinching, but Charlie could see the anger darkening her delicate features. "Leave her alone," he growled. "She's with me."

The soldier ignored him.

Charlie was forced to stand there at gunpoint and watch helplessly as the soldier continued his rough search of the young woman. He pulled a six-inch stiletto from a silk sheath tightly bound against Truin's calf, then yelled something to another soldier.

A sergeant replied and walked over to them. He took the knife from his soldier and examined it.

"What are you doing?" Charlie said, pushing against two soldiers, trying to reach Truin. But the soldiers still were able to box her in. "Leave her alone. Your superior officer will hear of this insult. I am an American on a diplomatic mission. The woman and the man accompany me."

At that moment, Major Hiroaka stepped out of the other vehicle. "Mr. Stanek," he called out. "You do not waste time, eh?" He bowed politely and spoke to his men in Japanese. They stepped away from Charlie but still held the two Vietnamese. The sergeant handed the knife to his commander and bowed.

"The British will hear of this," Charlie growled, indignant. "You have no jurisdiction here."

"Yes, Mr. Stanek, I do. I've been given authority to keep order in Saigon from General Gracey himself," he said proudly but respectfully.

Charlie was even more infuriated. "You, sir, are a prisoner of war, a soldier of a defeated nation. I demand that you let us go immediately."

"You have assisted me in capturing two suspects in my investigation of the killing of your American officer."

His soldiers began to take the two Vietnamese prisoners away to the truck. The Japanese major turned to the soldier still holding his rifle on Charlie's back, and nodded to release him. "Return his weapon," he ordered.

The soldier complied, handing Charlie back his pistol while bowing politely.

"I demand that you release the two prisoners," Charlie said, not holstering his weapon. He stood only inches from the smaller man. He was enraged. "They are assisting me, and officially assigned to the American diplomatic mission."

"Please. You are interfering in police work," the Japanese officer insisted. "They are now my prisoners."

Charlie couldn't take any more. "Major, must I remind you?" he hissed. "The war is over, and you lost. Now you take orders from me," he said sharply. "I am here representing the United States government. I will speak personally with General Gracey if you do not release these people to me immediately." Still only inches away, he stared at Major Hiroaka.

"As you command," the Japanese major said with a slight bow. His face was red from humiliation as he turned from Charlie and barked to his men, "Release them, now!"

The sergeant bowed and immediately released the two Vietnamese.

"Do you remember my warning, Mr. Stanek?" Hiroaka asked, holding his anger admirably. "Learn who your enemies are before they kill you too."

The Japanese cop did not give Charlie an opportunity to respond. He handed over the razor-sharp knife hilt first in his open palm, then bowed and turned on his heels to march back to the vehicle.

The Japanese soldiers crawled back into the truck, and both vehicles were gone up the street as quickly as they had arrived.

"Are you all right?" Charlie asked. He watched as Truin straightened her blouse. For a brief second, he saw rage ignite her calm, dark eyes. He was reminded of the Slavic peasant women who fought the Germans alongside their men.

"Thank you, Charlie," she said with a gracious bow. "I know Major Hiroaka and have seen the inside of their cells before. And have felt their methods of interrogation. But I can take care of myself."

"Yes, I can see that," he said softly, handing her the stiletto hilt first. She took it gracefully and, lifting her black cotton pantaloon to reveal her creamy white skin, returned it to the sheath.

They finally found where Old Man Quoc lived – a wooden boat used for ferrying people across the Saigon River. It was tied to a rickety old bamboo dock with a badly worn hemp line. The oars were neatly laid against the sides. Someone had recently scrubbed down the deck. Charlie saw dried soap residue on the wood planking. "This is the boat, I think," Truin said, carefully looking over the old hand-built wood craft. "It is where he said it would be." She again covered her mouth and nose with the silk handkerchief. The smells of rotting fish and something else filled his nostrils, but he didn't bother with his handkerchief again.

"The boat's cabin is empty," he said, peering through an open window into a single room. The only furnishings he saw were a single chair and a rolled mat against the starboard bulkhead. He looked down the shoreline and then up the steep bank. Above them, he saw smoke rising from a small, thatched shack sitting only a few feet back from the edge.

"Charlie! Up there," Truin said, squinting into the sun to point to the shack. "That could belong to the old man."

With Captain Nguyen's soldier leading, the three climbed a crude rock stairway to the top of the riverbank. The soldier called out when he reached the top and again when he stood directly in front of the shack. There was no response. The rotten stench of death was suddenly overpowering.

"Mr. Quoc. Mr. Quoc," Truin called, knocking on the door politely. Charlie already knew there was nothing alive inside. Motioning for Charlie and Truin to stand aside, the soldier tried the door, and the hinges groaned as it opened just slightly. He tried to force the door open by ramming it with his shoulder but succeeded only in opening it a few more inches. Something was blocking it from the inside.

Quickly stepping in front of Truin, Charlie added his weight to the soldier's and pushed hard against the door. It opened slowly, at first an inch, then several, and finally a full eight inches. Looking through the partially opened door, Charlie saw embers in a brazier still smoking. The smell of blood and rotting flesh hung in the heavy air. Refusing to give up, he motioned at the soldier, and they pushed harder. The soldier turned sideways to squeeze through the narrow space. In one final motion, he was inside. The door closed behind him. *"Eeeyi!"* he squealed loudly from behind the door.

"What is it?" Truin asked, her nose and mouth still covered with a silk handkerchief. She grabbed Charlie's arm.

The soldier spoke rapidly to Truin in Vietnamese through the closed door.

"Quickly, the body of a man..." she said, stepping around Charlie to enter. He followed.

The three, standing in the midday light that streamed in from the opened door, stared silently. A headless body lay on the dirt floor. It had partially blocked the door where it had fallen, but the soldier had moved it to allow entrance for Truin and Charlie. Smeared in blood long dried from multiple slashes and cuts, the bloated corpse was barely recognizable. A large pool of blood had collected and hardened on the dirt floor beside the corpse. It was already in an advanced state of decay, with maggots and other insects having devoured large sections of flesh. The soldier spoke while pointing to the back of the wood door, where hemp cord still dangled from a hook.

"Charlie, he says the man had been hung from the door but fell to the ground when the door was closed."

"I see that," Charlie replied, examining the door.

Truin pointed to a corner of the shack. "Charlie," she said.

Charlie looked into the corner where she pointed. There, propped on a simple stool, was the head. It was the heat-shrunken face of an old man, his eyes staring at them. A look of horror captured the moment of his death, with a gaping mouth and wide-open eyes. The head appeared to be cleanly struck from the torso.

"Did you know him?" Charlie asked, turning his back on the old man to look at the two Vietnamese. They stared at the head, its features masked by the shadows.

She looked at the soldier. They spoke. "Yes, Charlie," she said softly. "He was known to us. The old man is Mr. Quoc. That is his ferry we saw."

"Outside," Charlie ordered. Without argument, all three left in search of fresh air.

Truin spoke with the young soldier. "He thinks he was killed several days ago. In our climate, the body decays quickly."

"Any ideas who could have done this?"

"I think someone who discovered he supports our cause," she said.

"Like who? The French?"

"Perhaps," Truin said. "I am sorry. This is horrible for us, and for you."

"Why?"

"Only Mr. Quoc knew where he dumped your American's body in the river. Now I fear your colonel will never be found."

Charlie thought she was genuinely sad about the setback. "What kind of weapon do you think they used?"

She asked the soldier, who replied immediately. "He says a long knife, very sharp."

"Or a sword?"

"That is possible. He says, maybe a knife for cutting sugar cane."

Or maybe a Samurai sword, Charlie thought.

Chapter 8

The taxi pulled up in front of the Intercontinental and Charlie got out. He stood on the curb and watched the car disappear into the thoroughfare crowded with pedestrians and carts. When he entered the front lobby, Sergeant Joe Catledge waited there to greet him. "Well, well," he said. "How was your day, Mr. Stan-yak?"

"Hi, Sarge, did you get my message?" Charlie asked.

"I got it," he said with a little stiffness in his voice. "That's not the way we do business 'round here," Joe said, sounding more disappointed than angry. His large frame stood inches away. Charlie felt his breath against his face. "You took an unnecessary risk out on those streets alone. It's our job to protect you."

Charlie then noticed the Japanese major standing at the desk, talking with Khanh.

"I had reasons for going alone, Sergeant," Charlie said.

"What's the Jap cop doing here?" Joe asked.

"I don't know." Charlie watched as their driver pointed across the lobby toward them.

Major Hiroaka marched over to where they stood. "Where are your friends, Mr. Stanek?" he asked. "I must tell you that they are communists and very dangerous. Beware of their treachery," he added, not waiting for a response. "Especially the woman."

Charlie stared at him as Joe asked, obviously confused, "What are you talking about, Major?"

"Wait, Catledge. I can explain later," Charlie said, interrupting. "But first ... Major, I must report another death."

"Another death?"

"I've discovered the body of an old man along the river. He was hacked to death."

"An Annamese?"

"Yeah."

"The French Colonial police are now charged with investigating the death of natives, so the murder of this old man should be reported to them," Major Hiroaka said. "But I can report the incident to Inspector Fournier. I know him well, as I had the great honor of arresting him some time ago. A sad part of war, I'm afraid."

"Yes, but I think this death is connected to the murder of Lieutenant Colonel Dixon," Charlie tried to explain. "I can show you where the body is located."

"We go, Mr. Stanek," Hiroaka said. "Or should I address you as Major Stanek?"

"I am a soldier with a diplomatic mission," Charlie replied. "Did you think I was purposely deceiving you?"

"Things are never as they seem, are they, Major Stanek?"

"Can we go?"

"Follow me," the Japanese major said and turned for the door. Charlie and Joe followed closely behind.

Khanh watched the three foreigners from inside the hotel.

The scene at the shack along the river did not seem to have been disturbed since Charlie was there earlier. They got out of the Japanese Army truck and proceeded by a narrow path to the shack. Major Hiroaka ordered his driver and two others to stay in the truck.

"Stay here," the major ordered Joe and Charlie when they neared the shack. The smell of rotting flesh was overpowering in the still tropical heat. "I will investigate and collect evidence." Charlie and Joe watched from the edge of the clearing while the Japanese officer slowly surveyed the immediate area. With great attention to detail, he inspected every inch, often on his hands and knees. Anything he found was deposited in a small canvas bag he carried. Finally, when Hiroaka was finished examining the outside sufficiently, he entered the shack. He pulled a white handkerchief from his trouser pocket, tied it around his face, and opened the rough wood door. Ever so lightly, he stepped into the darkness. "Ayyyy," he growled loud enough for Charlie and Joe to hear. They smiled.

"It's a pretty gruesome scene," Charlie told Joe. "This man was probably the last person to see Dixon's body, and probably the one who disposed of his corpse."

"Is this what you've been doing all day?" Joe asked him.

"Truin took me here to talk with the old man," Charlie answered, not liking the sarcasm in Joe's voice. "That's when we discovered he had been murdered, tortured, and decapitated. This is all we seemed to have accomplished."

About twenty minutes later, Major Hiroaka re-emerged from the shack. To Charlie, it seemed like hours. The policeman removed his makeshift mask and breathed deeply of the fresh air when he cleared the smell of the shack. He was covered in perspiration. His fingers and knees were soiled.

"What do you think?" Charlie asked with a newfound respect for the diligent policeman.

At first the man, deep in thought, said nothing. Then he spoke. "I think the old man was tortured by professionals, determined men who always get what they want. I have seen this many times," he said. "Perhaps professional interrogators, and by their talent with the sword, I think they were Japanese." He grimaced when he said Japanese. "I am certain they were not ordinary street thieves, because they did not take anything of value or even search for valuables. They wanted something very specific."

Charlie and Joe listened intently.

"First we must look carefully at what the ferryman did for the native insurgents and for others as well," he said confidently. "Did you know that as payment for his services, he was allowed to keep anything – valuables, clothing, boots – found on the bodies?"

"I didn't know that," Charlie said.

"I found this gold ring in a hiding place under the cot," Major Hiroaka said, producing the shiny object from his pocket. "Do you recognize it? Look closely at the engraving inside." He handed it to Joe.

Joe examined it closely, turning it over and trying to read the inside letters. "L-o-v-e R-u-t-h," he said slowly. "Yeah, that belonged to the colonel. I remember he told me once his wife's name was Ruth."

"The crime scene tells me two things," the Japanese policeman said conclusively. "Someone believed that the ferryman held valuable information. He was tortured and killed by Japanese soldiers."

"Do you think they got what they were looking for?" Joe asked.

"That is a very good question, Sergeant."

"Major, who in your command ordered you to halt your investigation of the diamond heist?" Charlie asked, thinking of their conversation of the previous day.

"Major Ishitoro, an intelligence officer in Colonel Imano's command here in Saigon."

"Someone was determined to examine Dixon's body for valuables, or to discover what secrets he knew," Joe added, still staring at the ring in his hand.

Charlie noticed that Joe rubbed his right arm when he was preoccupied. "Football injury?" he asked, watching him.

"What? Yeah," Joe replied. "Fractured it my freshman year against Cal."

"You're searching for diamonds, aren't you?" Major Hiroaka said, directing his question to Charlie.

"It may be a motive for murder," Charlie replied, seeing the Japanese soldier growing more interested in his investigation. Charlie felt the investigator's eyes on him and didn't like the suspicious scrutiny.

Chapter 9

When Charlie and Joe returned to the Intercontinental, Major Blankston was waiting impatiently in the lobby. "Mr. Stanek, please come with me," he said, standing at the door to greet them. "I must know what you've been up to today. And what's with the Jap cop?" he asked, watching the military vehicle disappear up the crowded street.

"He's assisting us with the investigation, Major," Charlie said. He followed Major Blankston to his hotel room. Entering, he saw that it was strewn with papers and ammo, mostly boxes of .45 caliber. The embankment commander swept a corner of the bed with his arm. Loose papers went flying. He sat down and indicated a single chair in the room. "Please, sit down. We need to talk."

Charlie sat on the chair facing Blankston. The continuous street noise roared outside the closed balcony door. A table fan hummed monotonously on the desk, ruffling the papers but, doing little to moderate the stifling heat. Blankston held a rolled-up copy of the *Los Angeles Times* in his hand to swat flies.

Charlie quietly watched Blankston swing the paper. Yellowed and badly torn, it appeared to be at least several weeks old. 'MacArthur ... Tokyo Bay,' was the partial headline he saw. He figured it had something to do with the formal surrender of the Japanese back in early September.

"What's the status of your investigation, Stanek?" the major asked, swatting a fly off his knee.

Charlie quickly briefed him on the day's events, including every detail of Major Hiroaka's crime scene investigation. "Unless it's washed up onshore somewhere and we find it... Well, we may never retrieve Dixon's body, sir," he said.

"Beer?"

"Thank you."

"It's warm, I'm afraid," the major said, opening a brown bottle with his C-ration opener. He handed the bottle to Charlie. The beer frothed over but Charlie took a deep swallow anyway. The major watched, seemingly amused. "What's your next move then, Major Stanek?"

Charlie wiped his mouth with the back of his hand and shrugged. "I still have a couple of leads to follow before I can wrap it up."

"Like what?" Major Blankston asked, taking a deep swallow of his own beer.

"I need to talk with Dixon's contacts both in Saigon and outside the city – the men he met in the days before he died. Somewhere between Bien Hoa and Dalat, I gather. And, of course, the diamonds. What do you know about them, Major?"

"Not a damn thing," the Embankment Team Commander replied and took another deep swallow from his bottle.

"Nothing?" Charlie watched the other man. His response surprised him.

"First time I knew anything about them was when we opened the pouch."

"I'm assuming the diamonds had something to do with Dixon's being out in the country for three days. But is it routine for the Embankment Team Commander to head off on a mission without his second knowing why?"

The major finished the beer and belched loudly. "Dixon told me he was meeting with a Frenchman up on his rubber plantation."

"Why go there?"

"He told me that the planter was very influential with both the Vietnamese and the other French colonials in the area. Dixon was working with the British to stabilize the situation here in Cochin."

"What about diamonds?"

"No mention of any diamonds," Major Blankston said with a shrug. "If you like, I'll arrange for Sergeant Catledge to take you to both Gracey and LeClerc's headquarters. Probably won't learn much, but it's good to touch bases anyway." He opened two more beers with an opener hanging from his neck on his dog tag chain. He handed Charlie another one. They both caught the froth by placing their mouths over the opening.

"Thanks." Charlie took a big swig. The warm beer bubbled in his throat as it went down, not doing much to quench his thirst, but at least it was wet.

"One more thing, Stanek. It's not wise, since you're an important guest of ours, to go off by yourself with the natives. A good way to get yourself killed. No way we could help you," the major said slowly. "Especially if you have a run-in with the commies."

"Sorry," Charlie said with a shrug. "But I can take care of myself."

"I'm sure you can," Major Blankston said, watching him closely. "Had some experience working for yourself? Undercover?"

"A little."

"The short dossier I got on you, and I had to really work to even get that," he commented, "said..."

"Who the hell authorized you to look in my file, Major?"

"Sorry, but I had to know. Anyway, don't get all in a tizzy. All I learned is that you speak Russian and served in the European theater. And I think that was fed to me."

"Donovan wanted you to know that, eh?"

"Maybe," he said and took a long swallow of his beer. "You know about the commies, eh?"

"I know a little," Charlie said. "I think they're all different. I worked with the Czechs and Russians. Not the Vietnamese."

"They good fighters, those commies?"

"Pretty good. Tough. But if you saw what the Germans did to them, I wager you'd fight like hell, too."

"Hmm, yeah."

"What do you know of my mission, Major?" Charlie asked. He needed to know.

"Not very damn much. I've been ordered to give you my fullest cooperation. That's it."

"Good," Charlie said, giving Blankston a hard look. "And I'll expect just that."

"Who you think you're talking to?" the major replied, sounding irritated. "I'll do my job, Stanek. See that you do yours. I worked with Mac's intelligence boys for three years, so I know the routine here in East Asia." He opened another beer but didn't offer one to his guest.

"I understand."

Major Blankston appeared to be looking out the window but was, in fact, eyeing him closely. "I have to know what I'm gettin' involved in, don't I?" Major Blankston asked, finally turning to face Charlie.

"I've told you," Charlie said, sucking down the last of his second beer. When he finished it, he set it with the others on the cluttered desk. He stood and prepared to leave. "And anything else I tell you is on a need-to-know basis. You know the routine."

"Stanek, you're kinda high-strung, aren't you?" Major Blankston said.

"Major, I'm here to accomplish a mission, one of the highest priority," Charlie said, looking down on the other man. "And it will be done right."

"Right. The Army way." He held up the bottle of beer. "Cheers to that."

"My way," Charlie replied evenly. "And if you have no further questions?"

"Just one more thing, Mr. Stanek," Major Blankston said, a slight slur in his voice.

"Yeah?"

"An undercover American intelligence officer sent straight from Washington to snoop around, asking questions about the death of one soldier ... one damn soldier. Someone might think you're up to something. Are you?" he asked determined.

"I'm investigating Dixon's death. No more, no less, and like I said, anything more I tell you is on a need-to-know basis. Orders."

"Right, just as I thought," the major said with a smile, holding up the half-empty beer. "Oh, before I forget. Be nice to Sergeant Catledge. I think you hurt his feelings by leaving him behind today."

"I'll try to remember that," Charlie said from the corridor. He was relieved to be free of the small, desperately hot room.

Chapter 10

Charlie and Joe left for the rubber plantation run by the Frenchman, Rene Bocquât, early in the morning. Charlie sat quietly in the passenger seat of the jeep, thinking about what he would ask the Frenchman. He'd been told Bocquât was one of the last people to see Dixon alive and had apparently assisted him in some way on his still vague mission to the north.

The road to Xuan Loc – Route One – was open and free of mines, but British roadblocks still slowed them down. Charlie saw heavy civilian traffic, mostly bicycles and pedestrians, along with a few military vehicles from any of the armies now in the Saigon area. The plantation, a hundred acres of rubber trees, was just outside of town. After a couple of dead ends, and with the aid of a French-speaking Vietnamese, they finally found it. By mid-morning, they were passing through neatly manicured groves of rubber trees.

The plantation appeared to be untouched by the war. Charlie had never seen rubber trees before, and the sight of workers in their conical straw hats tapping the trees and collecting the sap from the small cups interested him.

"It takes a lot of workers to run a plantation this size," Joe commented as they reached the main house.

"Who gets the rubber?" Charlie asked.

"Michelin," Joe replied. "Who else?"

A middle-aged European man, slightly stooped and leaning on a cane, stood on the large veranda, waiting to greet them. He wore a large wide-brimmed Panama hat and a light silk shirt, both contrasting sharply with the man's deeply tanned skin. He was thin except for a paunch that pressed against the silk. He smoked a cigar.

"Ahh, Sergeant, *bon jour*," he said, grasping Catledge's hand before he stepped out of the jeep. "And you, sir, are...?" he asked, grabbing Charlie's hand and holding it tightly.

Charlie found himself looking at piercing blue eyes deep set in the small man's leathery brown face. "Charles Stanek, representing the Allied Control Commission for President Truman," he said.

"Mr. Stanek, this is *Monsieur* Bocquât," Joe said as an introduction. They shook hands.

"Welcome to my home, Mr. Stanek," the older man said with a slight bow. He continued to stare intently at Charlie. "Come in, come in. You must have a thirst, no?"

"Yes," Joe said.

"*Oui.* I know this about you," Bocquât said, slapping Catledge on the back.

"Truc, come, come," he called to an attractive Vietnamese woman who stood shyly in the doorway. "*Vin* for my guests, *s'il vous plaît.*"

She obeyed immediately without speaking.

"Sit down here," the Frenchman said, pointing to wicker chairs surrounding a large mahogany coffee table. The room with its dark mahogany paneling and deep-grained wood floors had a masculine feel. An oil painting of a Parisian street scene with the Eiffel Tower in the background hung on one wall. Bookshelves filled with bound volumes lined another. The rest of the room featured large open windows, three to a wall. A fan rotated slowly from the ceiling. Charlie and Joe sat down on the creaking but sturdy chairs. Bocquât joined them, sitting down to face them.

The woman quickly returned with an open bottle of wine, a pitcher of water, and six glasses on a serving tray. She set the tray down, bowed, and left the room. "My wife Truc, gentlemen." He poured water from the pitcher and handed each of them a filled glass.

"*Merci*," Joe said. He drank the water in several large swallows. Charlie sipped.

"*Monsieur* Stanek, when did you arrive here?" Rene Bocquât asked.

"Only two days ago ... from the Philippines."

"You are new then," he said slowly. "Will your work keep you here very long?"

"No, I expect to be on my way back to the States in several days. But we'll see."

"*Oui?* Do you come to assist the sergeant and the other Americans?" he asked with an open curiosity.

"Yes."

"So far, what do you think of my *Indochine*, eh?" the Frenchman asked with a wink. "Thanks to you Americans, we are finally rid of the Japanese. Yes, gentlemen, the last few years have been very difficult. The bastards. They came to my home only once, gentlemen. Once to demand that I sell only to them. I tell them to go to hell. I sell on the market."

"What did they do then?" Charlie asked, curious. *Of course, during the war, the Japanese controlled the world's rubber market, so he did sell only to them,* he thought, wondering if the man was mostly bluster.

"Then?" Rene said. "I had no problems until they seized the government from Vichy. They threatened to punish me if I did not obey them. My eldest son was imprisoned in Saigon for six months and tortured by those savages, eh? But I never gave in. I take my latex and destroy it. They arrest me – house arrest for five months. Then the war end. *Viva la France!*"

"You've had quite an ordeal," Charlie said.

"*Oui,*" he responded. "But yet, this is paradise, I think."

"I've been here only a very short time, *Monsieur* Bocquât, but it is an interesting place, and very beautiful. I'm beginning to understand why it has been fought over by so many."

"Soon General LeClerc will have his army here, and then we'll have our pearl back securely within our grasp," he said, visibly excited. "You know Saigon is our pearl, don't you? *Oui?*"

"The Vietnamese seem to have different ideas, sir," Charlie said, not wanting to provoke an argument. He wondered if this man represented the end of an era, or the vanguard of a new one. Charlie quickly remembered the determination and growing military capabilities of the Vietnamese that he had seen in Vung Tau. He decided it could easily be the former.

"Ha! Bandits! They are all bandits. Troublemakers." The cigar trembled between Rene's fingers. "Most natives desire the protection of France," he said, visibly agitated.

Joe poured wine for all three while the Frenchman spoke. "To the end of a horrible, bloody war," he toasted. "*Vive la France!*" Rene Bocquât proclaimed again loudly. Charlie and Joe echoed the toast, but more softly. The Frenchman smiled and drank his wine heartily. He filled the glasses again. "To Colonel Rolly Dixon, a brave soldier who will be missed." He held his glass high.

"Here, here," Joe replied enthusiastically, holding up his glass to touch Bocquât's.

"To Colonel Dixon," Charlie repeated, holding up his glass.

"Now, gentlemen, how can I assist you?" Bocquât asked.

"I'm trying to retrace Colonel Dixon's steps in the days before his death. That is, who he spoke with, what he was doing," Charlie explained slowly. "I understand *monsieur*, that you were one of the last to speak with him."

Truc brought in another bottle of wine, already opened.

Rene paused a moment to collect his memories while filling their glasses again. He closed his eyes to think. "Yes, three days before, I think," he said much more softly. "I helped him."

"Helped him?"

"*Oui*. I arranged for him to go to Dalat, north of here, in the mountains." He drank deeply from the glass. "He told me he must go to Dalat. 'Top secret,' he said, eh?"

"Did he tell you why?" Charlie asked and looked at Joe. He hoped he had found a break in the investigation.

"He says, 'Rene, it is a secret mission.' So I do not ask more. I find a man he can trust to take him to Dalat and bring him back. A Frenchman, eh?"

"A Frenchman? Who?"

"My friend, Andre Deloz. We come to *Indochine* together after the Great War. In 1919, we come here when we are discharged from the Army. He can be trusted and he is very loyal to me."

"I would like to speak with him. He would know where Dixon went, and maybe he knows who he met there. Where does your friend live?"

The Frenchman poured each another glass from the bottle. "My friend Andre is a poor man, yes? He lost his property during the World Depression. The bankers took all of it because of debts. He now lives alone in Xuan Loc. I can help him because we are friends, *non*? But he is a very proud man."

"Can you take me to him? Now?"

"I can do this, *Monsieur* Stanek," Rene said with a wink. "But first we must eat. Truc," he called. The woman reentered the room carrying a tray with three steaming cotton cloths. Two female servants followed her. "For cleaning your fingers, eh?" Rene said as Truc handed each man a cloth with bamboo tongs.

The servants set dishes with small fried rolls, large prawns, and sauces on the table. Truc filled each glass with more wine.

"How do we eat this?" Charlie asked, taken aback by the great bounty he saw spread out on the table. When he was briefed on Vietnam in the Philippines, he was told that famine gripped the country, a condition blamed on Japanese exploitation. *Rene certainly isn't starving*, he thought.

"With these, *monsieur*," Rene said good-naturedly, holding up his chopsticks. "Here, I show you. But it is not impolite to eat with your fingers." Meanwhile, the two servants brought more dishes as Truc supervised proudly. Beautifully painted ceramic plates held chicken, chopped into small pieces, and a steamed leafy green vegetable. Charlie thought it might be spinach. Steaming rice and three bowls with a noodle broth were finally squeezed onto the table.

Charlie watched Rene closely for clues on how to eat the food. "Like this, my friends," Rene said, placing the rice, a piece of chicken, a green leaf, and a bit of the red sauce into the bowl of broth and noodles. "We call this *pho*." After Charlie and Joe figured out how to use the chopsticks, they ate ravenously. Truc completed the meal with fresh pineapple and mangoes arranged as a lotus flower.

When they finished, Rene offered cigars and the three of them sat and smoked in silence. Finally, reaching for his cane, Rene said, "Now, we go."

"Good," Charlie said, looking to his sergeant. Joe nodded, cigar hanging from his lips.

The old man, cigar still in hand, took up a wide-brimmed straw hat and led the way to the jeep.

"When did you last see your friend, Rene?" Charlie asked as they walked to the jeep.

"Oh, I must think," Rene replied, getting in the passenger side. Charlie jumped in the back. "I think when he returned from Dalat after taking your colonel to Bien Hoa. Yes, strange."

"Strange? Why is that strange?" Charlie asked as the jeep roared down the long driveway through the groves of trees.

"Before, he comes to my house often. Two, three days a week. We play chess, you see," he said, turning to Charlie. "I don't see him this week. I think, 'hmm.'"

"Is that unusual?"

"When he returned from his trip with Colonel Dixon, we talk," Rene said, excited. "Andre said the colonel met with a Japanese war criminal. He tells me there were spies about. Yes, he felt their eyes everywhere. 'Spying on the American?' I ask him."

"Who were the spies?" Charlie asked.

"They were Vietnamese. But Andre did not think the Vietnamese spied on him and the American colonel. He said he believed that they also want this war criminal, but no one can harm him because this Japanese can buy protection in Dalat from other Japanese soldiers."

"What was this Jap criminal's name, Rene?" Charlie asked.

"I don't believe he said the name to me."

"Anything else?"

"Yes, one more thing." Rene paused to think. "Andre said soon he has enough money to pay off all his debts. I say, 'Andre, what do you mean?' And he tells me that a big deal was made between the American and the Jap war criminal. He said he was paid well for his help."

"Did he say what the deal was?" Charlie asked.

"He said only 'diamonds.'" Rene looked at the sergeant. "Hurry my friend! Hurry!" He tapped the cane against the door panel as if to make the jeep move faster. "I do not see my friend for two weeks. Oh, I am so stupid. I do not see that Andre is in danger."

Joe downshifted to make the turn onto the highway. Flooring it again, he shifted with a jerk, narrowly missing a young woman carrying wrapped bundles balanced on a pole from her shoulders. The red dust from the road blew over her.

"Stop! Here!" Rene said, pointing at a roadside café.

Joe slammed on the brakes, pitching all three of them forward.

"*Allons*," the Frenchman said, jumping out of the vehicle and rushing across the road. Charlie and Joe followed. He led them between two cinderblock and thatch-roof buildings, down a narrow alley.

Charlie noticed the Vietnamese men at a nearby cafe watching them with interest while they smoked and drank their green tea. The appearance of foreigners would no doubt give them something to talk about for several days.

"This is where Andre lives," Rene said, tapping on the wood door of an older brick home with his cane. "Andre, *Andre, vien. C'est Rene, mon ami.*" There was no answer. Rene tried again.

Finally, hearing the noise, an old woman came to an open doorway next to Andre's room. Stooping slightly and leaning against the doorframe, she observed them without saying a word. Her dark eyes, inset in her broad face, watched them closely, but she looked down each time they looked over to her.

Watching her, Charlie saw the deep wrinkles that furrowed her cheeks and forehead. Her faded black hair, streaked with gray, was pulled back tightly and tied in a knot. He thought she looked much older than she probably was. "Ask the woman, Rene," he finally said. "She might know something of value."

"*Oui,* of course," Rene replied. He spoke to her in Vietnamese, asking where Andre was. She answered him promptly. Rene then translated. "The old woman says Andre left with one suitcase about twelve days ago. He did not say where he was going or when he would return."

The woman smiled and nodded politely, revealing purple teeth stained from years of lacquering to enhance a beauty that had now faded.

"Is that unusual?" Charlie asked.

"*Oui,*" he answered quickly. "Andre, you have left without even a farewell to me, your *vieux copain,*" he cried with great emotion. "How can that be?"

Charlie said nothing for a moment, and then asked, "What else can she tell us?" He wanted to get into the room for a look. He studied the door.

Rene spoke to the woman. She listened closely, then answered him. She gestured with her hands as she spoke. He translated: "She say another Frenchman come a week ago looking for him. The man was not a soldier. He was dressed in a suit. Very handsome, she says to me, eh? And in a big black car with a Vietnamese driver."

"What else?"

The woman shrugged when Rene asked her the question. "That is all she knows about Andre," he said. "She says he does not owe her money." He lit his half-smoked cigar again and blew smoke from his lungs. An old hen, huddled in the deserted doorway to Andre's room, clucked and flapped its wings to get out of their way.

As Rene, Charlie, and Joe stood in front of the locked door to the room, the Vietnamese woman leaned against her doorframe, just watching them.

"I think that man must be Monsieur Bergier, a French banker in Saigon. I think it is him. He loans to planters and others at enormous rates. The *cochon*! So evil. I hate the bastard worse than the communists, I think." Rene spit. "He collaborates with the Japanese, eh? Anything for this." Rubbing his thumb and forefinger together, he held them in the air to indicate money.

"What bank?" Joe asked.

"Banque Nacional de France."

"Will she let us into his room?" Charlie asked.

Rene asked the woman politely for entrance. Charlie watched as he slipped her a *piastre* note. She nodded and pulled a key from beneath her black blouse. They stepped out of her way while she unlocked the ancient lock and opened the creaking door. The woman entered without hesitating. They followed.

The room was in complete disarray. The simple closet and dresser drawers stood open, their few contents strewn across the concrete floor. The wood-framed bed was turned upside down. The thin mattress was ripped open, straw hanging out in clumps. Angry, the old woman spoke rapidly, waving her fist in the air.

"She is cursing all foreigners ... and her dead husband for leaving her this pitiful building," Rene said indifferently, puffing his cigar.

Charlie still stood near the door. Leaning against the wall, he listened to the exchange between the Frenchman and the woman. Then, ignoring her outburst, he walked to the one window set in the rear wall. He noticed immediately that a pane was broken and the latch was undone. *Whoever searched the room entered and exited through the window,* he decided. *Probably a Vietnamese. It had to have been a Vietnamese. Anyone else would have been noticed and remembered,* he concluded. *Surely the old woman would have remembered any other foreigner snooping around.*

"Look here," he said, opening the window and peering outside. He scanned the ground and shrubs around the back of the building.

Rene and Joe walked to the window and looked out.

"Oh, what is *mon vieux*, my dear Andre, involved in?" Rene wailed.

"Let's get out of here. I've seen enough," Charlie said, looking at Joe. "Come, Rene." They left, but on the way out, Charlie slipped the old woman a five-dollar bill. "Tell her thank you for assisting the United States government in its investigation." Rene spoke to her, explaining.

Appearing to recognize the currency, she accepted it with a smile and bowed graciously, thanking him. Her anger quickly evaporated. She closed Andre's door without locking it and returned to her own doorway to watch them leave.

"Sarge, sure are a lot of pieces missing here," Charlie said, sitting in the lobby of the Intercontinental, watching Joe drink the last of his bourbon. He suspected Joe was holding something back. Charlie also knew he had to get on the sergeant's good side to get any answers. And if plying him with good bourbon was what it took, then so be it.

"You're tryin' too hard," Joe replied. "Jus' a poor Frenchie skippin' out for a better life somewhere else, now that the war is over. Probably no connection."

Charlie stared hard at him. "From what Rene said, Andre was working with Dixon on something. It sounds to me like Dixon, and maybe even the Vietnamese, were after the same thing. Diamonds?"

"Could be," the sergeant responded with a shrug, still enjoying the whiskey.

"Give me some help here, Catledge," Charlie said, beginning to lose patience. "This is an official investigation. Remember that."

"Listen, Major, I don't want no trouble," Joe said. "'Three more months, and I'm out of here. Back to the States. I don't need any cops-and-robbers shit. You understand?" He gave out a long sigh and finished his drink. "If you were smart, you'd wrap this thing up and get the hell out of here. Who the hell cares what happens way out here? You must have something to go back to. A girl? A hometown?"

"Right now, I have nothing better to do than sit in a hotel on the far side of the world and pump you for information. So give it to me."

"Pitiful, just pitiful," Joe said, shaking his head. "That sounds like my life back in California. I had a girl, though. So I guess I'm one up on you."

"You're not helping, Sergeant," Charlie replied. "You know more about Dixon's mission than you're telling me."

"I think you need to learn more about Dixon's background."

"Why don't you fill me in?"

"He was a Jap interrogator. Fluent in the language. He joined MacArthur's staff in Australia and stayed with him all the way to Manila. Was working there when the war ended. He was tracking war criminals for some big trial next year."

"I already know all that. It was in his record file. Tell me something I don't know," Charlie said. Anger had replaced impatience.

"Okay," Joe said defensively. "Let me think a minute."

"Do you think that Dixon's investigation of war criminals here in Indochina may be related to his death ... and with the mysterious diamonds?"

"Listen, I happen to know there are a lot of Japs they haven't rounded up yet, that they want to interrogate on suspicion of war crimes. Couple of real bad prisons here in Indochina. One is the Saigon Prison just around the corner from where we're sitting, and another one up north in the central highlands, at a place called Plei Toan. It is northwest of a French outpost at Pleiku."

"Keep talking. I'm listening," Charlie said.

"Remember Captain Suzuki that Jap cop mentioned?"

"I remember the name, yeah."

"He's the war criminal Rene mentioned. I know for a fact that he ordered the execution of six downed American flyers. Hell, had 'em shot even before they reached the POW camp. Dixon told me that's why he had to take him in. Suzuki was right at the top of his Indochina list. The Vietnamese called him the Butcher of Saigon. Everyone wants to get his hands on him. Dead or alive, it doesn't seem to matter...And Dixon told me himself that the man deserved to be hung."

"You think he's the man Dixon met with up in Dalat?"

"All I know is that Dixon had a meeting with the Japanese G-2 of the Southern Army, Colonel Imano, a day before he headed north. Imano called him to his office. Said it was urgent. You know, 'Important intelligence information.'"

"And?"

"That same day, Dixon told me only that he had to go to Dalat first thing in the morning ... alone. That he was meeting with the commander of the Japanese detachment there, I think. Imano may have told him that Suzuki or one of the others was at the Japanese garrison in Dalat."

"Joe, you still know more than you're telling me," Charlie said, pressing. "What is it?"

Joe considered. "Okay. I knew he was up to something. When he wouldn't take me along, I figured there was something else with Suzuki, something more than catching a war criminal. To bring him back here, he would have needed support. Too much for one man. He never requested it, so I knew something else was going on. I just didn't know what it was."

"Did you figure it out?"

"I didn't like Colonel Dixon much. I was his driver, and even in three weeks you can learn a lot about a man, driving for him every day."

"What did you learn?"

"Dixon wasn't easy to get along with. He didn't like me much, and the feeling was mutual. You understand?"

"I think so. Go on."

"He always seemed distracted. He seemed to me to have little interest in our mission here. Even Major Blankston commented on that. The guy stayed to himself, never had much contact even with the other Americans here."

"Was that a problem?"

Joe shrugged. "It created some tension. He acted like a man with a lot of secrets that he didn't want the rest of us to know.

From the moment we got off the plane and probably before we left Clark Airfield, it seemed like he was chasing something."

"How do you know that?"

"Just a hunch from the way he acted, but it makes sense when I think about it," the sergeant said. "He had a short list of Japanese suspected of war crimes, but he was primarily interested in Captain Suzuki. He had me drive him around, looking for anything he could dig up on this Suzuki and his whereabouts. He wrote everything down in his journal, and he took that journal everywhere"

"Journal? I haven't seen any journal."

"It's gone, too. Maybe it's under the Saigon River with his body."

"What do you think it all meant? Couldn't he have been just doing his job, collecting evidence on all the suspects for a trial?"

"Maybe, but I don't think so."

"Why not?"

"I asked him once if he was after other Japs wanted for war crimes here in Saigon. He told me they weren't important to him. Someone else would get them eventually. He was after one Jap in particular – Captain Suzuki."

"Did you ask to go with him to Dalat?"

"I sure did. Just going off on your own was not the way we were doing things here. Too damn dangerous," Joe said.

"What did he tell you?"

"Hell, I don't remember it word for word, but he said that going alone was the only way he could travel north without attracting attention. Any more foreigners traveling up there, and the Japs, the Vietnamese – hell, anyone – would know about it long before we ever arrived in Dalat. Surprise was important to him. He even got a set of civvies to wear as a disguise, as a French businessman. I know it sounds strange. But, hell, he was in command."

"And you accepted that explanation?"

Joe stopped talking and paused a moment before replying. "Major Stanek, I follow orders. What else could I do?"

"What did Blankston say about his plan?"

"Dixon made me swear not to tell him or anyone on the team. So, I didn't."

"Where did they think he was?"

"Onboard ship, working with the British. I heard him tell Major Blankston that he would be out on one of the Brits' destroyers anchored in the Saigon River. He said he was working with Major Clifton, their intelligence officer. No one was suspicious until I had to go pick him up, and the Vietnamese chose that day to try to seize the damn city," Joe said. "Blankston almost had a heart attack when I told him I had to drive to Bien Hoa to pick Dixon up. That was our designated rendezvous site – where Andre dropped him off after they returned from the trip north to Dalat."

"Dixon's behavior was unusual. His record file suggests he had a very good career in the Army, no problems of any kind. He appeared to be a man who followed orders, not real independent," Charlie replied, trying hard to put it together.

"I wouldn't know much about that."

"You could have told me all this yesterday."

"Hey, I'm just putting in the last couple of months, and then it's back to the States for my discharge. The last thing I want is to get bogged down in some high-level investigation. I thought you might strand me out here." He shrugged apologetically. "I figured I'd just play the GI bit, shuffle you around until you were satisfied you had enough for a report to Washington, then put you back on the plane."

"I understand you, I guess," Charlie said, not taking offense. "What the hell do you care about some report to Washington, eh?"

"It won't bring Dixon back, will it?" Joe replied. "And it won't get me home any sooner."

"And Andre, Rene's friend?" Charlie asked. "Tell me what you know about his role in all this."

"Andre was Dixon's driver and translator, nothing more. That's what I was told." Joe smiled and took a belt of his remaining bourbon. "You don't give up, do you?"

"Not easily." Charlie folded his hands in his lap and studied Joe. "Tell me the rest."

"Dixon paid him well, of course, for his services."

"To go alone without a backup when you had so many unknowns?" Charlie massaged his forehead gently, thinking it through. "How was he to contact you in an emergency?"

"Through the French. They have a good network here, especially south of Tourane."

"Did Dixon think the Japs would help him apprehend Suzuki?"

"He expected their full cooperation. Orders from MacArthur's headquarters state that all assets will be used, and that means Japanese airplanes, vehicles, and troops, if necessary. Dixon knew he could use them to transport prisoners back to Saigon and deliver them over to British troops. Tracking war criminals is a high priority for all Allied commands, so using Japanese troops easily fit in Dixon's plan. And they have no choice in the matter."

"How much of this did Rene know about?"

"Only what Andre told him," Joe said. "And you heard him."

"Do you think he may have suspected what Dixon was up to?"

"Anything is possible. The French colonials here are a small but incestuous bunch. Hard to keep secrets from."

"So now we have a dead American, his French accomplice gone without a trace, seventy-five thousand in diamonds from an unknown source, and no Jap war criminal. We don't even have Dixon's body to send to Manila."

"Yeah, that's about the long of it, Major Stanek. Is it still home before Christmas, you think?" Joe asked, polishing off his bourbon.

Chapter 11

The next morning, Charlie and Joe stood in a sandy field on the outskirts of the city. The sun had just broken through the cloud cover, but the smell of rain still hung in the dense air. They were surrounded by mostly Gurkha troops of the 20th Indian Division, which, Charlie was informed, had arrived in August to receive the Japanese surrender in Indochina.

Charlie said, "Major Blankston has scheduled us to meet with..." He consulted a slip of paper and read from it. "N. H. Chatham-Brown, Political Advisor to Major General Douglas Gracey, the commanding officer appointed by Lord Mountbatten, SEAC Supreme Commander, to head the Allied Control Commission in Indochina." He looked at Joe. "I think I got that right. So, Sarge, tell me again who this guy is."

"Chatham-Brown's the general's political advisor. Supposed to have a grasp of the political situation here in Saigon and the colonel's death may have something to do with politics, eh? Maybe he can explain what's going on 'round here for you."

"Good. I need some answers."

Joe led Charlie toward a dilapidated two-story villa. The British flag flew in front. Two Gurkha soldiers in crisply pressed uniforms stood at attention just outside the entrance. Charlie looked around at the military activity. An early morning cloudburst had turned the area into a sea of red mud pockmarked by pools of water. Deep ruts cut through the mud where tracked vehicles had passed.

They were greeted at the heavy wood front door and escorted in by a turbaned Sikh master sergeant. At the top of the steps, he led them into a small room. There, a tall lean man dressed in a pressed white shirt over khaki trousers greeted them. A British military officer stood beside him. Radio equipment, bound folders, and metal boxes were stacked on the desk and on a small table under the window. Charlie saw loose documents scattered about. The place had a general appearance of chaos.

"Thank you, Sergeant," the British officer said. The Sikh gave him a quick but snappy salute, stamping his foot, then turned and left without a word.

Both Charlie and Joe saluted the major. He reciprocated. "Gentlemen, please sit down. I'm Major Clifton, and this is Mr. Chatham-Brown, our political officer here." He looked at the civilian, who offered a clipped smile.

Charlie sat in a nearby chair, and Joe did the same. "Gentlemen, I'm Major Charles Stanek, representing President Truman on the Allied Control Commission, and this is my associate, Sergeant Joe Catledge, from the mission here in Saigon," he said, trying to sound official and mask his inexperience at diplomacy. "As you know, we're investigating the death of Lieutenant Colonel Roland Dixon, the mission commander killed during the recent disturbance with the Annamese. We have questions about the circumstances surrounding his death. Questions that I hope you can help me with."

Charlie didn't know much about the role of the British in Indochina and didn't have much experience working with them. He had spent two days in Gibraltar on his way back to the States, but most of that time he was sleeping, something he hadn't done much of while fighting in Eastern Europe. They had offered him a bed with a real mattress, and he, of course, couldn't refuse, even though it was inside the 'Rock' itself. For two years he had slept on the ground, on horseback, even in trees, but seldom in a bed. "I have a couple of questions and won't..."

Before he could finish speaking, the civilian, Chatham-Brown, spoke. "Major Stanek, I've been assigned by the P.M. to get this business with the Japanese over and provide some sort of political stability, so that things can eventually return to normal. That is, so civilian government can again be implemented here in Indochina." He studied Charlie, much like a college professor would a new student, which Charlie immediately resented. "I've asked Major Clifton to join us. He is our chief war crimes officer with the Allied Control Commission. He had corresponded extensively with Lieutenant Colonel Dixon. I thought, under the circumstances, he would be able to offer some information and insight with regard to your assignment."

Charlie kept his gaze on Chatham-Brown.

"I see from your face, Major Stanek, that you are confused."

"Mr. Chatham-Brown, I have been informed that Dixon was involved in the investigation of war crimes." Charlie looked hard at Joe, then back to the two Brits. "I have learned that he was tracking Japs here in Vietnam. But I've never been briefed on the extent to which we are trying to capture war criminals. Or how many there are to be caught."

"Major Stanek, I think we can provide some clarification on this matter," Chatham-Brown said patiently. An Indian private brought in a tray with tea and four small porcelain cups. "Tea, gentlemen?" he asked.

"Yeah, thank you," Joe answered for the two.

"Major Clifton worked closely with him on this very important issue. I'll let him explain our collaboration with Lieutenant Colonel Dixon."

"Dixon was my contact on General MacArthur's staff," Major Clifton began. "We have been involved in collecting statements and gathering names of Japanese who are suspected of committing war crimes against Allied soldiers. As a matter of fact, we have compiled quite a list of criminals still loose in Indochina. We continued that collaboration here in Saigon and met several times, actually."

"What was the result of that collaboration, sir?" Charlie asked.

"There are several Japs here in Indochina we should very much like to get our hands on. Would you like us to provide you with a copy of our list?"

"Yes, please," Charlie answered. "Anyone in particular who Dixon was interested in?" He sipped the tea and found it too sweet.

Clifton paused briefly. "Mostly we discussed the camps here. Try to understand that, with so many different armies here and with the local population demanding their independence, it has been difficult to focus our resources on criminals. It has been difficult enough just to maintain order here in Saigon. "

"I understand, Major."

"In Indochina, we currently have troops from three armies filling a power vacuum left by the Japanese. Five, if we count your detachment and that of the Russians. Everyone seems to be pursuing their own national agendas. Well, as you can see, the possibility of the criminal element slipping away is high, very high. Maintaining harmonious relations among all has proved a trifle difficult, I'm afraid," Clifton said.

"In Saigon, we have found ourselves in a very tenuous situation, one that escalated into serious fighting last month. The British Army is responsible for this region up to the 16th Parallel under the agreement forged at Potsdam. We have sixty thousand Jap troops who we have not disarmed. We've ordered them to assist us on many of the day-to-day details of keeping order here. There are two hundred thousand Chinese rampaging through the northern provinces of this country. When we arrived, we released thousands of French soldiers who had been imprisoned by the Japs. Unfortunately, the French, mostly Legionnaires, wasted no time seeking revenge, mostly on the Annamese here, and forcefully asserting what they believe to be their 'rights.' The Annamese, of course, disagree most vehemently. The Vietnamese want independence, the French want their colony back, and God alone knows what the Chinese intend. As we speak, General LeClerc continues his buildup of French forces. Any spark could set the whole damned mess off. It's our responsibility to put the fires out. We must keep these groups separated and maintain some sort of order. I hope I haven't sounded too dreadfully pessimistic, but we must face reality."

"I understand your position, Major. Anything else you could tell me that we might find helpful? Names of people that Dixon contacted? That sort of thing?" *The man sounds frustrated and a bit overwhelmed*, Charlie thought. Still, he expected their full cooperation with his mission.

"He mentioned a Japanese prison guard," Clifton said. "What was his name? Oh yes, Captain Suzuki, I think."

"What about this Suzuki, Major?" Charlie asked. "This man's name keeps popping up." He wondered if they were going to mention Suzuki's diamonds.

"Yes, well, we talked at great length regarding Suzuki. Dixon appeared to have rather a special interest in tracking him. But I didn't have much information to share, I'm afraid."

"Were you able to assist him in any way?"

"Assistance? Yes, we provided all we could give, sir," the major said. "We've been quite shorthanded. I must say, Major Stanek, we had our hands full last month just putting out fires.

No time left for chasing war criminals through the jungle. Wouldn't you say, Mr. Chatham-Brown?"

"Yes, quite so. A dreadful affair, that. And I'm afraid, Mr. Stanek, we just do not have the troops to do those things. But, in due course."

"What information did you provide Colonel Dixon that could have assisted him in his mission? Can you recall? It is very important to my investigation."

"Not much, I'm afraid. I did suggest that he contact certain Japanese intelligence agents here in Saigon. Those with the Southern Army. The Japs have been very helpful so far. And he spoke very passable Japanese."

"Do you think he contacted them?"

"I am told he did."

"Who did he contact?"

"Members of Colonel Imano's staff – G2," he said. "It's not a big city. And after the fighting last month, we've made it a point to know what's going on here."

"Major, what do you know about Dixon's mission to Dalat?"

"I assisted him with maps, who to contact, that sort of thing, so that he could conclude his mission without problems. He also requested current intelligence on the Jap detachment up there. But I'm afraid that's about the extent of British involvement."

"Sir, he did not tell you when he was traveling to that city, when he was returning, or anything about what he was going to do there?"

"No, Mr. Stanek, he did not."

"Thank you, sir. You've been very helpful." Charlie figured he had gotten about as much as he was going to get out of the two.

"Wait," Chatham-Brown said. He stood and leaned against the desk. "I think you may be pursuing rather a dead end here. Your man was killed during heavy fighting between our forces and local Annamese insurgents. Before reaching any conclusions, you must consider the military situation in Cochin as it existed in late September."

"You're right, sir. And I greatly appreciate your briefing," Charlie replied.

"The current situation has not much improved, so I would caution you on travel into the country."

"We will certainly heed your advice, sir." Charlie turned to Joe. "Well, Sergeant, we don't want to take up any more of their time. Let's get moving."

"Brigandage and disorders of all sorts have increased here in Cochin. All roads leading out of Saigon are considered unsafe. The French blame the Viet Minh, the Japs, and former convicts," Chatham-Brown continued.

"Do you believe that, sir?" Charlie asked, turning again to face the British civilian.

"They are partially responsible, of course, but the French must share part of the blame, certainly."

"Everyone seems to believe the French plan to reoccupy the country."

"I have no doubt, Mr. Stanek. But it is British policy to mediate between the French and the Annamese so that they can agree on an acceptable form of government. But first we must have a semblance of law and order here in Saigon and Cholon. We also need the French Army. Don't forget that."

"How will you use the French, sir?" Joe asked.

Everyone turned to stare at the sergeant.

"Because of their experience here, they will be best suited to disarm Jap troops in the countryside – Phnom Penh, Dalat, Cam Ranh Bay," Major Clifton replied, looking only at Charlie. "We simply do not, and will not, have sufficient strength to do that job." He paused briefly. "Remember, for us to retake the city last month, we were forced to fight pitched battles with well-organized Vietnamese insurgents. We fought over every major bridge. We had a disturbing number of casualties, gentlemen, and our forces here were stretched thin before the fighting erupted. Fires raged in the industrial and dock areas that alone took more than a week to extinguish. Naval oil stores were severely depleted by fire. Only recently have we been able to restore electric power and fresh water. Our army is not prepared to wage that type of warfare in Indochina. Do I make myself clear?" He still looked only at Charlie.

"Who started the fighting?" Charlie asked.

"Who?" Major Clifton repeated. "I fear it was overzealous French soldiers supporting their civilians."

"Who rearmed them?"

"Mostly their own weapons," the major continued. "Admiral Mountbatten ordered us to return their weapons to them. They are our allies, after all," he said.

"Then what happened?"

"French civilians and soldiers went on a rampage, beating up locals, destroying shops. A considerable number of Annamese were killed. Then the Viet Minh forces intervened in considerable numbers. They, of course, have their own agenda."

"What do you know about the Viet Minh, sir?" Charlie asked, directing his question at the civilian advisor.

"They are one of the strongest Vietnamese factions. In the early thirties, a number of left-wing groups united to form a single organization to fight for independence, dominated by the communists and led by a man called Ho Chi Minh. They get their marching orders via the Third International."

"Are you saying they are controlled by Moscow?"

"Yes, they take orders from our Red allies," Chatham-Brown said, sounding to Charlie like he was convinced of their politics. "They are determined communists, it would seem."

Indochina is a long way from Moscow, Charlie thought. "Did the Japs play any role in the fighting last month?"

"Ah, yes, the Japanese, our prisoners," Chatham-Brown said.

"Gentlemen, we have proof their junior officers and men are supporting the Annamese. Some have even joined their forces. The Viet Minh are now armed mostly with weapons and equipment given to them by the Japanese here," Major Clifton added. "A very dicey situation, but we must use the Japs. We have no choice. Currently, we have no one to replace them, and without their presence in the city, we would be unable to maintain any sort of control. They also know this." Charlie immediately detected the concern in his voice as he continued. "With a buildup of French troops, of course, that will change. And we've found that some of the Japs are actually trustworthy and quite efficient at their jobs."

"I see," Charlie said, filing the information away. "Mr. Chatham-Brown, Major Clifton, you have been very helpful." *Politics*, he thought.

"If there is anything else we can do to assist you, pop on in," the Chatham-Brown said.

As Charlie and Joe stood and prepared to leave, Charlie said, "Thank you. Oh, one more thing. Lieutenant Colonel Dixon was carrying thousands of dollars in diamonds when he was killed. Do you have any idea where he found them and what he was doing with them?"

The two Brits looked at each other. A momentary silence fell on the small room. "Major Stanek, I don't know anything about diamonds," Chatham-Brown stated definitively. "Do you, Major?" he asked Clifton.

"Nothing at all, sir," Major Clifton replied.

Charlie had hoped for more information on the diamonds. But it was clear that the two men knew nothing of diamonds, or were not about to give up any information they did have.

"Have you spoken with the French here, yet?" the major asked. "They may have some helpful information. I will contact Major Verger. He is attached to E Group, Allied Control Commission. I'm sure he would be more than willing to assist you with your investigation."

"Yes, thank you, sir. I'd appreciate that."

"What do you think, Sarge?" Charlie asked later during the jeep ride back to town.

"I think Dixon used the Brits for his own purposes."

"I think so, too," he said. "And they don't seem to know anything about the diamonds Dixon was carrying."

"I'm thinking that something was worked out when Dixon was in the Central Highlands ... alone," Joe added. "And he didn't bother to keep the Brits informed."

"I'm still uneasy about trusting our security here to the Japanese Army. It doesn't seem right," Charlie said as they passed a marching formation of armed Japanese soldiers.

"What choices do we have?"

"Then there's Major Hiroaka. He may prove very helpful in our investigation. I hope he stays on the case."

"Our investigation?" Joe said, giving Charlie a hard look. "The Jap is a dedicated cop. He'll stay with us unless..."

"Unless what?"

"Unless his superiors take him off it again."

"That's what I'm thinking," Charlie said. "We have to remember that members of his own army were involved with Dixon in this."

"Right," Joe said, smiling. "This isn't the States. These people think different from us, and they run things different."

"So I keep being told."

"With the Orientals, it's all about face," Joe advised.

"What?"

"Hiroaka believes it's his job to find Dixon and solve the crime. He's doing it for us. If he fails, he loses face. Keeping our respect is very important to him. I've learned that from being out here in Asia for two years."

"But his commander, on the other hand, probably doesn't give a damn about our investigation," Charlie replied. "Or he may have his own reasons for covering it up."

Joe raised his brows. "You're talking conspiracy."

"We can't rule out anyone or anything. At least not yet."

Chapter 12

It was late, well past midnight. Charlie had just lain down to try to sleep when he heard a knock at his door. "Who is it?" he asked, standing by the closed door with his .45 in hand.

"Captain Francois Beauvolet of the French *Deuxieme* Bureau. I apologize for the most dreadful hour, *monsieur,*" his late-night visitor said with a heavy French accent, "but I received word only now from Major Verger. I was told it was urgent that I speak with you, *oui*?"

"*Oui.*" Charlie opened the door cautiously and was greeted by a short thin man a few years older than himself. The man wore US Army fatigues and boots and a Vietnamese black cotton shirt with a red scarf tied loosely around his neck. A revolver was strapped to his waist. The colorful combination amused Charlie.

Captain Beauvolet stepped into the room and closed the door softly behind him. "I am now traveling to Tourane and will not return for some weeks, so..."

"Have a seat, Captain," Charlie said. He clicked the safety on his gun and offered the man the single chair in his room. "Sorry, I don't have any refreshments on hand–"

"But I do, *oui*?" Beauvolet pulled a metal flask from his shirt. "A little brandy to warm the heart on a lonely night."

Charlie smiled.

"Do tell me how I may assist you, *monsieur*."

When Charlie finished relating his earlier conversation with the British about the war crimes investigation, Beauvolet groused, "*Sacre bleu*. The English. They always know everything, even here in *Indochine* . They think they are so noble." He took a swig from his flask. "The British should stay out of *Indochine*. It belongs to us. General DeGaulle says so, *oui*?"

"Hmm, yes. But Captain?"

"Capitan Beauvolet, sir."

"Capitan Beauvolet, I'm here to investigate the death of one of our team. Did Major Verger explain that?"

"*Oui, monsieur. Monsieur...*?" he asked.

"Stanek."

"I know all about Colonel Dixon. Killed by the communists, *non*?"

"But we want to know *why* he was killed."

"Why? Why, *Monsieur* Stanek?" The Frenchman seemed surprised by the question. "Because they are communists, and you, like we French, are their enemies. The French Army is now preparing for the new struggle against the communists. We are allies."

Charlie ignored the harangue. "So you think they shot him deliberately because he was an American?"

"*Oui, mais certainment*. Why else, *monsieur*?"

"No other possibilities?" Charlie sat on his cot, clad only in cotton shorts. He studied the Frenchman. Judging by the look of him, Beauvolet had been in Indochina for a while. His skin was dark and leathery, dried out by many years in a tropical sun.

As an agent of the Deuxieme Bureau, the French equivalent of the OSS, he should have a good handle on local politics. I just hope he has ears in the street too.

"Something other than politics, *monsieur*?" the French soldier asked, a sudden look of curiosity on his face. "You have other ideas?" He paid full attention for the first time.

"We are neutral, *Capitan*, and the Annamese want our support."

"They believe they can defeat us without it, I think."

"How long have you been in Indochina?" Charlie asked, abruptly changing the subject.

"I was born in Tourane. You know the city?"

"No, never been there," he said. "How long have you worked for France?" he asked, thinking that if anyone knew anything about the diamonds, it should be him.

"Since before the war," the Frenchman answered.

"I see. And you survived the Japanese occupation?"

"As a soldier of France, my duty is to follow orders, but it was very difficult. When the Japanese took control and arrested everyone, I fled to the jungle ... in Laos. I knew the war would end eventually with the Japanese defeated."

"You fought the Japs from there?"

"I survived," he said simply. "Major Verger told me that you need information on the terrible tragedy of Colonel Dixon. That is so?"

"I want to know about diamonds, *Capitan*. Diamonds that are here in Indochina," Charlie said slowly, watching the man for a reaction.

"Diamonds? Yes, diamonds," the Frenchman replied carefully. "What do you know about diamonds?"

"It seems that Dixon was carrying about seventy-five thousand worth when he was ambushed on the streets of Saigon. I was told in Washington that they were mined here in French Indochina. What do you know about that?"

The Frenchman looked hard at him, then slowly looked around as if he were searching out other spies hidden somewhere in the small room. "That type of information is a state secret, *monsieur*," he said in a whisper.

"Not any longer, it seems."

For a very long moment, the Frenchman hesitated, saying nothing. "For almost four years we hid this valuable secret from the Japanese, but in the end, we failed. It was the Vietnamese traitors, *les sale brutes*, who tell them about *les diamants*. In April, I think. *Oui,* I know this." He paused to scratch his day-old beard. "*Les diamants*, they belong *to Industrie Colonial de France*, not the Japanese or the Vietnamese. We must protect the property of France, *non*?"

"Why do you think the Vietnamese did that?"

"Who knows why they do such things? These people are of simple minds. That is why they need us to protect them. Perhaps, *Monsieur* Stanek, they bargain with the Japanese for a deal, a share for themselves. And to harm us, eh?"

That doesn't make a lot of sense, based on what I already know about them. "Who do you mean by us, exactly?"

"French interests here, *naturellement.* When the French Army is imprisoned, my people are at the mercy of the Japanese."

"Where do the diamonds come from?"

Captain Beauvolet looked hard at Charlie. "This I do not know."

He's lying, Charlie thought but didn't say anything. "So, now that the war is over, can't you demand the Japs return them?" he asked.

"*Monsieur,*" the Frenchman said with a sigh. "When my government demands their return, the Japanese general here in *Indochine*, he say, 'I know nothing.'"

"What was the total value of the diamonds stolen?"

"I do not know such things."

Again he lies. "Which bank were they taken from, exactly?"

"*Banque Nacional de France.* In Saigon. The Japanese bastards came and took them out. We could do nothing to stop them. The criminals."

"And you think the Vietnamese told the Japanese that they were kept there?"

"*Oui.* Who else, eh?"

"They then took them and shipped them to Japan?"

"Ha!" the Frenchman said with a laugh. "To Japan? *Ma fois,* I think not. These are actions by clever thieves, not the Japanese government. The jewels are still in Vietnam. I am sure of it."

"You think those Japanese soldiers – the thieves – kept all the diamonds for themselves?"

"We believe this," the Frenchman said. "What have you discovered about the identity of these bandits, *monsieur?* Any information you can provide that can help recover this national treasure would be greatly appreciated."

"I'm sorry, *Capitan,* but I don't have anything that would help."

"I humbly request that President Truman assist us with their safe return," the Frenchman said. "What more do you know, *monsieur?* I beg you to tell me what you know."

"I know nothing that can help you, *Capitan.* But I'm sure the Americans will do all they can here to help in your own investigation," Charlie said.

"*Merci, Monsieur* Stanek."

"Is there anything else you can tell me about Colonel Dixon's death?"

"I am sorry, but no, *monsieur,*" The Frenchman said, his eyes down. "But I must warn you. The Annamese here follow the movements of foreigners very closely. They watch carefully when you travel outside this city. Maybe, they learn that your colonel had *les diamants.* It is possible that they followed him."

"Possible," Charlie repeated. "Then they killed him – ambushed him – to get hold of them? Is that what you mean?"

"Oh, *non, non,* my American friend. Tran Van Giau may have suspected that he carried valuable diamonds, but he was not killed for the crystals."

"Then why?"

"Like I tell you before, the Vietnamese have more important reasons for killing Americans. Don't you see this?"

"No, *Capitan* Beauvolet. I don't understand your meaning."

"They are communists, eh? Always, you must remember this. They want you to believe an accident, or that the Japanese are to blame for his death." He prepared to leave. "We are allies, *monsieur,* and must work together. When you have information for me, please contact me at this address." He handed a small slip of paper to Charlie. Then he was gone.

Chapter 13

"*M*onsieur Bergier, thank you for seeing us on such short notice," Charlie said as he and Joe sat down in the French banker's palatial office in his Saigon bank. His office, like the bank itself, showed no evidence that war had as recently as several weeks ago raged through the streets of Saigon. The high-ceilinged room was trimmed in mahogany with furnishings to match. In addition to clerks and guards, the banker was attended by personal servants. Charlie noted one, a younger Vietnamese man dressed in a dark suit, standing immediately behind the banker.

"*Monsieur* Stanek, I thank you," Bergier said with a bow, "for liberating France and ridding *Indochine* of those hated Japanese. We owe the Americans much."

"Yes, *Monsieur* Bergier," Charlie said, quickly sizing up the Frenchman. He guessed Bergier to be about thirty-five, with light, thinning hair that he wore long but neatly trimmed. He wore thick glasses over his watery blue eyes. Easily six feet tall, the man was impeccably dressed in a white silk suit. Shaking his hand, Charlie felt a soft fleshiness. *No dirt under this man's fingernails*, he thought. Bergier was the only European in the bank, as far as he could see. "You've done well," he said, still looking around.

"Thank you," Bergier said proudly. "I came to this wilderness fifteen years ago, just out of university in Paris. I was determined to make my fortune. I've worked very hard."

"The Japanese did not arrest you with the others, sir?"

"No, *monsieur*," he replied directly. "I am a businessman, not a soldier or government official. And I learned how to work with the Japanese."

"So it seems, *monsieur*," Charlie said. "But still, it must have been difficult with the Japanese occupation."

"The Japanese too needed the commerce that we in *Indochine* offered, *monsieur*. They needed rubber, rice, and oil. My position was to facilitate that process. And to make a profit for my bank, no? Remember, we French were not at war with the Japanese Empire until only last year."

"*Monsieur*, I wish to talk about diamonds."

"Diamonds?"

"Yes, French diamonds that were stolen from your bank earlier this year," Charlie said, not wasting any time with the banker.

Joe listened quietly to the exchange.

"You know of this terrible thing, *monsieur*? You are investigating this crime?"

"Yes, it seems a few of these gems were found," Charlie answered, watching the banker's response closely.

"I did not know of this," Bergier said, acting surprised. "It was the Japanese who did this robbery. But, of course, you already know."

"Were you here when the bank was robbed?"

"No," the banker said curtly.

"No?"

"I was at home, *monsieur.* Sick. Yes, I was ill with a sudden fever."

Charlie nodded, accepting the banker's response, although it did seem a little too convenient. "Please, *monsieur*, would you tell me the exact value of the heist?"

"Heist?" he said with a nervous smile. "The value in francs, *monsieur*, is about twenty million. I would call it a simple robbery by brigands. There is no security here to protect commerce since the end of the war. Now there is fighting everywhere and looting."

"Do you have any idea how an American soldier may have picked up a few of the diamonds?"

"An American soldier with our diamonds? Why do you ask me this? I know nothing about that," Bergier said, sounding defensive.

"Please, *monsieur*, any information you have that could aid in our investigation of the dead American would be appreciated," Charlie said. "Have more of the gems showed up in the city?"

"No, but I only know what the gendarmes and the soldiers tell me," Bergier said. "An American soldier was carrying diamonds? How?"

"We don't have an answer to that question, *monsieur*," Charlie said patiently.

"What role do you have in investigating this horrible crime? Our Council General has not contacted me. Nor has Major Hiroaka of the Japanese Army said anything to me about you, sir."

"I have been sent by the President of the United States to investigate the death of Lieutenant Colonel Rolly Dixon, United States Army. Diamonds were found with him after he was killed in the fighting last month," Charlie said. "Your full cooperation is expected, sir." Charlie clearly stressed the part about the president. He was beginning to enjoy his official duties. "I don't care what the Japanese Army has to say."

"What business does the United States Government have taking diamonds out of our *Indochine*?"

"None, sir, but it seems that it's becoming my business," Charlie replied curtly. "I wonder if General LeClerc would be interested in knowing of your close relationship with the Japanese Army. Shall we ask him, *Monsieur* Bergier?"

"I've had to work with the Japs to survive, *monsieur*, but only to survive."

"And I think you've done a very good job of it. Surviving, I mean."

"Those diamonds belong to France, *monsieur*. I want them back," the banker said.

"Of course you do. But please, don't insult my intelligence."

"I only mean, sir, that I must represent France here in the colonies."

"I am here only to investigate the death of Colonel Dixon. He died under mysterious circumstances, and those circumstances involved diamonds. That is our primary interest in the matter."

The banker paused to stare at Charlie, which Charlie interpreted as taking time to formulate a good lie. "I am aware that he was killed during the disturbance last month. How very unfortunate, *monsieur*," the banker said. He tapped his fingers on the large mahogany desk. "But I don't understand. How am I able to assist with this? I know nothing of his involvement in our loss of the gems."

"I need information, sir," Charlie said patiently. "I simply want to ask you several questions regarding one of his acquaintances. That's all I need from you."

"Acquaintances?"

"Yes, a *Monsieur* Andre Deloz. Do you know him?" Charlie asked.

"I know him. He is a customer of *le Banque Nacional*," Bergier replied. "Is Andre in the service of the United States Army?"

"Not exactly, but he has assisted the US Army ... under contract."

"You paid him, yes?"

"Dixon did," Charlie replied. "But that's not what I want to talk about. We are unable to locate Mr. Deloz. And it appears that you, sir, were one of the last people to visit his home and see him alive, perhaps." He waited for a reaction, but didn't get one, so he continued. "You paid Mr. Deloz a visit about five days ago. Is that not correct?"

"*Oui*. On October fourth, I think, I visited him. But he was not at home."

"Why did you wish to speak with him?"

"Please, *monsieur*. It is bank business," he said. "But I will tell you. One week before my visit, Andre came to my office and said he could finally make payment on his debt. You see, he owes us much money. Since 1936, we have waited for payment, but he does not pay. Then he came to me and said, 'I will pay off my debt in full tomorrow. Please renew my credit.' His credit? Ha!"

"Yes?" Charlie asked, waiting for Bergier to continue.

"He never returned, so I went to his apartment to speak with him, but he was not there."

"Did Mr. Deloz happen to mention diamonds during your meeting with him?"

"Diamonds? Certainly not," Bergier replied immediately. He stopped tapping his fingers on the desk.

"I see," Charlie said. *Just a little too quick*, he thought.

"Did you hire someone to search his room?" Joe interjected. Charlie and the banker both turned to look at him.

"No, of course not," the banker stated defensively.

"Do you have any idea where he could have gone?" Joe asked.

"*Monsieur* Deloz is a very solitary man. I think he has many creditors, but only one friend."

"*Monsieur* Bocquât?" Charlie answered.

"*Oui*. And Andre also owes him much money, eh?"

"Are you suggesting that...?"

"Oh, no, no, no. I am merely saying that if Andre came into a sum of money, he may have thought it prudent to pay his debts to his friend. Have you spoken with *Monsieur* Bocquât?"

"Yes, we have."

Charlie thanked Bergier for his time, and he and Joe left the man's office.

"The son of a bitch is lying," Joe said as they walked toward the huge wood doors of the bank. "He knows a hell of a lot more about the diamonds and disappearance of Andre than he is letting on."

Two Vietnamese men, unarmed and wearing simple uniforms, held the doors open for them. They bowed when Charlie and Joe passed.

"I agree," Charlie said. "But why is he lying? And what is he lying about?"

They got in the jeep and returned to the hotel. Once settled at a corner table in the now vacant lobby, Joe said, "This is beginning to look more and more like a Raymond Chandler who-done-it, isn't it?"

Drinking coffee, Charlie shrugged.

Joe rose from his chair. "I think I'll call it a day and turn in. How about you?"

"I'm going to stay up awhile," Charlie said, preoccupied. "We'll take another look at it in the morning?"

Joe nodded and took his leave.

Silently, Charlie looked out the window down *Rue de la Liberté*. What he saw there belonged half a world away, and he foolishly wanted to believe, buried deep in the past. But as he already knew, the past was still very much alive.

In his mind, he drifted back to the mountain hiding place forward of German lines. From there he could hear the loud whistle of their trains. Night and day, they transported prisoners to permanent camps still operating in southern Poland. Black smoke from the locomotives darkened the skies. He had asked any and all survivors he found, but no one knew anything ... no one had seen her. He blamed himself. He should have stopped her from fighting with the partisans against the German Army.

He pushed the coffee cup away, rising slowly from his window seat. As he climbed the wide marble staircase to his second-floor room, his broad shoulders slumped forward slightly.

Khanh called to him from the lobby. "Mr. Stanek, a message for you from my cousin," he said as he caught up to him.

Charlie stopped and waited for the young man. "From Truin? Give it to me," he said, holding out his hand.

"It is here. Much safer," Khanh said, tapping his head.

"What's her message then?" he asked, feeling weary and sick, down deep in his soul.

"She says meet her in the *Café Indochine* now – tonight. She has important information. She says to come alone."

He thought for a moment. "How do I get there?"

"I will get you a driver, a bicycle cab. It is fast and cheap."

"How much to the *Café Indochine*?"

"Maybe ten cents, American. No more."

"Call the cab," Charlie said, more anxious than curious. *Anything to drive away the bad memories.*

They quickly left the hotel. Khanh waved to a man standing nearby, next to his vehicle. The man immediately responded with a wave. Charlie walked over and stepped into the narrow cab. The young Vietnamese cabbie mounted the bicycle, and they were off down *Rue de la Liberté*.

The driver easily found the café, hidden away on a side street only blocks from the hotel. Getting out, Charlie saw Europeans, most likely French, crowded around small round tables dotting the sidewalk in front. They sipped wine and chatted. Only a small metal plaque inserted into the wall next to the door identified the café by name.

Young Vietnamese women scurried among the patrons, bowing and taking orders. Truin was nowhere to be seen. Charlie paid his driver and walked toward the open doorway. A large menu on an easel beside the door announced the evening's offerings. It was written in French. Before Charlie reached it, a young woman called to him quietly. She seemed to step out of nowhere.

"*Monsieur* Stanek?" she asked, bowing. The woman was dressed in the traditional *ao dai*.

"*Oui*," he responded, wondering how he had been recognized. He was dressed casually in rumpled civilian attire, not much different from the others there.

"Please, follow me," she said in good English. "A woman waits for you inside." The attractive young woman led him inside and into the darkness.

At a far corner in the back of a large room near an exit, she stopped at a table lit by a single candle. Charlie saw a woman sitting there, also dressed in a white *ao dai*, sipping a glass of wine. She did not look up.

"Wine, monsieur?" the attendant asked and patiently waited for his response.

"*Oui*," he said, still standing. "Truin, how lovely to see you," he said, recognizing her when she looked up. Only her eyes were illuminated by the light of the candle. Charlie easily remembered how beautiful she was with her rich dark hair and porcelain skin.

"Charlie, please join me," she said, smiling.

Charlie sat down and immediately appreciated their intimacy. He admired the soft silk of the traditional dress and how her breasts pressed tightly against the fabric, a small red turtle carefully embroidered above each breast. The white of the *ao dai* contrasted perfectly with her dark eyes and black hair, which she now wore long to her waist. Above her right ear was a freshly cut lotus blossom. Her delicate hands rested on the white tablecloth. *Everything about her seems so out of place, out of time. Or is it me?*

"Here, there are fewer eyes," she said as if she were reading his mind. "That is better for me and, I think, for you."

"Thank you," he said softly, still looking at her. The attendant returned with a glass of wine. "Another, *Mademoiselle du Vire?*" she asked Truin in French.

"*Oui,*" she said.

"*Mademoiselle du Vire?*" Charlie asked. His eyes found hers. He held her gaze until she grew embarrassed and looked down. "Is that your name?"

"It is a name I use when I must be discreet," she said with great modesty. She nervously smoothed an invisible wrinkle on her dress. "He gave it to me."

Tonight, she is dressed much differently. I wonder if she carries a weapon. That would ruin everything, he thought. "Discreet?" he asked, confused. He could not take his eyes off her.

"You see, I am a member of the Emperor's family, Emperor Bao Dai. He is my father's cousin. Please understand, eyes are everywhere. When I need to go out without others knowing, I am *Mademoiselle du Vire*, a Frenchman's native whore. We're a common sight in Saigon. Last year, I was banned from the court in Hue, our royal city, because of my political views, but I kept the name. I have found it very useful."

"Now you work with the communists?"

"I work for the freedom and independence of my people, Charlie. Bao Dai supported the return of the French. I could never accept that arrangement."

"Didn't Bao Dai abdicate? I thought I read that he's no longer Emperor."

"You are correct. On August twenty-fifth." The young attendant returned to replace the small candle, then left. "My cousin has spent too much time in France and has been corrupted by their decadence."

"I see." He sipped the wine without tasting it, enjoying watching her. *Each movement seems so graceful, so practiced and refined.* "You said you have a message for me?" he asked finally.

She smiled. "You are very impatient tonight, Charlie."

"Yes," he said seriously. Then he smiled. "I am uncomfortable being in the company of such a beautiful woman. I'm not used to such luxury. I've spent much of the last few years only in the company of men. Or alone." That sudden, candid statement surprised him.

"You honor me," she said, flattered, and held up the glass. "To the success of your mission."

"To truth."

"But be wary, *monsieur,*" Truin said with a smile and touched his glass again. "In Vietnam, the truth is never one thing ... and its possession comes at a very high price." To Charlie, her smile seemed enigmatic and distant.

"Sometimes it's worth the price," Charlie replied, wondering where the conversation was headed.

"Char-lie," she repeated syllable by syllable. "I like that name. It seems so American."

"I was named after an uncle," he said simply.

Truin closed her eyes, trying to embrace the strength she felt in him. "Why have you not married, Charlie?" she asked. She knew that question was too direct, but strangely, it felt important to ask.

"Probably because of the war."

"Yes, I understand. Does that mean you've never loved?"

"No, I have loved. Briefly," he answered.

"In war, we must avoid love," she said softly, trying to carry the conversation. She sensed the deep sadness in this strange, tall man and guessed the cause.

"I learned that too late, I'm afraid," Charlie replied. "In war, there can be no place for love. Passion, maybe. But love, never." His voice sounded flat and uncertain to her.

"That is wise to say. And, in that way, you have escaped tragedy?" she asked.

"I didn't say that," he replied softly.

"And now you will never love again? Is that how you feel?" she asked delicately.

"No, never again," he said. "Have you ever been in love?" he asked.

"Ah, Charlie, never ask a woman of love," she said, her smile warm. "But I will tell you. I have loved many times. Yes, but my heart is still not full. My life is not complete."

"Love is easy for you then?"

She smiled. "Once I loved a man more than anything else in the world. He was a Frenchman, a diplomat. He told me he loved me, too. And he would do anything for me, even give up his life. Ah, it was so romantic. He was why I had my French name ... for our secret meetings."

"Have we both been wounded then?" he asked.

"Wounded? I think I was wounded, but not damaged, Charlie. I believe I will love again."

"What happened?" he asked.

"When the Japanese came, he fled. To England, I think. To fight for the free French, he said. Now, I wonder. Does he fight against the Vietnamese people?"

"He left you to face the Japanese?"

"He left me in Saigon, alone and without the resources of my family," she answered. "But that was not the worst."

"What do you mean?"

"I discovered later from a friend that he was married. He had a wife and child in Paris." She felt her anger darken the moment and looked down.

"I'm sorry," he said softly.

"I will be no man's servant. And never again to a Frenchman."

"I can understand that. Those scars," he said, pointing to reddish purple lines across both wrists. "Did the Japanese do that to you?"

"No Charlie. I did it."

"Why?"

"I wanted to die."

"Because of him?"

She looked directly at him, her heart suddenly hard and full of fire. "He hurt me, and I didn't want to live any longer."

"What?" Charlie said.

"He betrayed me. I loved him, and he lied to me, Charlie," she stated coldly. She could not mask the hurt she still felt. "I would have given my life for him, but to him, I was only his Vietnamese whore. A diversion while serving in the colonies."

"I'm sorry," he said.

"The French are arrogant bastards. I hate them," she said, feeling it was her right to do so.

"I'm sorry," he said again. "I know that kind of love."

Truin touched his hand. *We share something, a sadness that won't go away*, she sensed, and knew they had connected in some emotional way. "Life is not fair, Charlie," she told him softly. "I have learned this from a thousand generations of suffering."

"Do you want to punish your lover for what he did to you?"

She smiled at him. "If I looked for vengeance because of a man's crime, I would have nothing left to give to Vietnam. Which, then, would be the greater crime?"

Charlie's brows furrowed. "That sounds like revenge to me."

"For each one of us, there is a destiny that must be fulfilled," she said slowly, wanting him to understand. "We Vietnamese know this. That is our greatness." She forced a smile. "There is no place in my heart for revenge, Charlie."

"You are strong," he said. "I don't think I could say that."

"For each of us there is a star. One waits for you, Charlie. It will take you where you must go." She reached across the table with both hands and cupped his hand in hers.

"I didn't know I would discover such a wise young woman when I came here. I'll think about what you've said. A star, eh?" He smiled.

She looked at him, returning his smile. "So now you begin to see, Charlie Stan-yak. This is a very old story."

"And now you think you serve a great cause," he said.

"Yes," she replied unequivocally.

"But be careful," he cautioned her. "Your friends, the Russians, have long since betrayed their own revolution. Don't let them betray yours."

"We are not as simple as you may believe," she said, withdrawing her hands, assuming a more formal posture.

"I didn't mean to say you are," he said.

"No, Charlie, it is not the great cause that I seek," Truin said, as if she had picked up his thought. "I fight only to be free, like you."

"Free of the French?"

"Of them, yes, but it is much more. I want to be free to choose how I live my life. In Vietnam, we do not have that right, Charlie. Do you believe, like the cynical conceited Europeans who say we are incapable of ruling ourselves?"

"I believe everyone should have the right to choose their own destiny," he said.

"Yet, you have doubts. I see it in your eyes."

"I've seen the horrors we've created in the name of freedom, Truin. The war was about that, I think. Fascism, communism, nationalism. Each is someone's idea of liberty and freedom," he said. Truin thought his voice sounded harsh, masking anger. "And tens of millions of people have carried those banners to their death. We've been fighting over abstractions and symbols, half-truths and outright lies. We've all been manipulated by tyrants, both large and small. Don't be fooled." He finished the wine, and their attendant quickly refilled the glass.

"But aren't ideas important?" she asked. "Don't they bind us together? Like your Declaration of Independence, aren't they sometimes worth dying for?"

"Sometimes, but most ideas are just things we talk about in dark cafés when we've had too much to drink."

"I don't think you mean what you say, Charlie." She watched him take another sip.

"We Americans are individualists. We are proud of that," he said. "Do you know what that means? To be an individualist?"

Truin looked at him, thoughtful. "In-di-vi-du-al-ist," she repeated slowly. "I don't understand that word. Is that another abstraction for you to consider?" she asked, teasing. "I think you are a complicated man, Charlie."

"I've learned that it's best if I just try to take care of myself. Yes, that's it. I survive and I endure. It's easier that way."

She smiled and shook her head. "You Americans have the luxury of enough freedom to believe in such nonsense." She reached out to touch his hand again with her fingertips.

"What I meant was I think I've wasted too much time fighting to save the world from itself."

Americans are much too complicated, she thought, but she felt something for this man.

"Yet you come all the way to Vietnam to investigate the death of one man, a man who is not even very important. Why?" She looked directly into his eyes.

"Truin, that's not what's important. Discovering the truth, that's the issue here."

"You believe it is your duty. As I, too, have a duty to my country."

"Of course," Charlie said. He began to laugh.

"Americans," she said, laughing with him. "You think too much. It confuses things for you."

"Have you known many Americans?"

"I know only you, Charlie. But I have seen movies about America. Hollywood, yes?"

"Hmm, yes, Hollywood," he said. "But then you did meet the American, Dixon. Isn't that right?"

"Yes."

"So, here we are ... back to Colonel Dixon," he said.

"Yes. And you want information," she said, letting go of his hand.

He nodded. "I want information. That's my job."

"A soldier who was in Dalat saw him on September twenty-first. He did not know he was an American. He described a tall man with blond hair. He was not in uniform, so the soldier thought maybe he was a Frenchman doing business with the Japanese."

"Now, why do you think the businessman was Dixon?"

"We spoke with his driver, who we know. This man, Andre Deloz, told us many things. The French, they talk very much."

"What happened to Deloz? After you spoke with him?" Charlie asked. "He seems to have disappeared."

"Disappeared? I did not know this," she replied, surprised. "We spoke with him in Dalat."

"What did he tell you?"

"He said that the American was hunting for the Butcher."

"Suzuki?"

"Yes, he is the one."

"Did he say if he found him?"

"He found him."

"And?"

"The Frenchman said that Dixon made a deal with the Butcher for his freedom. A deal that involved diamonds."

"Your people followed them to Dalat. Why?"

"We heard from our sources that foreigners – we did not know which foreigners – were traveling to Dalat. We had to know if they were French and why they were meeting with Japanese soldiers," she said, very careful with her words. "We watch foreigners very closely, and the French closer still. I think you know already that we are preparing for war with the French."

"Dixon was an American and a neutral," Charlie said. "You are not telling me everything, are you?"

"We think you will support the French, so we watch. Our spies are everywhere, and we watch everything."

"Did you know about the diamonds?"

"Of course."

"Where is the Frenchman now, Truin?"

"He is gone, I think. Maybe to Paris or Marseilles."

"Or maybe at the bottom of the Saigon River beside Rolly Dixon?" Charlie replied. "How convenient."

Does he think I am one of his soldiers? she thought. "We are not responsible for the lives of Americans, Charlie."

Charlie did not respond.

"One more thing," she said. "He told us the Butcher is now held in a hotel there and is guarded by well-armed Japanese soldiers."

"To guard him or protect him?"

"We do not know, but it is too dangerous for us to get him."

"When will the Japanese be relieved there?" he asked.

"When the French Army is strong enough to garrison the city. Two or three months, perhaps a little longer. We trade one master for another. Again."

"I see."

"Charlie, another thing I must tell you," she said carefully. "Comrade Giau has told me that the Russians have agreed to help us in our fight for freedom."

"How will they help?"

"They will give us weapons, big guns they took from the Japanese. Now I must know, Charlie. What will your President Truman offer us?"

"I can't answer that question, Truin. I don't know."

She looked down, averting his eyes. "A Major Zerenowsky told Comrade Giau that you have come to our country for more reasons than the death of your soldier. Is that true?"

"Major Gregor Zerenowsky? How does Comrade Giau know him?"

"He is part of the Russian delegation meeting with Ho Chi Minh in Hanoi," she explained. "I think the major is following your visit here with great interest. Do you know him?" She watched him.

"He was someone I knew during the war," Charlie said, but Truin could easily tell there was much more. "I've already warned you about the Russians, Truin."

"I will remember what you said."

"Now, back to the Butcher. So he hides in Dalat. I must go there," he said. "Soon."

"I will take you," she told him.

"Why the hell take the woman?" Joe asked early the next morning. "What do we need her for?"

"She can get us safely through Viet Minh-held areas," Charlie argued. "Her people have spies everywhere in Dalat. And, I think it's a good idea to have her close. To keep an eye on her."

"I don't trust her."

"I don't either. She has her own agenda," Charlie replied. *And I'm still not certain how much I should trust anyone around here,* he thought.

"What's Major Blankston say about your scheme?"

"He likes it. He thinks tracing Dixon's final days is the only way we can wrap up this investigation and get me out of town," Charlie said. "He said he'll contact the Jap commander of the

Southern Army immediately to get us our visit with the officer-in-charge up there. But Sergeant, it's my call, not his. So let's get moving."

"Okay," Joe said with a shrug. "I'll start getting the gear organized."

"We'll need guns and ammo," Charlie said, already planning. "Truin will be here tomorrow at dawn."

"Hey, what do we do with the war criminal? If we catch him, I mean."

Charlie didn't respond. He had no answer ... yet.

Chapter 14

Studying a French map provided by Major Blankston, Charlie figured it was about two hundred miles to Phan Rang, traveling on French Highway 1, and another seventy miles up the mountains to the resort town of Dalat on Highway 20.

Charlie learned that Dalat, tucked into the mountains about 4,400 feet above the sea, was considered to be the most pleasant and beautiful city in all of Vietnam. Truin told him that this route was the only way to reach Dalat without fear of ambush by local bandits. The Japanese no longer patrolled the mountain roads, and neither the Vietnamese nor the French were yet strong enough to take over those duties. Neither road was hard surface, but the bridges were passable, according to Truin.

They began their trip at dawn, taking the jeep, a radio, two M3 submachine guns with plenty of ammo, and ten extra gallons of gas. Charlie brought extra green backs for food and lodging.

They traveled across a land of rice paddies, rubber plantations, and ancient ruins. Small villages and hamlets lined the road for much of the trip. Most of the homes were built of thatch, but they occasionally passed concrete and mud-brick houses. Charlie was amazed by the beauty of the Vietnamese countryside – sharp vistas with mountains and deep valleys. The green of rice paddies spread out as far as they could see, disappearing into the mist of distant mountains.

With Truin interpreting for them, they were provided with whatever they needed when they stopped. They soon discovered, however, that there was very little to eat in the villages. The war had caused a terrible famine, Truin told them. She blamed the Japanese. "More than a million of my people died during the war. They starved," she said sadly. "The Japanese took all the rice. The French sold it to them."

To break the monotony of the long trip, Charlie and Joe took turns driving. Truin spoke little while Joe drove, but became very talkative and informative when Charlie was beside her.

"The Vietnamese people settled this part of the country only several hundred years ago. Before us, the Champa people from the sea. Cambodians, and Thai peoples, all lived here and claimed Cochin China for themselves. It was then, maybe a hundred years ago, that the French started coming. Always, the Vietnamese people must fight foreigners to be free and independent. We fought the Chinese for hundreds of years, we drove out the Cambodians, then the Japanese, and now the French come again," she lectured Charlie while he drove.

"The Nguyen Dynasty has ruled all of Vietnam for the past one hundred and fifty years. I am a direct descendant of the first Nguyen Emperor," she said. "But now I serve the people," she added. "Bao Dai lost his mandate from heaven. He has betrayed his family, and so has forfeited his right to rule."

"You serve Ho Chi Minh," Charlie said flatly.

"Yes, Charlie, I serve Ho Chi Minh proudly like you serve your President Truman. Ho Chi Minh knows the heart of the Vietnamese people, and that is why I follow him." Charlie saw she was convinced of the rightness of her cause, and he had to respect that, even if he didn't entirely trust the one on whom she focused her dedication.

There were deep ruts in the road, the terrible red dust, and the enervating heat to contend with. But Truin never voiced a word of complaint and seemed to be enjoying the trip. She wore a conical straw hat and a silk scarf tied tightly around her mouth and nose to protect her from dust and sun. Her arms were wrapped in cotton sheaths. Toward evening, they approached Phan Rang and the South China Sea. When the road neared the ocean, they saw waves of deep blue crested white, touching the fine sand of spectacularly beautiful beaches.

"There is a place near here where we will stay tonight," Truin announced suddenly.

"Is it part of the plan?" Joe asked, looking to Charlie.

"Don't worry," Charlie assured him. "We talked about it. The French villa on the beach, right?" he asked her.

"Yes, very private and very safe."

"Hey, Sarge," Charlie said, turning so that Catledge could hear. "A survivor from the Saigon Prison will be there who knows Suzuki well. I want to hear his story for myself and make sure the Control Commission gets his complete testimony. Truin suggested it and sent word for him to meet with us."

"Nguyen Ngoc Tran," Truin added, "a member of the Southern Committee, was imprisoned at Plei Toan for three years. First captured and tortured by the French collaborators, then later by the Japanese Army for political activities. He knows the French and Japanese well."

"Do we really need to hear his story?" Joe growled. "I think we know what they're capable of."

"He's also an important member of the Viet Minh," Charlie added.

"What does that mean?" Joe asked.

Charlie detected the concern in his voice. "They may be the only government out here – for the time being, anyway. As a representative of the US government, I'm obligated to meet local functionaries. And he might have something to add to our investigation. Don't worry. It should be routine."

"They seem to be everywhere, eh?" Joe said, looking at Charlie.

"Our talk with Tran may be helpful – more info on Suzuki."

"You're damn thorough, aren't you? I just hope you're not digging us a hole we can't get out of," Joe growled. "Remember, I'm down to a few weeks, and then I'm outta here."

Several hours later, after darkness set in, Nguyen Ngoc Tran came to visit them as Charlie had requested. The middle-aged man told them of his internment in the Japanese camp. He related how Suzuki seemed to take delight in the torture of prisoners, especially the British and Americans.

Charlie was surprised to learn that a team from the Control Commission had already visited Tran. They had taken his testimony in a written statement early in September. But when Charlie had gone through Dixon's files, he found no statement from him, or any reference to this important witness or even his name anywhere among Dixon's belongings. *Had Dixon destroyed any record that referred to Suzuki? But why?*

"Truin, ask Mr. Tran what he knows about diamonds."

She did as he asked.

Charlie watched the man's expression when she spoke with him. He saw something in Tran's face change. "Tell him I must know about the stolen diamonds."

Truin frowned but again did as he requested. "The Butcher learned of them while at the camp, he says." Charlie noted the man's anger rising as he spoke. "Comrade Tran says the Japanese soldier knows where the diamonds are hidden," she said, translating. "They belong to the Vietnamese people."

Without any prompting, the man pulled up his shirt to reveal long pink scars crisscrossing his back. "He says Suzuki did this to him. Comrade Tran says if the Americans do not take him, he will." Truin paused. "A very bad man," she said.

"The sadistic bastard," Charlie said softly to himself. "We'll bring him in."

"Hey, Stanek, you're on military orders, not some mission from God," Joe cautioned.

"Where exactly is he now?" Charlie asked Tran, with Truin still translating.

"He is still being guarded by the commander of the Japanese soldiers in Dalat," she said, "surrounded by heavily armed soldiers."

The Vietnamese man held Charlie's gaze. "Beware of him," he said to Truin. She translated. "At the camp I saw him murder prisoners for no reason. Like this." He made a chopping motion with his hand and arm. "Tell the American this." He motioned emphatically to Charlie.

"Yet you survived," Charlie replied.

"The diamonds bought my freedom. But others – my friends – who also knew about the diamonds hidden in the French vault were shot. The Butcher lined them against the wall and shot them before my eyes. Then he says, 'Tell me where the diamonds are kept, or I will kill everyone in your family.'" Truin translated it word-for-word.

"Thank him for telling us his story," Charlie replied, looking directly at Tran. "Tell him that the Japanese will pay for this crime."

Truin did as she was instructed.

Tran bowed to Charlie and Joe. He smiled softly at Truin, turned and departed, limping out the door with the aid of a cane. They watched him leave in silence.

"I will go to my room," Truin said, looking only at Charlie.

"Is chasing war criminals and diamonds part of your investigation now, Major Stanek?" Joe said after she had left the room.

"I think we'll finish Dixon's work. Take the Jap in," Charlie replied without hesitating.

"You want to take Suzuki in?" Joe said, surprised. "That's what you've decided?"

"Yeah, that's right," he said. "We better do it now, or he's going to run." He stood and began to pace about the dimly lit room, with one side facing to the ocean. "Let's take a walk. Where we can talk."

Charlie noticed the proprietor, an older woman, was watching them as they left.

They walked across a broad swath of sand. The rumbling sound of the surf overwhelmed the other night noises. Like a freight train, the surf rolled and broke against the broad beach. They stood side by side, staring over the crests of the waves. At first, neither spoke nor moved. Finally, Charlie stepped directly into the surf and looked up into the star-studded sky. "You think there're a couple for us, Joe?" he asked, pointing upward. "To guide us, I mean."

Standing at the edge of the surf, Joe stared at Charlie. "I don't think about it much."

Sea foam circled Charlie's shoes, then the tip of a wave washed over them. Still he stood there, looking up into the starry darkness. "You don't think much of my idea, do you?"

"You're not a soldier here," Joe called above the crashing waves.

Charlie turned to Joe. "It'll work out," he said. "But we need a plan. Come on, let's walk."

They strolled further down the beach. Charlie, his brows furled, looked hard at Joe. "You think the Jap commander in Dalat will help us take Suzuki back to Saigon?" The tide crept up on them, touching the soles of their shoes, and then receded again.

"Suzuki has been there since the end of the war. I just hope the commander hasn't been bought off, too."

"We need to find that out right away," Charlie replied, deep in thought. "When we meet with him."

"How do we do that? Ask him?"

"If we have to," he said. "Listen, everyone has a price? The commander is probably ready to go home, back to a devastated homeland. He could use a few extra bucks."

"Keep talking."

"It fits, doesn't it? This guy has probably been living like a king up there. No one's been able to reach him because the garrison commander's protecting him. For a price."

They continued to walk side by side along the dark deserted beach. Only a few scattered lights from Phan Rang could be seen on the right.

"You think Dixon came up here chasing Suzuki and got bought like the Jap commander?"

"That or he came here specifically looking for a payoff," Charlie explained. "Perhaps Dixon had already discovered that the Japs took the diamonds. He probably didn't know how great their value was, but he somehow figured out who had them."

"That doesn't make sense." Joe stopped dead in his tracks. "How did he know?"

"I went through Dixon's papers. After talking with the French banker, I got access to Dixon's things again and took a closer look."

"What'd Major Blankston say about that?"

"He doesn't know."

"So, what did you find?"

"Nothing, nothing at all," he said. "That's what was so surprising. I found undeciphered cablegrams from the Kandy headquarters in Ceylon, and the list of names you mentioned, but nothing else."

"Nothing about Suzuki or diamonds?"

"That's right. He was covering his tracks real good."

"You think he destroyed the records, everything about Suzuki?"

"I think he had prepared his mission well, done all the background. Commander of the Embankment Team was just Dixon's cover. He came to Indochina for diamonds. After all, they were already stolen. He was just going to cut himself in for a share."

"That's a long shot, isn't it? Where's your proof?"

"You're right. It's just a hunch."

"I think you're out on a limb on this one," Joe growled. "I don't know how Dixon knew who heisted the gems when no one else here did."

"I think he discovered Nguyen Tran's written statement to the War Crimes Commission. It may have been one of the first documents he got hold of when he first met with the Brits. Hell, maybe he got a copy when he was still in the Philippines before he arrived in Saigon. Remember, he was a member of that war crimes investigation."

"Those people were here even before we arrived on September fourth."

"But I think Dixon already knew about the stolen diamonds. He learned through deciphered Japanese Army cablegrams much earlier in the summer. He just didn't know who had them."

"He was still a soldier in the United States Army. You can't forget that."

"A soldier's pay isn't all that great. Maybe Dixon needed something extra to sweeten his retirement. And diamonds are pretty damn easy to sell, especially if they have no history," Charlie reasoned.

"Maybe, but I still think it's a stretch."

"I'm just working a theory here."

"Do you think we were ambushed to get those diamonds?" Joe asked.

"I didn't say that. I think the Vietnamese, as well as the Japs, wanted the diamonds, but I don't know if that's the reason Dixon was killed. I don't even know if anyone knew he carried them at that point. That's what we need to find out in Dalat. What Jap intelligence there knows."

"Now I'm confused. You saying that no one knew Dixon was carrying the diamonds when he was killed?"

"I'm saying I don't know." Charlie looked back to the villa where they were staying. The walled, three-story house was dark except for a few windows. He wondered about Truin, or rather *Mademoiselle du Vire*.

"And the woman?" Joe asked, verbalizing Charlie's thoughts.

"She knows all about Suzuki and his treasure."

"Will she help us get Suzuki back to Saigon, you think?"

"That's a very good question. I need to find out ... tonight," he said. "She's along on this trip for her own reasons. The Viet Minh are working their own agenda, and I hope it doesn't involve us. But if it doesn't, then why is she here?"

"We need to keep a close eye on her."

"Yeah," Charlie said.

"I told you not to trust her."

"I think, Sergeant, we need to fit all the pieces together," Charlie replied. "We probably already know who the main players are."

Returning to the house, Joe went off to his small room. But Charlie remained on the patio, listening to waves crash against the beach. He waited, then quietly approached Truin's room. Softly, he knocked on her door.

"Charlie?" He heard her voice through the door.

"Yes," he said. "May I come in?"

"*Oui*. Come, come," she said, opening the door to him. In the dim candlelight, Charlie saw that she was clad only in a sheet, wrapped tightly around her. He was not expecting that and looked at her in surprise. After he entered, she quickly closed the door. "Charlie, I've waited for you." She allowed the sheet to drop to the floor then bent to extinguish the flame.

"Truin?" he said. But before he could say more, she grabbed his hand and led him to the bed. He stopped to pull her to him. They embraced. Charlie ran his hands over her back and down her thighs, feeling the cool nakedness of her body. In such a hot land, he was surprised that she should feel so cool to his touch.

With practiced hands, she undid the buttons on his shirt, then his trousers. "You want me, Charlie?" she asked.

"I want you," he said, remembering how long it had been since he had felt such passion. He picked her up, burying his head in her small but firm breasts. Truin wrapped her legs around his waist and shuddered.

He laid her gently on the bed. Quickly, he stripped off the remainder of his clothes and lay down beside her. With his right hand, he massaged her body, first her breasts, stomach, and finally touching between her thighs.

Truin turned so that she could run her hand down his body. "Now," she said softly and lay back to pull him on top. She moaned softly in his ear. "Charlie," she whispered, opening her legs for him.

They made love that was passionate and physical.

Later, they made love again. Finally, both expended, they lay together in the darkness. Charlie held her close in his arms on the small bed. Neither spoke.

"Was she pretty?" she finally asked.

"Who?"

"The one you lost in the European war."

"Yes," he replied, the memory of Marie's face suddenly fresh in his mind. He sat up. "I better go," he said abruptly. He kissed her on the forehead, not knowing why, but it seemed to fit. "But first I have to ask you something." He moved to sit on the edge of the bed where he could see her face.

Truin reached out to touch his hand. "Ask me," she replied softly.

He looked at her, still lying on the bed, not embarrassed by her nakedness. Unable to resist, he bent down and kissed her right breast. "What do you want from me?"

She looked at him. "We ask nothing from you but consideration for our cause. From your president."

"What else do you want to tell me?"

For a few seconds, Truin hesitated, then spoke. "The Japanese criminal must receive justice for his crimes, but I think others can take him. It doesn't have to be you," she replied. "I am worried ... for you."

"Worried? Why?"

"Charlie, Dalat is too dangerous. We must go back to Saigon. In the morning. Or I cannot guarantee your safety," she said, fear in her voice. "Please."

"Truin, what is it you haven't told me?"

"Everywhere you have enemies. They watch us," she said.

"Do you know of a plot against me ... by the Viet Minh or others?"

"No, Charlie," she said, still holding his hand. "The risk you take with the Japanese, for Suzuki, is unnecessary. We must return to Saigon."

"Tell me what you know about the diamonds. There's something you're not telling me. Why was it so important that you come with us?"

"I was ordered to ... and I wanted to come. I don't want anything to happen to you, Charlie. We like Americans," she said. "I know nothing of diamonds in Dalat."

He smiled, appreciating her concern for their well-being. "Don't worry," he said. "Sergeant Catledge and I can handle it." Grabbing his shoes, he abruptly stood and walked to the door.

"Charlie. Please. Don't leave."

He gently closed the door behind him.

Early the next morning, Charlie walked out onto the second-story balcony to watch the sun rise over the South China Sea. Hearing noises below, he looked down and saw Truin washing her long dark hair at a brick well on the patio. She was naked to the waist. Watching intently while she lathered and stroked her hair, he realized he wanted her again. He couldn't get enough of the woman and thought of the previous night. *I haven't learned anything of value from her except that I have feelings for her, and I can expect treachery in the mountain city.* He felt almost out of focus, trying to balance everything in his mind.

Looking up at him, Truin smiled. A young girl poured water from a bucket to rinse her raven hair while she squeezed out the suds. She made no effort to shield her nakedness from him.

"We are going on to Dalat?" she asked later that morning as they drank tea at a small shop nearby.

"Yes," he replied.

"Then you must be prepared for anything," she whispered. "And I can no longer protect you."

Charlie looked at her, hearing the fear in her voice. "We will have a plan," he said.

Before she could respond, Joe sat down at the small table. "Everything's ready," he said.

At 0800 hours, the three resumed their trip to Dalat. As they rose steadily into the mountainous Lam Vien Highland, the climate slowly cooled. About midday, they reached Ngoan Muc Pass. The road narrowed through high, rocky outcroppings. Now surrounded by forests of tall evergreens, they continued the steep ascent.

A perfect place for an ambush, Charlie thought as the road narrowed further. "How far to Dalat?" he asked Joe.

"About two hours," Joe replied.

The tall evergreen forest and cool fresh air reminded him of the Wisconsin of his childhood. Every summer his father would take him north to the shore of Lake Superior for a week of camping. At night, under the stars, he would tell him about Bohemia and the struggles of the Czech people to be free of the Austrians and the nobility who had cursed both the land and the people.

"Can we expect trouble from bandits or from your people, Truin?" Joe asked, breaking the silence. Charlie looked over at Joe behind the wheel.

"Dalat is a very quiet town. Vietnamese respect its beauty and peacefulness."

"What about the Japs?" Charlie asked.

"Major Blankston said we can expect full cooperation from Colonel Hamura," Joe said, wrestling with the wheel.

"I see there's a good airfield," Charlie said, studying the map. "They have any planes there?"

"I don't know."

Charlie automatically checked their weapons again to ensure they had plenty of ammo. "Get ready for anything," he suddenly said, pulling back the bolt on the M-3 and peering down the chamber. His late-night conversation with Truin was still on his mind. "If any local group is going to ambush us, this is the place."

"The commies or the Japs?" Joe asked.

"Truin was worried last night about something," he said, blowing sand and red dust off boxes of .45 caliber rounds.

The woman's eyes were closed as she took in the cooler air.

"What was she worried about?" Joe asked, not surprised.

"She wouldn't tell me," Charlie replied, looking over at her. "Evidently, a lot of people want this Suzuki," he said, "including the Vietnamese. They may not want us to take him.." He reached out to touch Truin's arm.

Truin's eyes opened immediately. "There is no police authority here, so we travel at our own risk," she announced, as if she had been listening. Then she closed her eyes again.

"The Japs have been ordered to stay garrisoned, and the Brits have no real authority this far north of Saigon," Joe informed him, to explain what Truin had just stated. He downshifted quickly to make the grade. The jeep jumped.

"Keep your eyes open." Charlie pointed the M-3 out the side of the vehicle, prepared to act if necessary.

"I think we need to make a quick grab on Suzuki. Get him and go," Joe said, his eyes glued to the road. "Remember, no heroics."

"I agree," Charlie replied. "But we still have to prepare for one night in town."

"We got enough ammo to hold out?" Joe asked, then shifted again.

"Depends. As long as we don't have to battle the Japs, we can make a stand," Charlie said, not very reassuringly. "A few insurgents. I think we could hold them off for a while. How long would it take the Brits to get to us?"

"By air, half a day to put together a force and get up here. With a bit of luck."

"Well, let's pray for some luck, then."

"I figured you'd say that," Joe replied. "I guess it's just you and me."

"You're not too happy with the plan, are you?"

"Nope."

Truin, with her eyes still closed, said nothing.

Colonel Hamura was waiting for them on the concrete landing strip in front of his headquarters when the three arrived. No flag flew from the pole. A large formation of troops stood at attention. Aircraft were lined up behind the soldiers, who he saw were still armed.

Colonel Hamura was not an old man. He stood proud and erect in a neatly pressed uniform and polished boots. But the years of war had apparently taken their toll. His face was deeply lined, and his full head of hair had gone gray. He seemed gaunt. When they were close, Charlie noticed a slight tremble in his neck that became more obvious when the man stood directly in front of them. Positioned between two junior officers, Hamura saluted them. He wore his ceremonial sword.

Charlie quickly scanned the base, surrounded by low, dark green mountains. Originally an old French outpost, the current occupants had attempted to keep back the jungle growth. But Charlie saw that here and there the jungle was returning. Vines had wrapped themselves around and through the high barbed-wire fence surrounding the entire area.

Several two-story barracks-type wood buildings and about a half dozen one-story brick structures stood immediately behind the formation. All the buildings had tile roofs and were painted beige. Their windows were open wide. A few palm trees dotted the base, but mostly red dirt and gravel streets linked the buildings. Solid one-story concrete bunkers with gun slits facing outward lined the perimeter at spaced intervals. He saw a large terminal at the far south end.

Charlie was told by the Brits that when the war ended, Colonel Hamura set up his temporary quarters at the airfield and waited to be repatriated. According to Major Clifton, a British military delegation arrived in late August to accept his surrender. At that time, they ordered him to stand by until the Allied Control Commission could remove his troops and assume responsibility for the region. He was directed to maintain order until then.

Charlie knew that, for the colonel, the war was over. The Emperor had decreed it. But he looked at the formation of armed soldiers standing at attention in front of him and wondered.

Charlie and Joe stood at attention in front of the detachment commander. Colonel Hamura saluted smartly and bowed. He then ceremoniously drew his sword and scabbard and presented them to Charlie. Charlie accepted them, acknowledging Japanese submission. He then returned them to the colonel, who accepted them with a bow.

Truin watched, amused, from the jeep.

"Welcome," Colonel Hamura said in halting English. "Come and we talk." In Japanese, he ordered his subordinate to dismiss the troops still standing at attention on the airfield before leading Charlie and Joe to his quarters. Charlie waved to Truin to join them. Hesitating at first, she got out of the jeep and followed.

"Nakajima Dragon Swallowers," Joe whispered, seeing Charlie stop and look at the planes. "They're converted bombers. Too easy for us to shoot 'em down, so they converted them to transports."

Charlie, Joe, and Truin entered Hamura's sparse office, following close behind the Japanese officer. A picture of the Emperor still hung on the wall above his desk in prominent view. But the top of the soldier's desk was clean. *One thing about defeat,* Charlie thought. *It wiped the slate clean. With victory comes a future filled with many, often complex, choices. For the defeated, there is only survival.* Charlie thought about what General Donovan had told him.

"I am Charles Stanek," Charlie announced, "representing the United States on the Allied Control Commission in Indochina. Sergeant Joe Catledge."

Truin bowed politely to the commanding officer. "She is *Mademoiselle du Vire,* who will be assisting us as guide and interpreter." Charlie thought her French name would sound more impressive to the Japanese officer, and he couldn't remember all of her Vietnamese name anyway.

Colonel Hamura bowed politely. "Please sit," he said and pointed to three chairs. Tea was brought and served in tiny porcelain cups. "I have been ordered to assist you," he said in heavily accented English.

"We are investigating the death of an American officer, Lieutenant Colonel Rolly Dixon. I believe he was here several weeks ago."

The Japanese paused. *Considering his reply,* Charlie thought. "Yes, Mr. Stanek. He was here. We assist him."

"How?" Charlie asked.

"We have a man arrested here in Dalat near the airfield. He is wanted by Allies. Yes?"

"Captain Suzuki?"

"Yes. Lieutenant Colonel Dixon of American Army ordered us to arrest him and hold him until new orders arrived from him. Those were his words. We did as ordered."

"Then?"

"Those were his last words to me before he left with a Frenchman."

"Did he meet with Captain Suzuki?"

"He meet with Captain Suzuki. The captain was brought here under arrest. You understand?" the Japanese officer asked, uncomfortable with his English. "Your colonel ordered that he stay under arrest."

"What else did you and Colonel Dixon talk about?" Charlie asked.

"He talk about Captain Suzuki. He say he is a very dangerous man. That it is very important that he not escape."

"Did he explain why?"

"Only that the captain committed crimes that he must be punished for. After a trial," Colonel Hamura said. "I understand this. We are a defeated army and subject to your laws."

"It's good that you understand that," Charlie said. "Did he ask you about diamonds?"

"No, Mr. Stanek."

"Do you know anything about lost diamonds here in Indochina?"

"I know nothing about diamonds."

Charlie sensed that he was telling the truth. "Do you know what Colonel Dixon and Captain Suzuki talked about when they met?"

"No, nothing," he said flatly. "I have told you all that I know about his visit."

"Who else did Dixon meet with? Other Japanese soldiers? Vietnamese?"

"He was here for two days," the colonel said politely. "He spoke Japanese. He talk with my officers and with Colonel Imano's men."

"Colonel Imano's men?"

"Major Ishitoro. He and one of his men assign to my command from Saigon in September. They come several days after Captain Suzuki join us from camp at Plei Toan. Yesterday another come."

"What are their duties here, Colonel? Surely, since the war is over, your army has no need for intelligence gathering."

"Their orders say they are here in Dalat to look at documents for the Allied Control Commission."

"I see," Charlie replied with growing interest. "What kind of documents have they been reviewing?"

Colonel Hamura smiled softly. "Camp records at Plei Toan. All records from camps in highlands must be brought here for transport to Saigon."

"And records regarding Captain Suzuki?"

"Yes, on the captain as well. They have spoken to him many times."

"You allowed that, Colonel?"

"I have done as ordered. Captain Suzuki is detained," the colonel said with dignity. "Orders allow Major Ishitoro and his men to review documents."

"You have followed orders," Charlie said. *No more, no less,* he thought. "What else can you tell me?" he asked.

"Major Ishitoro and his men made several trips to the camp."

"Where is this camp located?"

"North, in Central Highlands. Two or three hours north of Pleiku."

"Are there still Japanese soldiers at this camp, Colonel?"

"It is deserted. Emptied of all documents, equipment, weapons. I have seen to that."

"I see," Charlie said. "Then, if the documents are here and the prisoners are freed and repatriated, why do they still travel to the camp?"

"Major Ishitoro say he must retrace Captain Suzuki's movements since leaving the camp ... in case he hid documents along the way. I think this very strange."

"I would like to speak with Major Ishitoro," Charlie said.

"I will arrange it, sir. When would you like to meet with them?"

"Early in the morning. Right now, I want to see Suzuki."

"What else do you need, sir?" the colonel asked.

"Tomorrow after the fog lifts, I must have a plane ready to go, with a pilot and armed guards, for a flight to Saigon. Also, I must have a detail of at least a squad of your most loyal soldiers, so that we can transport Captain Suzuki from his cell to the airport," Charlie ordered, clear and precise. "Can that be arranged?"

"That will be done, sir," the Japanese said, bowing slightly from the waist.

Charlie turned to Joe and Truin. "Let's go."

The colonel stood, bowed again. He then gave orders to the subordinates who stood beside his desk, one at each corner.

"So, what do we do now?" Joe asked after they left the colonel's office.

"Stand by," Charlie said, sounding more like a military officer than a civilian diplomat.

Truin followed closely behind, listening to every word. "Charlie, please, we must talk."

Charlie saw that she had purposely waited until the sergeant had walked around the vehicle before making her request.

"This evening. It is very important," she said softly before stepping into the jeep.

"Tonight, at dinner," Charlie answered, distracted.

Charlie and Joe were both surprised by the quarters where the war criminal was being held. It was not a cell but a suite in the Dalat Hill Resort. The same hotel where they were to stay. Security included two Japanese soldiers at Suzuki's door and, as far as Charlie could tell, at least a company guarding the hotel grounds with heavy machine guns. To keep Suzuki in or intruders out wasn't exactly clear to him.

Joe unloaded their gear, while Truin located their rooms.

With a Japanese guard at his side, Charlie entered the prisoner's suite.

"Captain Isoruku Suzuki of the Imperial Japanese Army," the prisoner introduced himself in very good English, and then bowed. "And you, sir?" He stood facing the door.

"Charles Stanek, United States Representative to the Allied Control Commission," he said, not returning the bow. He already hated the man. The guard remained standing near the door, while Charlie followed the prisoner into the large room.

Suzuki's quarters appeared to be very comfortable, almost luxurious. The spacious suite, dressed in teak and mahogany, had French doors leading to a balcony. The furnishings were French Empire and tastefully arranged about the room. The adjoining room was attached by double doors and appeared to be equally well furnished.

"Please sit, Mr. Stanek," the prisoner said, gesturing to a well-cushioned couch. "How can I be of service to you?" The officer was impeccably dressed in his formal uniform, his dark goatee neatly trimmed. He stood erect while an aide stood stiffly beside the entrance to the other room. "Tea," the officer ordered in Japanese. He sat down in a chair directly facing Charlie.

Charlie was surprised by Suzuki's youth. He didn't look thirty years of age. "Captain, as you know, under the Geneva Convention you are being charged with crimes of cruel and inhumane treatment of prisoners, torture, and murder. Specifically, according to my records, you summarily executed six Americans." He waited for some response, received none, and continued. "I am here to expedite your transfer to the British Navy for transport to Manila to stand trial. You will travel alone." Charlie enjoyed saying that.

"Mr. Stanek, I am astonished."

"You will be accorded justice." This man reminded him of Gestapo officers he had captured toward the end of the war. "Just doing my duty," they said when asked about wholesale shootings of civilians. They, too, had always demanded to be treated with dignity and respect.

Tea was brought and served in porcelain by the aide, a small thin man, much older than Suzuki, and also impeccably dressed in his uniform. He bowed politely and offered the tea.

Charlie declined. "Captain Suzuki, I am surprised to find you here rather than in a cell ... under guard at the camp."

"And I am surprised, sir, that you came all this way just for me. Lieutenant Colonel Dixon had assured me that I would not be detained for any great period."

"Not detained?" Charlie asked, surprised by his statement.

"Yes. When the British finally ordered Colonel Hamura to withdraw south, I expected I would be left behind. Simply forgotten, perhaps?" Suzuki said, watching Charlie closely for some reaction. "This is what your colonel assured me."

"How much did such an expectation cost?"

"I suspect that you already know."

"What does Major Ishitoro want from you?" Charlie asked, abruptly changing the subject.

Suzuki smiled, his cold brown eyes leveled at Charlie. "What everyone wants, sir."

"Did you give them to him?"

"That man is troublesome and very dangerous, and worse, unreliable."

"So you didn't give him what he wants?"

"His price was much too high, Mr. Stanek," Suzuki said. "I prefer to sit and wait ... for now."

"Here where you are protected by Colonel Hamura, under orders from the Allies."

"It isn't such a bad place, is it?" he said.

"No, it isn't. But you and I will depart tomorrow for Saigon. I don't believe you need much preparation," Charlie told him.

"Like you, Lieutenant Colonel Dixon at first threatened he would take me to Saigon."

"But?"

"We are reasonable men, sir. He and I reached an accommodation. Why not you and I?" Suzuki said with a smile.

"Tell me about your diamonds, Captain," Charlie said directly, changing the subject.

The man raised his eyes again and smiled. "Yes, the diamonds. Everyone seeks wealth, Mr. Stanek. It is truly what rules the world, isn't it?" He nodded then stood, obviously believing that he still held a measure of power. "Prisons hold many secrets, sir, and the hiding place of rare Annamese gems may be one of them."

"I must know where the stolen gems are hidden. Will you tell me?" Charlie asked as pleasantly as he could.

"I am a flexible man, sir, and, it seems that you have me in a delicate position," the prisoner said. "I think we can reach some type of arrangement."

"What is your price?"

"Well, sir, I'm still prepared to make you an offer, a much better offer. Even a partnership," he said. "I respect a man of your abilities and determination."

"I see," Charlie nodded, fighting to hold back his disgust. *The man's arrogance astounds me.* "You sound very brave for a man facing a trial by his enemies, and perhaps a long rope," he said with a cold smile. "Tell me the location of the gems and I will ensure, in writing, to the Adjutant General that your cooperation was extended to our investigation. It could keep you off the gallows, Captain."

"I still hold almost twenty million francs worth of the gems hidden where no one will ever find them. The French and the Vietnamese want them and will offer fair terms to get their hands on them. Even others here in the Japanese Army want them. So as you can see, I am not quite desperate yet," he said, smiling.

"You think I can be bought? Just like that, and I'm your partner?" Charlie replied, barely masking his contempt. "If I agree, I'm no better than you, am I?"

"Mr. Stanek, please," Suzuki said. "I did not mean to insult. But we all have our price. That line over which even our honor can be bought. Didn't this war, this horrible war, teach you anything?

Charlie said nothing.

"Let's discuss an arrangement, perhaps over dinner?" the captain said, sounding very confident.

"Over dinner, Captain Suzuki? I think not. I will give you until tomorrow morning at 0730 hours to tell me where the diamonds are located," Charlie said dismissively.

"And if I do not agree to those terms?"

"At 0800 hours, I will march you out of your quarters and into an airplane for a short ride to Saigon."

"I see," Suzuki said with growing anxiety. "Sir, why do I think you will do that even if I tell you their location?"

"Those are my terms, Captain," Charlie said, standing abruptly. "Please think them over carefully." He prepared to leave. "Be prepared to travel early in the morning. Without your aide." He looked to the man who stood by the door impassively.

"I will consider your offer," Suzuki said, standing also.

Charlie stood in the hall and watched as the guard locked the door. He inspected both guards then retired to his room, one floor below Suzuki's suite.

He planned to contact Major Clifton early in the morning by radio to notify him of his decision to immediately transport the prisoner to Saigon, where he would be turned over to the Allied Control Commission. He decided he would personally accompany Suzuki to the airstrip and ensure he got on one of the Japanese aircraft for the short flight to Saigon. *Let the Brits interrogate him and track down the lost diamonds,* he thought. He was surprised that no one – the Vietnamese, French or Brits – had yet attempted to spring Suzuki from Colonel Hamura's custody, but Suzuki was probably right. *Diamonds buy a lot of time, protection, and silence. And those Jap machine guns outside prove it,* he thought.

Later that evening, following a splendid four-course dinner with Sergeant Catledge not unlike the meal they had eaten with the Frenchman on his plantation, he knocked on Truin's door. He thought it was unusual that she had not joined them. "It's Charlie," he said through the dark wood panels. "You said we had to talk."

"No!" she answered through the door. "Not now, please, Charlie."

"Let me in," he demanded with growing concern. He thought he heard another voice in the room.

The door opened several inches. "Charlie? No. You must leave, now," Truin whispered through the narrow space.

Charlie pushed his shoulder into the door.

"Go away."

She braced herself against the door, but he easily overpowered her. With a push and two quick steps, the door was open, and he was in the room.

"No! No, Charlie...," she said, fighting against his superior strength. She tried futilely to push him back outside.

He grabbed her arms. He held them tightly while eyeing the dimly lit room. He saw no one. Then he noticed a dark shadow move across the light wood floor to his right. He began to turn but was too late. A hard blow struck the side of his head. His eyes lost focus, his knees buckled, and he fell.

Charlie floated away on a cushion of air heavy with the scent of pine, jasmine, and something else. Something sweetly aromatic. Finally, darkness closed in all around...

Chapter 15

*F*ames roared, dancing in the dark underbrush of the forest. Higher and higher they leaped. The inferno engulfed and then consumed her in its blazing sweep. Her beautiful face with its dark eyes and delicate features dissolved into something grotesque – a putrefying skull as flesh melted away. Her clothes were fiery rags wrapped around her. She turned one last time. "Charles," she mouthed silently, then she was gone.*

"No! Marie!" Charlie screamed into the darkness. He felt sharp pain, seemed on fire. He jerked awake on wet concrete, his body drenched in fear. His head throbbed as he looked around frantically to find something, anything, recognizable. *I'm buried in my own tomb*, he thought, lying in complete darkness, unnerved by the nightmare. *And Marie ... where's Marie?*

He looked around again, trying to calm himself. Slowly and with difficulty, he moved his legs, first one and then the other. His head pounded with his pulse. His throat was parched, and he had difficulty swallowing. With the tips of his fingers, he slowly felt his head. Nose, teeth, bones, all seemed okay.

Moving his hand around his neck, he located the source of the pain – behind his left ear. It was bandaged. *So they don't want me dead just yet,* he thought coldly.

My shirt? Shoes? They took everything but my trousers. "Where are my orders?" he whispered, searching his pockets.

He tried to sit up, straining to roll to his side, but failed. Something held down his legs and feet. At first, he was too weak and shaky to struggle against it. But he tried again and succeeded in raising himself up. By using one arm to brace himself, he could use the other to feel his way down his legs. His ankles were shackled to the floor in heavy steel manacles. Charlie felt that he was lying on an incline, with his feet slightly higher than his head, on a damp, musty-smelling concrete floor. He fell backward.

Struggling up again to a sitting position, he felt for walls, then saw a sliver of light. *A door?* He realized he was imprisoned within concrete walls. Counting by using his outstretched hands, he estimated that the room was about seven feet by seven feet, just enough room for him to lie there. While measuring, he accidentally bumped into a bucket. He felt it. Wood. *What's in it? Water. They must want me to drink. That's good. But who are they?*

Everything smelled of dampness, mildew, and old death. He heard a constant drip coming from just outside the door. It seemed to echo against the concrete, the sound magnified in the silence.

"Hey," he yelled weakly. "Anybody there?" There was no response, but he refused to give up. "Hey out there! I'm hungry! Hey! Hey!" Still, no response.

Then, from the far end of the cell block, he thought he heard a noise. "Hey! Let me out of here!" he yelled again.

Suddenly, there was a pounding on the door. Then a loud male voice spoke in Vietnamese, but Charlie had no idea what the man said.

"American! Let me go!" he tried again.

The man uttered the same words as before. Charlie heard his footsteps slowly walking down the corridor away from him. *The bastard probably told me to shut up,* he thought.

The cell block was quiet. Time passed, but very slowly. *How long have I been in this place?* he wondered, realizing he had no idea how much time had passed.

As more time slowly creeped by, he heard voices and movement outside the door to his cell. A guard opened his door to check on him, and later, so did another. His guards were older Vietnamese men wearing worn khaki uniforms and simple straw sandals. Speaking in rough French, Charlie attempted to communicate with them. He received very little information, but did learn that they served the government of Vietnam. "Ho Chi Minh," they replied. He guessed that the guards had been doing their jobs for years and had served many masters – the French, the Japanese, and now the Viet Minh.

He began to call his regular guard 'Old Man' because he looked the most senior, with his white chin whiskers and gaunt, slightly stooped hobble in and out of the cell each day.

When it came, food was a simple gruel. A ball of rice placed in a tin bowl in his cell through a long, three-inch-wide slit in the lower part of a door. He was also given a tin cup. His captors fed him twice a day, early in the morning and later in the evening. Once a day, he was taken from his cell in shackles and walked in a small, inner courtyard – a brick walkway around a grassy center area, while two guards swabbed out the cell. There was no slop bucket, only the small wooden one that held his drinking water. The light only improved slightly when the sun crept across the sky to shine through a corridor window just outside his cell. The rest of the time, Charlie lived in shadowy twilight or total darkness. It felt like weeks had passed.

During the first outing from his cell, Old Man took him to a central room in what Charlie perceived to be a large compound. There, from the street noise he heard outside the walls, he thought he might be in the middle of an urban area. In the center of the room was a high guillotine, its wide steel blade tied in the up position at the top of the wood frame. A thatched wicker basket sat alongside a bench where the blade's blindfolded victims probably lay. Old Man allowed Charlie a close look. *First, they try intimidation*, he thought.

The simple efficiency of a machine designed solely to kill human beings quickly sent chills through his weakened frame. Charlie dreamed of the killing machine that night. The intimidation worked.

By slapping and kicking him, the other guards let Charlie know that talking was against the rules. But Old Man never laid a hand on him. On the third day, he finally got one of the guards, a man he thought to be at least sixty, to answer a simple question he asked repeatedly in French: "Where am I?"

The man replied in a whisper, "Hanoi."

"Jesi Cristo! What the hell am I doing in Hanoi?" Charlie said partly in Czech, shocked. *Someone has kidnapped and transported me almost eight hundred miles. Why?*

On a later outing from the dark confines of his cell, he saw others – a long line of seemingly frail men of varying ages, all Vietnamese, shackled together ankle to ankle, wearing gray pajamas but barefoot. They shuffled along around the inner courtyard. Two guards, carrying long sticks, yelled at them while they circled the grass. Charlie had not seen any of the guards armed with weapons.

He counted three days based on his routine since he had regained consciousness. He was not tortured, but the thought of spending what remained of his life in this place frightened him even more. To take his mind off it, he spent the long hours trying to unravel the puzzle of his predicament and to plan an escape. He tried to eat, conserve his strength, and wait for an opportunity – any opportunity.

He thought long and hard about who might have put him in this place. *The last person I saw was Truin. She had to have been involved. After all, I was slugged in her room. But who had been in the room with her?*

Charlie wondered how or if his kidnapping was connected to the Japanese, or with the investigation of Dixon's death. But he was convinced that the diamonds were somehow involved. *Everyone wants those diamonds*, he thought, but maybe something more. *Why would they take me as far as Hanoi and then throw me in this dungeon? They must have known that I didn't have any diamonds in my possession. And they have no way of knowing how cooperative I would be, even if I knew where they were. My kidnapping must have something to do with their struggle for independence.* He tried to reason it all out. *No, it's the diamonds*, he decided.

In the dark, he carefully loosened the brittle tin stay wrapped around the side of the water bucket and worked a six-inch end back and forth until it snapped off. Feverishly, he scraped the soft metal against the concrete floor to sharpen a point. Back and forth he dragged the edge, feeling the heat on his fingers and beside his leg. He worked the tin in the darkness. *I must act quickly, before Old Man brings rice in the morning. Then I'll wait for an opportunity to use it. Old Man is my best chance of getting out of this hole. If I could get word to the American team on the ground here, that might be my best option. Yes, they would insist that I be freed.* He caught himself and fought to repress feelings of his growing desperation.

Early the morning of the fourth day, Charlie heard a voice just outside the door. *It's Old Man!* He heard the key turn in the ancient lock. The door swung open, and the old guard entered with the rice. He studied him closely as he went about his daily routine. *I will bribe him to take a message to the Americans or British here. That might work*, he decided.

Charlie moved but only slightly. "I want to die quickly," he said in French. "I cannot live in this place. Will you help me, Old Man?" he asked, watching his guard closely.

The old man said nothing, but carefully looked him over. "Be quiet," he finally said in French and prepared to leave.

"A message? To tell my poor mother I'm still alive. You would be rewarded handsomely if you would deliver a simple message to the Americans here in Hanoi."

The old man ignored him. The heavy metal door slammed shut. *At least he didn't tell me to shut up again,* Charlie thought, trying to put a bright face on it.

Later that day, he heard shouting coming from down the dark corridor. The words, echoing off the walls, were in both Vietnamese and French. "*Vive la liberté!*" he heard.

Silence soon returned. Charlie thought he could hear the thud of heavy boots on the concrete. *Soldiers coming for me? Yes, I'm certain,* he thought, but not hopeful anyone would ever free him.

"Open this door. I order you," the strong voice said in Russian.

Soon Charlie heard the lock turn and as quickly, in the shadows of the dim sunshine stood Major Gregor Zerenowsky.

"Free him," he ordered the old man and he complied. "I have orders from Colonel Andre Pavlov."

Hearing the name, Pavlov, caused Charlie to react by withdrawing quickly to a far corner. "No, not that brute."

"I free you from this stench, comrade," Zerenowsky said, helping Charlie to his feet but also having a firm grasp of him.

"Take me to an embassy, any embassy, I beg you," Charlie growled weakly, having to force out each word.

"Come. We go." Zerenowsky drug Charlie out the doorway, down the wet concrete corridor and through the courtyard to a waiting car. He threw Charlie in the back of an old Peugeot and slid in with him. "To the mission," he ordered the driver. They were accompanied by two Russian soldiers to ensure that orders were followed. Pavlov was determined the clever American would not escape his clutches.

"Colonel," Zerenowsky said, presenting the prisoner to him at the small Russian Mission in Hanoi. "What are your plans for him? Remember sir, if you kill him, we will learn nothing about Rasputin."

Pavlov stared at the Ukrainian. "You think me a fool, Major? I've been doing this since before you were born, so do not tell me my business."

"The prisoner is weak. I worry his heart may not take torture."

Pavlov only stared at the junior officer. "Sergeant, he called to one of his guards. "Take the prisoner to the large room and tie him into the chair. Then leave him."

"Yes sir," a short man with Asian features replied. He took another man and went to get Charlie.

"Do you wish to assist me, Major? You may find my methods most educational." Pavlov blew a long stream of cigarette smoke from his lungs, then smiled deviously.

"When you are finished, I will come in and remove the prisoner," Zerenowsky replied hesitantly. "I am confident you will have the identity of Rasputin by then. He forced a smile.

"If not today, tomorrow, or the next. No matter," he said. "Patience. We must have patience." Pavlov saw immediately that Zerenowsky had no stomach for this kind of work. *He won't last long in our business,* he thought, feeling only contempt for the younger man.

Charlie sat in a chair, hands and ankles bound tightly. He still had little understanding for why he was here, but he knew well the Russians, and their methods for extracting information. He thought back to his last meeting with the NKVD officer one year earlier on the far side of the world. His unit had reached forward elements of the Red Army of the Second Ukrainian front midday of November sixth. He learned that NKVD units already were briefed on their impending arrival and were waiting to interrogate everyone.

Charlie called the three surviving Americans together. "Tell the Russians that you are US Army, here rescuing downed pilots," he explained carefully. "You must say that you were trapped during the fighting. Do not, I repeat, do not say anything more. Last night, I radioed my contact in the NKVD to get clearances so that you can pass through their lines safely." He knew that even though the Russians had granted them permission well in advance of their operation, his men would be safer if he radioed the Russian command before reaching their lines.

"Captain," Sergeant Donleavy called. "The radio. They're responding to your call. It's in Russian. I can't understand all of it."

"All Americans will be allowed to enter Russian lines. End of message."

"Let's go," Charlie said as a Russian truck arrived for them about midday. But before any of the Americans understood what was happening, they were closely surrounded by six Ukrainians. Pointing their machine guns threateningly, the Ukrainians quickly herded them against the side of the truck and disarmed them.

The leader looked each American over closely, then singled Charlie out from the others. "You go. But him, no. We take with us," he said in broken English to Donleavy and the other Americans. Charlie's hands were bound securely behind his back, and he was forcibly separated from the others.

"Go! Do as they say," he called to Donleavy. "I'll be okay. Just a little misunderstanding."

"Be quiet," the Ukrainian leader said. His men leveled their weapons at the other Americans. The other Americans quickly jumped into the back of the truck.

"You," the man said after the other Americans had departed. He still held his Tokarev at Charlie's head. "I am ordered to kill you, Captain Stanek."

"Who gave the order?" Charlie demanded.

"A high officer in our security police has ordered it," he said, lighting a cigarette and trying to stick it in Charlie's mouth.

"His name? Tell me the name of the bastard," Charlie again demanded, struggling against the rope.

The Russian smiled. "Tie him to that tree," he ordered two of his subordinates.

Their leader, a small thin man with eyes like a cat, always smiling, blindfolded Charlie. He was certain he was going to die, and prepared for that final moment, for the shots that would kill him. But nothing. He was shocked. Finally, he heard another voice, one that he recognized. "Cut him loose," the voice ordered in Russian. When they removed the blindfold, he saw that it was Major Zerenowsky.

"Now Comrade Stanek, the debt has been repaid," Zerenowsky said. "Go back to the mountains with your men." Then he turned and walked away. He got back in his vehicle and departed even before Charlie was freed.

The bastard, Major Zerenowsky, staged the entire incident for my benefit. I'm sure of it, Charlie thought, waiting for his impending fate at the hands of the two Russians. *But why?* His mind screamed for an answer.

Chapter 16

Torture at the hands of Colonel Andre Pavlov was not pleasant. For the remainder of the day the Russian NKVD agent had his way with Charlie, attempting to extract the information he wanted. Charlie gave him nothing and Pavlov swore he would continue as long as it took for him to reveal the identity of Rasputin. "Then you will go to Siberia for the remainder of your short life," he growled, blowing smoke in Charlie's face. "Tomorrow we do it again, but now I will rest and think." He smiled, turned, and left with the soldiers.

After Pavlov left the room heading to his upstairs office, Major Zerenowsky entered with a doctor in tow. "Comrade, he is dying. We must take him to the dispensary."

The older man quickly gave Charlie the once-over, and then nodded. "Take him."

"I will untie him and take him to your office," Zerenowsky said. "Go. I will meet you there."

The doctor turned and left the room.

"We go, comrade. Quickly and quietly." He untied Charlie, lifted him onto his shoulders, and made for the door, into the empty lobby and out the front door. A taxi with a Vietnamese driver waited.

"You are a strong man, Stan –yak, and I have taken a great risk for freedom."

Within minutes, they were racing across Hanoi in a bid to escape. Charlie had no idea what was happening, and in great pain. He fought to stay conscious. The trip through the city and across the Red River to Hanoi's French-built airfield was fast. They passed through two roadblocks manned by Chinese Kuomintang troops before reaching the single large hangar on the edge of the field. The soldiers allowed passage when Gregor told them in Russian that they were with the Allied Control Commission and confidently flashed his papers at them.

The airfield consisted of one concrete runway, the large hangar of corrugated steel, and a steel-framed control tower, not unlike the one in Dalat. They found a few of the Chinese soldiers hanging about near the planes parked alongside the hangar. Charlie counted four planes – one with Russian markings, one with Chinese, and two with the Rising Sun clearly visible.

"Gregor, where are we going?" Charlie asked, not comprehending what was happening. "Where are you taking me?"

"To America."

"To America? Is this a trick of yours, Zerenowsky? I know what you're capable of." Charlie kept looking behind him, expecting something. This turn of events was still unfathomable.

"A trick? No, we must leave this place, comrade." He pointed to several planes parked in the middle of the group. "There," he said to the driver, pointing.

"Is that plane one of ours?" Charlie asked, seeing it was American built.

"Can you fly it?" Gregor asked intently. "Quickly. Time is running out for us. Can you?"

"You mean we have to steal it and fly it ourselves?"

"Yes. You are a pilot."

"That one. Curtis C-46. I can fly it," Charlie replied quickly, pointing at the American plane with Chinese markings. "I hope they don't mind us borrowing their airplane."

Gregor motioned for the driver to pull alongside and let them out. He jumped from the vehicle and ran to Charlie's door. "Come, quickly."

With the Russian's aid, he got out. At first hesitant and suspicious that he was walking into another trap, he then sensed the urgency in Gregor's actions and knew he had to act quickly. "Okay, let's go."

"Take this. You may need it," Gregor said, handing him another Tokarev pistol. Charlie looked it over, pulled the magazine. Full. He reinserted it and dropped the weapon in a front pocket of his trousers.

"You will act like you are my prisoner. We will march directly past the guards to the middle plane, just like it is ours to ride in. Let's go," Gregor ordered in a whisper. They walked directly to the plane with the Chinese markings. Gregor pointed his gun in the middle of Charlie's back. He smiled and bowed politely to the Chinese. "To Kunming," he yelled in Chinese, "with this traitor." He quickly opened the cargo bay door and helped Charlie in. The guards stared but no one made any move to stop them.

"Empty. Good, good. I didn't know for certain. Yesterday, I came out here to investigate the airplanes. I spoke with the Chinese," Gregor explained, peering around the fuselage and into the cockpit. "My American brother, the pilot. Go," he said and pointed forward.

Charlie sat down in the left-hand pilot seat and began checking over the instruments and controls. *Lucky,* he thought, *they're in English.* He was running on pure adrenaline. Still shoeless, he was clad only in trousers and the torn wool tunic. "The old bird has fuel," he said. "Get up here!"

"I'm coming," Gregor called, closing the cargo door. "Start it, and we fly to America."

Charlie hoped they could get to an American or British airfield with the fuel they had.

"If we can get out of here, General Donovan will rescue us," Gregor said, sounding confident.

"But first, we must take off," Charlie reminded him. Scanning the field, he looked for any sign of trouble. From behind the hangar, he saw soldiers running toward them.

Gregor saw them too. "Hurry, comrade. They see it is a trick."

Charlie cranked an engine. Nothing. He tried again. Still nothing. The third time, it fired, slowly spinning up, first one engine then the second. The soldiers were getting closer. He saw that they were Chinese. The planes' guards still had not moved but watched the others. *Would they shoot at their own airplane?* he wondered.

He taxied the plane onto the runway, heading for the far end of the field, away from the soldiers. They saw a car cross the field and turn directly at them. "Quickly, to America," Gregor yelled. He opened the side window of the cockpit and fired off three shots at the Chinese soldiers rapidly approaching at a dead run. Hearing the gunfire, they dived for cover, but the black sedan still raced across the field at a ninety-degree angle to intercept.

"Buckle up," Charlie ordered. He concentrated on the control panel.

"We must stop them," Gregor said. This time he fired off more rounds at the sedan, aiming at the driver. The car zigzagged but still kept coming. "Damn Pavlov," he cursed. "Fuck his mother."

Charlie advanced the throttles. The engines screamed as the RPMs spiked. Rattling and shaking, the plane lumbered down the runway, slowly picking up speed. They were on a collision course with the car. The two rushed toward each other from the far ends of the airstrip.

Gregor reloaded his pistol and prepared to fire again.

The C-46 accelerated faster under Charlie's steady hand with the throttles firewalled. "Hold on," he yelled, now tightly gripping the yoke.

The Russian fired in the general direction of the car, emptying the magazine.

At the last second, the old Peugeot swerved out of the way. The plane roared past. They heard the twang of bullets puncturing the fuselage. Charlie pulled the yoke back and they lifted slowly off the ground. He gained altitude and banked. The plane headed south-southeast. "To Manila," Zerenowsky ordered. "I think it is the closest American field."

"No, to Saigon, Major," Charlie replied. "I have unfinished business." His chest burned.

"That is very dangerous for both of us, I think."

"Why, comrade? And why have you rescued me from Russian security?"

"The NKVD look for spies everywhere," Gregor said slowly. "I think they would have killed you, and I could not allow that to happen. Now we must get away from them."

"Yes. I know you've taken a great risk for me," Charlie said, extending his hand. They shook. "Now, see if there's anything on board. Clothing, weapons, anything useful."

"I will go and see what is here," Gregor mumbled, obviously not happy with Charlie's change of plan to fly to Saigon. He exited the cockpit.

A few minutes later, he returned. "Some rice in back, but no weapons or clothing. I did find a first-aid kit, and in English, too."

"Let me see," Charlie said, rifling through the metal box. "I can use this." He removed band-aids and burn ointment. Gregor helped him apply the band-aid. "I think of Wisconsin and its great forests, just like in my Ukraine. I remember your stories, my friend, from our first meeting in Tehran. I can never go home again, so maybe I go to Wisconsin."

"Wisconsin, eh?" Charlie remarked, amused. The pilot on his trip from Manila had told him that the only aircraft flying in the South China Sea were British and American. All Japanese aircraft were grounded unless given permission on a case-by-case basis. With this plane's Chinese markings, he knew they would not be disturbed. He looked down, saw the inky blackness of the ocean, and banked the plane to follow the coastline south.

"Set a course for Manila. Please," Gregor pleaded. "I think that is safer."

Safer for who, Charlie wondered. "We are going to Saigon, comrade," he repeated. He looked straight ahead.

The Russian stared sullenly out the window.

"I have to get to Saigon."

"To do what?"

"Solve a mystery," Charlie answered. "And..."

"You do not know the NKVD like I do, my American friend. They will hunt me down, and Saigon is much too close," he said, the worry apparent in his voice. "What mystery could be so important?"

"I'm going to catch a murderer."

"There are so many to catch," Gregor answered sadly. "Why just one?"

Charlie thought he could cover the distance to Saigon in about three hours. He looked over to the Russian, who was sound to sleep, his chin resting against his burly chest. He still found it difficult to believe that Zerenowsky would risk his own life to save his. Where the Russians were concerned, nothing was simple. It seemed that duplicity and betrayal always lay around the next corner.

The sun was breaking the horizon when they reached the Mekong River delta. They were almost out of fuel. Charlie knew they would have to land on the airstrip outside of Saigon immediately, without circling. He had practiced that landing before while in flight school in Louisiana. But during a routine training flight, the aircraft had malfunctioned. His right engine had sputtered then died. The plane had lost altitude, forcing him to make an emergency landing on a dirt road ninety miles from Baton Rouge. The natural skill and quick thinking he demonstrated had helped earn him his wings, but he had decided then and there that he never wanted to repeat the exercise.

Two hundred miles out, he had finally made radio contact with a British radio operator at Tan Son Nhat.

"I see the airstrip," Gregor announced, excited. "I see no other planes in the air. That is good, eh?"

"Yeah, good," Charlie replied, concentrating on the impending landing.

"No one must know, Major," Gregor insisted. "You must tell no one that I am on this airplane."

"But..." Charlie began. He gave in when he realized that Gregor was right. Having a defecting Russian NKVD officer onboard was not something he needed to announce. And he was too busy at the moment to argue, so he complied with his wishes.

He did not mention he had a Russian defector onboard and requested that only Sergeant Catledge of the American Embankment Team be notified of his arrival. Charlie gave the radioman a message for Catledge that he hoped only Joe would understand. 'Tell no one. Bring top cop and come at once.'

Gregor tried to monitor the message, but with little grasp of the English language, he understood clearly that his fate was in Charlie's hands.

"Sure you don't want to bail out?" Charlie asked, looking straight ahead.

"Ha! I take my chances with you, my comrade. I do not trust Chinese parachutes."

They made their approach from the northeast without circling the field. He lowered the landing gear. Now they could see vehicles on standby, the white crosses visible on the tops of some. Slowly, Charlie throttled back. "Hold on. Here we go."

Suddenly both engines began to sputter. He increased the fuel mixture to give them more fuel and keep them running just a minute more. The entire cabin shook as the engines still coughed and spit. They were two hundred meters from the runway and closing. Finally, engine one and then engine two coughed one last time and died.

The plane touched ground to Charlie's relief. He kept the C-46 under control. Within seconds, they were coasting to a stop about 700 feet from the terminal. Charlie thought he saw Catledge standing by his jeep waiting for his arrival.

"Who is waiting for us? Just your sergeant? I must know now if there will be others."

"Sergeant Catledge and a Japanese soldier will meet us here. You can trust Catledge, and the Jap won't give us any trouble. But still, we'll tell them nothing until we come up with a plan."

"Good," Gregor replied uneasily. He gripped the butt of his automatic. "But quickly, I need a cover."

"You're right. I'll think of something."

"It will be several days before others discover where I am and come for me from Hanoi. So we have some time to operate. But, then we must get out of here quickly. They want you, too. Don't forget that."

"I understand," he said, looking Gregor over carefully. "Let me do the talking. I will tell them that you are a Russian soldier from the delegation in Hanoi on a routine mission to Saigon to consult with your allies. I'll say that you intervened to clear up a misunderstanding regarding my arrest. That's your cover for the time being."

"Yes, good." Gregor said, smiling, satisfied. He patted Charlie on the back.

"Oh, yeah, don't call me 'major.' I'm traveling as a civilian," Charlie said.

"Yes, that is so. Always, we deceive, eh?" He laughed and patted him again, this time harder.

"Ouch! Be careful, I'm still hurting from your buddy's pounding," he growled.

"Yes," Gregor said, suddenly looking concerned. "I follow you."

"We'll come up with some type of workable plan that'll get you out of here," he said, massaging the back of his neck. "But first, I must deal with Captain Suzuki."

Chapter 17

A delegation of three – Joe Catledge, Major Hiroaka, and a representative of the Chinese government – waited to greet them. The Chinese officer was there to safeguard the return of his property. Charlie knew that the C-46 was invaluable to them. When he stepped off the plane with the big Russian, Joe was taken aback.

Gregor still wore his uniform, that of a major in the Russian Army. Charlie, in obvious pain from his wounds, was still dressed only in his Russian-issue tunic. He was barefooted. The gash across his neck still oozed blood through his improvised compress. It had trickled down his shoulder and back before hardening on his bare skin. He knew the wound would require stitches. Dried, caked blood also was visible from the gash on his cheek. But that wound looked worse than it actually was.

Joe rushed to Charlie. "You okay?" he asked, wrapping his large arm around him. "I didn't think I'd see you again." He hugged him tightly.

"Careful," Charlie said with a grimace. "For a while there, I didn't think I'd be back either."

"The woman said Cao Dai extremists had captured you. She said you were probably dead." He tried to help Charlie walk by bracing him against his shoulder. "So much for Russian hospitality."

"Who did she say captured me?"

"Cao Dai extremists. They're some sort of religious group north of here. They're fighting to be independent of the French too. But they hate the commies," Joe continued. "A revenge killing, I think is the way she worded it." He held on to Charlie. "I didn't believe it. She was blaming a group she didn't like. But we searched everywhere. Nothing."

"We?"

"Yeah, the Brits and the Japanese helped," Joe replied, looking at the Japanese soldier standing beside him. "We couldn't allow our special envoy to just disappear without a trace," he said, still holding on to him. "As you requested in your message, I found the major here and brought him along. But what's going on?"

"I'll explain everything. Just hold on."

Major Hiroaka bowed. "Good to see you again, Mr. Stanek, alive," he said calmly. "I have important information for you on your investigation." He looked the Russian over carefully.

"Good, good," Charlie replied. "I had hoped you would. As soon as I get a doc to sew me up, we can talk."

"That colonel up in Dalat is still sending progress reports," Joe said, hugging him again. "Hey," he asked, pointing to Charlie's companion walking beside them. "Who's the guerilla?"

"A long story, Sarge," Charlie said, glad to be back with the football player. "He's a Russian soldier who helped clear up the mess in Hanoi. Major Gregor Zerenowsky, this is Sergeant Joe Catledge, Major Hiroaka." The Russian shook hands with both men. "He's here to see the British, but first..."

Charlie looked around for other vehicles. "Sarge, you didn't tell Blankston or anyone that I was returning, did you?"

"No, just like you requested," Joe said, confused. "But he's commanding here. I don't feel right keeping this from him. Why the secrecy?"

"I think someone is trying very hard to stop our investigation. We need to move quickly before anyone knows I'm back. We don't need to tell Blankston about the Russian just yet. It'll just confuse things."

"I don't know about that," Joe mumbled under his breath.

"Major, is there a place we can meet ... in private?" Charlie asked the Japanese policeman.

"Yes, come with me." He led the three to a private room in the airport where they saw only Japanese soldiers. "They are my men who guard our airplanes." He carefully looked at Charlie's wounds. "I have ordered a doctor, a Japanese doctor, for your wounds, Mr. Stanek."

"Thank you," Charlie said. "Now, what do you have for me?"

"I have bad news, Mr. Stanek," the major said. "The criminal, Suzuki, has escaped."

"When?"

"Early this morning ... in the darkness."

"How?"

"I was told by Colonel Hamura that Major Ishitoro and two of his men smuggled him out of the hotel, right under their noses, it seems. According to the colonel, Ishitoro had been investigating the captain. They knew he had stolen the diamonds."

The doctor, a man, well into his fifties, Charlie guessed, with thick bifocals and the uniform of a colonel, arrived. Without a word, he began to examine him. He was thin, almost frail looking, but his hands were quick and agile, like those of a surgeon.

"I think they cut a deal that Suzuki couldn't refuse, eh?" Joe added.

"Yeah, but we knew it was just a matter of time. Suzuki knew time was running short for him, and he had to act."

The doctor removed a suturing needle and thin thread from his bag and began to work carefully on Charlie's wound.

"Who else knows of Suzuki's escape, Major?" Charlie asked, feeling the pain from the needle. "Ouch," he growled at the doctor. The doctor nodded that he heard and understood.

"I don't know, but soon everyone will know," Joe said. "And that includes the Vietnamese."

"Yes, the Viet Minh," Charlie replied, his brows furrowing. "*Mademoiselle du Vire* warned me that something would happen. She probably learned in Dalat that Major Ishitoro was determined to get the gems for himself."

"I suspect one of Suzuki's accomplices killed the ferryman, Mr. Stanek," Major Hiroaka said.

"I agree with you, Major." *Did they also kill the Frenchman?* Charlie wondered. *Or was it the Vietnamese? And what is Truin's role in all this?* He had many questions and damn few answers.

"There was a rumor that the British were preparing to remove Suzuki to Saigon today," Major Hiroaka said.

"Word travels fast around here," Charlie said. "Where will Suzuki and Ishitoro go now?"

"I don't know for certain, but I suspect they will flee for Laos with their stolen gems," the policeman said. "I am told that they are well armed."

"What about the British?" Joe asked. "Will they go after them?"

"I have told Major Clifton about the escape," the Japanese policeman replied. "He notified General Hawakawa of Southern Japanese Command that the British Army cannot spare any soldiers. He said the Japanese Army will be held responsible for their capture. If we fail, British and French members of the Allied Control Commission will inform General MacArthur that we have violated the terms of the peace treaty. General Hawakawa told me as much."

Charlie thought about that. "What do you think their escape route is?"

"They travel north to Pleiku. I suspect the diamonds are hidden somewhere between Pleiku and the prison camp at PleiToan. Perhaps along the highway, because Suzuki has not left that area since he stole them. But when they retrieve the diamonds, they will flee into the jungles of Laos. There they can hide until it is safe to move about."

"I knew the bastard would run," Joe growled.

"I must go after them, Mr. Stanek. Their capture has become my responsibility."

"Sarge, I must go with the major. I have to finish this job. I will not allow this murderer to go free with a fortune in diamonds," Charlie said, having made up his mind.

"I'm with you," Joe said without hesitation. "Let's get to work on it. We gotta move before they get too much of a head start on us."

The doctor, having finished, bowed politely and left.

"I go prepare," Major Hiroaka announced and abruptly left the room.

Major Zerenowsky listened to the discussion quietly from the corner of the room. "Stanek, what are we doing?"

The Russian, he suddenly remembered. "Sarge, we need to get Major Zerenowsky to Manila ASAP." He repeated it in Russian for Gregor's benefit.

"What? Why?" Joe asked, surprised.

"Defector," Charlie said softly under his breath. "Can we do it, today?"

"No problem. There's a bird on the tarmac now," he said, looking out the window. "DC-3 on the Manila run warming up."

"Comrade, I cannot leave without you," Gregor said, looking worried.

"I know what we discussed, but we can't protect you here. If you come with us, every Viet Minh in the country will be trying to get you. Your allies, remember?"

"I must warn you. There is a traitor high in your organization," the Russian said, speaking softly only to Charlie in Russian. "I know him only as 'Attila,' and he has been supplying us with intelligence since 1943. So tell your man to be careful, not to trust anyone. We cannot cable General Donovan. It is too risky."

"Things are starting to make more sense. Is that how they tracked me here in Indochina?" *Another piece of the puzzle*, Charlie thought, still not trusting the Russian. "I have a plan that doesn't involve Washington, and we get you out of here quickly."

"What is your plan?" Gregor asked, giving in.

"We will get you to Clark Field where you will be protected until I arrive. I will write a letter of introduction to the base commander on behalf of President Truman and the Allied Control Commission to explain your status. There, you'll be out of reach of the NKVD. We'll stress the importance of your mission to the commander and swear him to secrecy."

"I'll go talk with the pilot," Joe said, then got up and quickly departed. He left Charlie and the Russian in the room alone.

I will never be safe from the Russians. This I know, Charlie thought, considering Major Zerenowsky and his importance to the United States.

Chapter 18

"Welcome back, Major," Major Blankston said when Charlie entered his small room. "We thought you were a goner."

"Major, the bastards kidnapped and tortured me. I'm going to lodge a formal complaint with the Russian Embassy. I request you do the same with the Vietnamese here in Saigon."

"I agree," Major Blankston replied. He looked Charlie over slowly. Wrinkling his nose, he indicated to Charlie that he smelled badly. "I see you found a doctor," he commented, observing the sutured wounds.

"A Japanese doctor at the airfield patched me up."

"I must hear all about your capture and especially your heroic escape. For my report to Washington." Major Blankston scowled. "You notified Sergeant Catledge through the British, I was told. Why was I not directly notified?"

"Major Blankston, I have come to trust Catledge and know that he can be relied upon to assist me. I did not purposely exclude you from the loop," Charlie said, thinking quickly. "There have been numerous security leaks. I simply wanted to ensure that an American received the message ASAP. I thought of Catledge."

"Do you think I'm a security risk, Major Stanek?"

"No, of course not, sir," he said, defensively. "Major, as a diplomat outside the chain of command here, I sometimes must operate as circumstances dictate. I apologize for any appearance of disrespect."

Major Blankston stared at him. "I suggest you get cleaned up, get a bath. A nap wouldn't hurt either. And a change of clothes would help. Then we'll talk again."

"I'm heading there now." Charlie left the room with a sigh of relief. *I think we'll manage to get the Russian out of the country discreetly,* he decided. *But after that, who knows?*

"I have to let Washington know you've returned," Major Blankston said. He wrote out a short cryptic note on tablet paper, folded it, and placed it in a courier pouch. "Sergeant Eddleton," he said to the quiet, dour man who stood behind him in the doorway. "Take this to British command and transmit. Do it yourself. It's classified."

Eddleton took the message and immediately left.

"We have to relay our messages through the British Far East Fleet, since the Embankment Team has no other way of communicating directly with our command in Ceylon ... or anywhere else for that matter."

Later that evening, Blankston made Charlie tell his story again in more detail for his report to Washington.

"I find it all very difficult to believe," he said when Charlie finished. "Why would the Reds go to all that trouble to take you? Are you that damn important to them?" he asked, almost incredulous. "There's a piece still missing, Major."

"Those are my thoughts exactly, Major Blankston," Charlie replied with a shrug. He could not help but smile, seeing a look of utter confusion on Blankston's face.

"Have you heard about the Jap criminal, Suzuki? He has escaped," Major Blankston finally said.

Charlie stood and prepared to return to his room. "I was told by Major Hiroaka. That just makes my job more difficult."

"What do you mean?"

"I'm going to get him, Major," Charlie said flatly.

The major gave him a look. "It would be better for you if you got the hell out of Indochina. Let someone else worry about the Jap."

"I was sent here to do a job, Major," Charlie said.

"Your job doesn't involve chasing a war criminal across Indochina, Major."

"Let's just call it wrapping up unfinished business."

"Yeah, right," the embankment commander said, giving up on persuading him to leave. "I'm sending Catledge along then. If something happens to you, Stanek, I'll be the first one they blame."

"I better leave right away. I'd appreciate it if you could coordinate with the Brits. We'll need a ride to Pleiku."

"I can do that. Get some rest," the major said, sounding genuinely concerned.

"We'll leave at dawn," Charlie said as he left.

"I'll tell Clifton."

Who am I fooling? Charlie asked himself, walking back to his room. *I just want to get the son of a bitch before he escapes for good.*

Chapter 19

C harlie lay on the thin mattress, exhausted. Light from a tropical sky streamed through the French doors opened to the small balcony to capture an evening breeze. He closed his eyes and tried to sleep.

In the deep of night, several hours before dawn, a slight figure quietly turned the lock on his door. Someone entered the room, moving soundlessly. Charlie pretended to be asleep, but he had heard the click of the lock. The intruder crept stealthily toward the bed.

When Truin reached him, she stood silently over him. Only the soft rhythm of his breathing broke the silence. She slid out of her sandals and pulled the cord that held up her black pants, allowing them to fall to the floor. Quickly, she threw off the cotton blouse. Now, also naked, she bent toward him. Aroused, Charlie watched through half-closed eyes.

Abruptly he reached up and grabbed her wrist, pulling her into the bed. With his other arm, he reached across her naked thigh and down to her calf. He found the stiletto and tossed it across the floor. "I remembered," he said softly in her ear. Her deep black hair fell across both their faces like a perfumed curtain. "Have you come to finish the job?" he whispered in her ear.

Truin turned on her right side. "Charlie," she said, pressing her small firm breasts and thigh into his body. "You are alive. I'm so happy."

"Yes, I'm alive," he whispered and rolled on top of her, pinning both her arms against the mattress. "I should kill you," he said, smiling down on her. "That's what you deserve."

"Kill me then," she whispered. "But I did not come to harm you, as you can see."

"I want information," he replied, still pressing her wrists against the mattress. "Tell me who arranged for my kidnapping."

"Let me go," the young princess said, struggling. "I demand that you let me go. You're hurting me."

"Tell me who kidnapped me."

"It was part of the agreement between us and the Russians."

"For the guns?"

"Yes, for the guns," she said, squirming to free herself against his superior strength.

"Who hit me?"

"It was Nguyen Ngoc Tran who you met in Phan Rang. He gave you to the Russians. One of his men hit you," she replied hesitantly. "Now let me go, or you will regret it."

"You betrayed me. It was all a trap to lure me to Dalat, wasn't it?"

"Yes," she said simply. "But I tried to warn you, Charlie. I wanted you to escape. That night, I pleaded with Comrade Tran not to harm you, but it was too late."

"Why did you warn me?"

She stopped struggling. "Because I love you. That night I realized that I loved you."

"Tell me the name of the Russian who had arranged for my kidnapping?"

"Major Zerenowsky."

"Zerenowsky? That doesn't make sense." Charlie's back tensed. *Lies, Major Zerenowsky, always you tell me lies. I wonder what kind of betrayal I should expect from you next.*

"If you do not believe me, then go ahead, Charlie, kill me. Shoot me with your pistol."

Charlie thought she was giving in too easily. He didn't take his eyes off her. "I believe you," he finally said. "They tortured me, threatened to kill me." He stared down at her. "Did you know that?"

"If you tell me it is true, *oui*, I believe you."

"Maybe I should do that to you, Comrade Truin or *Mademoiselle du Vire* or whatever name you are currently using."

"I don't think that's what you want to do," she said with a smile. She relaxed under his weight. "I am called Madame Thieu by my countrymen."

"That works...Madame Thieu."

"Why did you come here?" He released her left arm to run his hand across her breasts, touching then circling her nipples with the tip of his index finger. With both hands he stroked her breasts, but the action was rough. He saw fear in her eyes and enjoyed the power he had over her.

"Do you want to hurt me, Charlie?" Truin asked, looking hard into his eyes. "I see your anger, but you are not an evil man. This I know."

"You are a dangerous woman, but I can't keep from touching you," he said, suddenly smiling. But he removed his hands from her breasts.

"I want to show you, to prove to you, that I love you," she said, rubbing her hands along his shoulders and arms. "I want to feel you. That's why I came."

"First you must tell me about Major Zerenowsky," Charlie said. "How do you know this man?"

"I do not know him. But he contacted our government in Hanoi. He said that you were an important agent working against his government. We had to assist him by capturing you."

"How did you get involved?"

"Comrade Giau ordered me to assist the Russians," she said, raising her head to kiss him on top of his left hand, then on each finger. "It was my duty. I had to obey."

"Even when you knew I was not spying on them?" He pushed her head back down hard against the mattress.

"I do not know that. You could be an American spy, Charlie."

"A spy?" He pressed both hands against her cheeks. "You betrayed me for what?" he asked, again thinking of how Nazis and NKVD agents had tried to destroy him.

"I must tell you one thing, and you must believe me." She pushed against his chest to free herself, but he was too strong, and finally she gave in to his superior strength. Again she looked into his eyes for a sign. "What will you do now?"

"Don't talk anymore," he ordered. He kissed first her right then left breast. He saw that her eyes were closed.

"I must say this. You must know."

"Then tell me."

"I could never hurt you, Charlie," she said. "I tried to protect you."

His tongue touched her nipple. He raised his mouth to find her lips. They kissed.

"I love you," Truin whispered in his ear. She raised both legs and tightened them around his waist.

Slowly but forcefully he thrust himself into her. Truin responded fiercely.

Later, they lay together on the narrow bed. She touched his face, and he opened his eyes. "Oh, Charlie, I can never give you up. But I must," she whispered, her hand still on his face. She leaned over him and softly kissed the small scar above his eye. Her face was wet with tears.

Charlie felt them on his cheek and knew they were real. He wrapped his arms around her to draw her close. "I don't know what to believe, but right now it doesn't matter." He held her tightly in his arms. "Truin, you and me ... we're just a passing moment of passion, aren't we?" he said, gently kissing her on the cheek.

Truin listened to his words. "I'm so sad for us, Charlie," she whispered and buried her head in his chest.

"When I found you, I found a part of myself," Charlie told her. He began to caress her thigh and back.

"Yes?" Truin said. She slowly rolled on top, straddling him between her thighs. She reached down with both hands to touch him. "You feel so good," she said, gently stroking him. Again, they made love slowly in the early-morning darkness, their passion exploding in a single and final moment of union.

Chapter 20

Joe arranged to borrow a small reconnaissance plane and pilot from the British in Saigon to take the three of them as far as Pleiku in the Central Highlands. From there they would be on their own. The only troops in the region were the small detachment of Japanese that kept the Pleiku airfield open.

Charlie accepted an offer from Truin to arrange for a car and driver to travel to Plei Toan from Pleiku. He would later return them to the coast. He suspected that the driver was also a Viet Minh soldier, and by his name – Nguyen Pham Khanh – another cousin. As Charlie requested the previous day, Major Hiroaka showed up exactly on time at Tan Son Nhut airfield, prepared to accompany them. Charlie wondered how that was going to work.

They would have to travel narrow dirt roads that had been carved out of the mountainsides between the wars by the French using local peasants as slave labor. Seeing the car they would be riding in, Charlie recognized it as a '35 Citroen Traction Avant. The black French sedan was parked alongside Pleiku's runway.

With its front-wheel drive and sufficient power, Charlie knew it would get them where they needed to go.

The driver, standing by his vehicle, waved as they stepped out of the small plane. When the four approached, he bowed, then opened the door for them.

Charlie recognized him immediately. He had been in Saigon and knew well Madame Thieu. *His name...what was his name?* That was important since they would be traveling together.

"Name?" Charlie asked the driver when he was seated. "Your name?" he repeated. "Me Char-lie," Charlie said, pointing at himself with his thumb. He noticed the shiny chrome shifter extending from the dash and appreciated the man for his taste in automobiles.

"*Toi?*" the man asked. "Me Khanh. You Char-lie." He smiled and shook Charlie's hand, nodding profusely.

"Khanh? I think I'll call you Bob. You know Bob Hope?" Charlie said. "It's simple and easy to say. He recalled the young hotel clerk and wondered how many cousins Truin had.

"Yes, Bob okay. No matter," he said with a slight bow.

Suddenly, a heavy downpour interrupted their preparations, forcing them to find shelter and wait the rain out. As quickly as it began, the rain stopped. The four men packed their equipment into the small sedan and departed. The heat and humidity quickly became brutally oppressive as steam rose from the vegetation around them.

"What happens when we catch this guy?" Joe asked.

"We get Suzuki, go to Quy Nhon on the coast, and the Brits will pick us up by boat," Charlie answered so that everyone would hear. "We've got three days to take care of business."

That same day, several hours after the three men had flown out of Tan Son Nhut airfield, Major Blankston received a radio message delivered to him by dutiful Sergeant Eddleton, who had received it from the British only minutes before. The message was stamped 'URGENT, TOP SECRET.' The sender was General Bill Donovan. The team commander took a deep breath and opened the sealed message. He read:

Must fly CS out on earliest available flight. His mission in Indo over. William Donovan, Commanding.

"Shit," was all Major Blankston could find to say. *I have to send someone after them. But who?* He considered. *I have no one.* "His mission and my career," he mumbled, then handed the message to Eddleton. "File it," he ordered.

Sergeant Eddleton did as he was directed.

Not taking any chances, Charlie made sure they were heavily armed. In addition to side arms, Joe and Charlie each carried an M3 'grease gun.' The sergeant threw in a box of M26 fragmentation grenades. Hiroaka carried only his Nambu automatic. Bob, a small man whom Charlie guessed to be about forty, told them he operated a sheet metal as well as a taxi business in Saigon. He was in Pleiku visiting family. They conversed in French, a language each realized the other understood. Bob watched their every action and seemed curious about each item of weaponry. His interest convinced Charlie that the man was a Viet Minh spy. *The guy pops up everywhere,* he thought. *Probably his job to keep an eye on foreigners.*

About midday, Bob offered them lunch from the trunk of his car – steamed rice and vegetables held in a light flour wrapping. The last rain shower had stopped about an hour earlier. They stopped along the road while he prepared the food on a hastily built fire. He served them hot green tea with the meal. All three were ravenous.

"I don't know what the hell it is, but it's tasty," Joe said, shoveling it in.

Bob nodded in agreement, even though it was obvious he had no idea what Joe had said. He still watched Charlie carefully, but always gave him a broad smile when Charlie looked over to him.

"His chow's better than army C rations," Joe said, still gulping down the rice.

When they finished eating, Bob cleaned up, hustled everyone into the sedan, and started the engine. "Yes?" he said. "Plei Toan." He threw the engine in gear, and they rumbled down the muddy road.

"Hey," Joe said, scratching his head. "What do we do with Bob if Suzuki decides to make a fight of it?"

"We'll park him out of the way somewhere. Truin gave him specific directions about that. He understands that there may be gunfire."

"Specific directions? Right," Joe grumbled and shook his head. "This woman had you kidnapped just a few days ago, and now she's your pal? I don't get it, Stanek."

Hiroaka said little during the meal. "Mr. Stanek?" he finally asked. "We must consider the four men armed and very dangerous. They have everything to gain by killing us. It must be by surprise when we meet."

"I agree," Charlie said. "And don't call me Mr. Stanek. Stanek will do just fine."

"That is your family's name? Stanek?" Major Hiroaka asked. "It is not appropriate for me to address you as only 'Stanek,' sir."

"Then call me major. Hell, why not. The game is up anyway."

"Yes, you are an officer in the United States Army," he said. "I understand. Yes, Major," he repeated with a smile.

"Yes," Charlie agreed. "What do I call you? Major?"

The man looked at him, then at Catledge. "Yes, I am still an officer in the Japanese Imperial Army. Please continue to address me as major."

"Of course, Major."

Sergeant Catledge listened quietly to the exchange. "And you can address me as Mr. Catledge, as I'm almost a civilian," he said.

"I have been given jurisdiction here, Major Stanek, by the British Army. I am responsible for returning the criminals to Saigon," Major Hiroaka said.

"We don't have a problem with that, as long as they are placed behind bars," Charlie replied.

"Then we understand each other," the Japanese soldier said, staring straight ahead.

They reached the small village of Plei Toan around dusk of the first day. The ragged dress of its inhabitants and the village's crumbling homes showed it to be very poor.

Bob pulled the car over to a roadside stand in the village center and quickly jumped out. While the village children swarmed the car, the adults held back. They stood in the shadows of their thatched homes, watching the strangers. Charlie could read the fear in their faces.

After looking over the area through the car window, he got out and was immediately swamped by kids, some begging and others just hanging on to his trousers. Joe just shook his head.

"Sarge, got any candy? From the C-rats?" Charlie called.

Joe opened the trunk. He rifled through the rations until he had enough to hand out. "Here we go," he said with a laugh, giving out Chiclets, one per child. "This is the best part of the mission." The children swarmed around the big friendly man, laughing.

Major Hiroaka stayed in the car, smoking and watching Charlie and Joe.

Charlie walked down the single muddy, unpaved street. A younger woman holding an infant she was breast-feeding stepped out of the shadows to hold out her hand to him. He understood what she wanted but didn't know how to respond to her. "Hey, Joe, give this woman a box, will you?" he called out again, pointing to her. But he kept walking.

Where are the young men? Charlie wondered. He saw only old men, women, and children. The houses stood two deep beside the road, with narrow walkways linking them. Flooded garden plots surrounded the entire village. He saw that everything – paddies, garden plots, households – was intricately woven together into a single entity.

Bob spoke to an old man. Charlie watched the exchange from a distance. He saw the old man became very animated, motioning with his hands. After five more minutes of conversation, their driver nodded politely, tipped the man, and returned to the car.

"What was that about?" Charlie asked.

"No good," Bob said. "Four Japs stay at fort, he say. Take two young men from Plei Toan this morning for work detail." All four crawled back in the Citroen and slammed the doors. "We go this way." He pointed at the road in front of them, then started the engine, and moved slowly through the mud in the direction of the fort.

"Are they still there?" Charlie asked.

"Old man says men not return to village. He sees nothing since then."

It started to rain again just as they left the village. The car struggled up a steep incline. The sudden downpour reduced visibility to less than twenty meters. Bob shifted, and then was forced to downshift as the rain steadily worsened, and the car began to lose traction. The mud grew deeper. The heavy rain had washed away tracks, but the men could still make out deep ruts that would be the road.

As they rounded a curve, Charlie caught a glimpse of something dark ahead. "What's that?" he asked. "Up ahead. See it?"

Major Hiroaka and Joe leaned forward and squinted, trying to see through the curtain of rain.

"Yes, yes," Bob said, excited.

"Stop over there," Charlie ordered, pointing to a wide spot against the embankment where the road turned for the final approach to the gate. "We'll walk the rest of the way."

"What's the plan?" Joe asked.

Charlie looked at the sergeant, then at the Japanese major. "We'll wait for the rain to stop. Then we walk up, when it's getting dark. If we're lucky we might surprise them. If not, well at least we'll have some cover along the road."

"They're probably gone. They've been here since this morning," Major Hiroaka said. He silently stared down the road into the sheet of rain.

"They don't know we're after them," Charlie said, reconsidering his plan. "And they know they're not more than a four- or five-hour drive from the deep jungles of Laos and freedom."

"They know we are chasing them," the Japanese major said, disagreeing. "He is not a fool, Major."

"We'll see," Joe said, fingering his weapon.

"We'll take a look at the place before we go in. I still believe, Major, that we can surprise them," Charlie said. "But we won't take any chances. Check your weapon and take extra ammo."

"Yes," Major Hiroaka agreed.

The clouds thinned. Within a few minutes the rain slowed to a drizzle. All three men jumped out of the car. They opened the trunk to pull out the M3's and pick up extra ammo. Joe opened the box of grenades and passed some around.

Charlie was expertly working the action on the grease gun. Bob watched them.

"What about him?" Joe asked, pointing to the Vietnamese.

Charlie looked over to Bob. "Bob, you stay with the car," he said in French.

"No, I go," Bob insisted. He returned to the car and reached under the front seat. He pulled out an old pistol. "I go, eh?" He held up an ancient .38 caliber Smith and Wesson. He reached under again and pulled out a handful of extra ammo.

"Jesus, look at that cannon, would ya?" Joe said with a whistle. "It's almost bigger than he is."

"I'm ready for the Japanese," he said, loading the revolver.

The Japanese policeman watched him without saying a word. But Charlie could see the concern written on his face. "Be damn careful," Charlie warned, giving in. "Listen. We split up. Sarge, you and Bob stick together. The major and I, we'll move up slowly. Stop when you see the gates. Four of them, all soldiers, according to the major here. Any questions?"

The drizzle continued, with low clouds reducing visibility.

Major Hiroaka nodded. "Let's go."

"Watch for an ambush," Charlie added.

"We're ready," Joe replied.

"Move out."

The four of them split up, two on each side of the road. They headed slowly upward into the gray, misting rain. They walked about twenty-five meters before Charlie saw the metal and wood detail of the large road gate clearly. It was open. Moving closer carefully, he could make out concrete blockhouses used as cells sitting silently in the shadows twenty meters beyond the entrance. Deep tracks gutted the road in front of the gate. Barbed wire lay twisted and rusting in the ditch alongside.

Charlie waved to Major Hiroaka, then turned and motioned for Joe to get down.

Joe touched Bob's shoulder and both men knelt in the tall grass adjacent to the road about ten meters from the gate. Charlie and Major Hiroaka slowly inched forward. When they had stepped just inside the gate, Charlie signaled that he would move forward alone.

He crept ahead slowly, holding the grease gun in front of him. He reached the center of the compound by following a recently trampled path through the tall grass. Nature was already reclaiming the abused plot of ground after only two short months without human habitation. The heavy wooden gates creaked in the breeze. The place, even in the cleansing rain, smelled foul. The darkness was quiet except for the patter of rain against the crumbling tile roofs of the concrete buildings.

Charlie walked about ten meters in and raised his arm, motioning for Major Hiroaka to move up. He in turn waved for the other two. Charlie saw tire tracks dug into the brown mud in an almost circular pattern where some type of vehicle had turned around. "A vehicle turned here and left, following the same track," he announced when the others reached his position. "See how the grass over here is trampled? They must have walked over to that building and entered it."

"This is the registration office," Major Hiroaka said. He walked to the doorway of the building and looked in. "Records were kept here."

"How do you know that?" Joe asked.

"Sergeant, I have been here before," he replied. "To pick up prisoners and take them to Saigon. British prisoners."

"Then what happened to them?" Joe asked.

"I am a policeman. Transporting and keeping prisoners is part of my job."

"Was. Was part of your job," Joe corrected him.

"The war is over," Charlie interjected. "Let's search the place, follow any tracks. But be careful. We don't know who's here. And watch out for booby traps." He remembered how the Germans had rigged booby traps as they retreated.

The four again went off in pairs to search the camp. For the next thirty minutes they walked the grounds, going in and out of abandoned concrete buildings already stripped of usable wood and metal by the villagers. They found the building where several people had eaten. The room was littered with bottles, cartons, and cans. "They were eating British rations," Joe said, examining the debris.

Major Hiroaka climbed to the top of one of the four guard towers to get a better view. At first, he saw nothing. Then, excited, he waved to Charlie.

"Major," he said to Charlie, when he stood immediately below him. "Look! Over there!" he pointed to a small building closest to the wall but still inside the wire. "I see a large mound of earth. Freshly dug, I think."

"What is it?" Charlie answered, looking in the direction Hiroaka pointed. He saw only green vegetation.

"Someone has dug a large hole."

Charlie called to Joe and Bob, and then walked to the spot. The hole, about three feet deep, had already begun to fill with rainwater, murky, discolored water. They saw two large log-shaped objects floating in the water.

Bob reached in to grab one. "Major!" he yelled, pulling it to the side. "Look!"

Charlie and Joe saw the object at the same time. It was the headless torso of a man. Assisting Bob, they pulled the other body to the side. Charlie scanned the area and saw the missing heads sitting side by side near a clump of tall grass that had been trampled down. Four liquid eyes stared back at him.

"Vietnamese," Bob whispered, without looking up.

Both heads seemed to be cleanly severed from the bodies. Charlie didn't see any bullet holes or other wounds. *Like the Saigon ferryman*, he thought.

"Japs do this," Bob said, barely suppressing his anger. "We get them, yes?"

"Criminals did this," Major Hiroaka corrected him.

"We'll get 'em," Charlie said.

"What do you make of it?" Joe asked.

"I don't know," Charlie replied, and then looked at the Vietnamese. "Bob, go tell the villagers so that they can take the bodies." He turned to look at Major Hiroaka.

"I go now." Bob turned and left at a trot.

"The Vietnamese served their purpose," the policeman said. "And now, they cannot be witnesses."

"What were they looking for here?"

"I think this is where Captain Suzuki hid his diamonds," the major replied, still inspecting the hole. "It makes sense. When we evacuate from here, he hides them, thinking no one will disturb them."

"Good theory, Major. They commandeered the two villagers to dig 'em up, and then executed them on the spot," Joe said. "Isn't that the way you do business?"

"No, Sergeant," Major Hiroaka replied calmly. "That is the way murderers do business."

"Major, come here," Charlie called, bent over one of the dead men. "Look."

Major Hiroaka knelt down and looked where he pointed. Charlie saw a bullet hole in the lower back. "Entrance wound, I'd say," Charlie observed. "I missed that earlier."

"Yes," the Japanese major agreed. "He tried to escape, so they shot him. But he was not dead, so they used their sword on him. And on the other man, too."

Charlie nodded.

"That's believable," Joe said, standing beside Charlie.

"The sword is an honorable weapon, Sergeant. In expert hands, it is quick and painless. But the men who did this are not honorable," Major Hiroaka said, staring at the victim.

"When Bob returns, we'll get the hell out of here. This place reminds me of a Nazi death camp," Charlie commented.

"Where we going next?" Joe asked.

"After them. Only two ways out of here, and they didn't pass us. They used the same track in and out. And the villagers never saw them leave," Charlie concluded. "So what direction does that leave?"

"North," Joe replied.

"North to Kontum," Charlie added. "They had to have taken the turn back there, right after the village. We gotta catch them before they can escape into Laos."

"How far ahead of us do you think they are?" Joe asked Hiroaka.

"I think it could be less than several hours, no more. Major, what do you think?" Major Hiroaka asked Charlie.

"I agree. In the rain, maybe we are fifty kilometers from Kontum. But the roads aren't good," Charlie answered, while trying to study the map in the growing darkness. "If our driver knows these roads, maybe we can catch them."

"Let's go, Major," Major Hiroaka said. "Time is being wasted."

They turned and walked in the shadowy mist down the mountain toward the car, then waited silently for Bob to return.

"Kontum," Charlie asked their Vietnamese driver when he returned. "How fast can you drive it?"

"*Oui,* very fast. I know this place," Bob answered, turning the car around. "We kill Japs, yes?" he said in English.

Major Hiroaka sat in the front seat beside the driver. He closed his eyes.

Charlie continued to speak with the driver in French. "Don't worry, Bob. We'll get them one way or another. And if we have to cross into Laos, we will," he said, looking straight ahead down the road.

The Vietnamese said nothing more as the old Citroen roared down the rough, muddy road.

It was apparent Bob knew his way. He handled the Citroen adeptly on the curving roads. Charlie was beginning to believe they had a good chance of catching up to Suzuki and the other Japanese soldiers. At a roadside coffee stand in the small village of La Khuoi, he learned from the old proprietor that the four Japanese had stopped there within the hour.

"They drink rice wine. Maybe they are drunk," Bob told him. "The old man say they go north to Kontum."

"What time is it?" Joe asked a short time later. He now sat beside the driver. They took turns watching the road ahead.

"About 2300 hours," Charlie replied, staring at his watch in the dark. "Why? You have a late-night appointment?"

"Just two more months. Two more months and it's back to the States for me," Joe said. He turned to Charlie with a hopeful look. "But we gotta be very careful. I'm too damn short to die out here."

Charlie nodded his agreement, half asleep.

Each knew that capturing the Japanese meant they had to spot them quickly without giving away their own position, so they were forced to drive without their headlights. Their constant vigilance blended with the monotony of a long ride as they bounced over potholed and rutted roads across undulating hills on the mountain plateau.

"I'll get a job and make some money. Maybe find some dame," the sergeant rambled on to pass the time. "What about you?"

"Don't know," Charlie answered. He rubbed his eyes and shook his head to stay awake.

Joe looked at the Japanese policeman. "What will you do, Major, when you return to your country?"

The major looked up, surprised at the question. "I will see my family for the first time in three years. I, too, will get out of the army. But..." he shrugged. "I don't know. For my country, the future is not so bright."

"A lot of devastation, I've read," Joe said.

Bob suddenly braked the car in the middle of the road and turned off the engine. Without saying a word, he opened the door and jumped out.

"What's the problem?" Charlie asked, now fully alert.

"More petrol," he said, and opened the trunk to get the last can of fuel out.

Everyone got out and stretched. Walking out to the side of the road to relieve himself, Joe froze in his tracks. "Look," he called out, pointing toward the north where the road seemed to straighten out.

Charlie stared out over the narrow valley. "I see something."

Major Hiroaka turned to look.

"Headlights. It might be them," Charlie said, still looking into the darkness. "How far ahead of us are they?"

"A couple of miles at the most," Joe estimated. He finished his task and buttoned up his trousers.

"Kontum? How far?" Charlie asked Bob after they had returned to the car.

"Ten kilometers," he replied, quickly shoving the French sedan into gear. They roared off down the road.

"We'll catch Suzuki north of Kontum then," Charlie said.

"I don't think they know we're behind 'em," Joe said, sounding hopeful. "Kontum big city?" he asked Bob.

"Kontum big, yes," Bob replied. "I know short way to north road. We take, yes?"

"Are we certain they're going that way?" Joe asked. Charlie repeated the question to Bob in French.

"Two roads only," Bob replied. "One north to Laos and one east to ocean."

"We'll take the shortcut," Charlie quickly decided.

Within less than an hour, they had passed through the city. They traveled over rough paths, around paddies, along dikes. Several times everyone got out to push. The worst was when the old Citroen bounced through potholes up to its axles. Still the city slept. Only an occasional barking dog disturbed the peace.

Finally, they reached the northern outskirts where the highway turned toward the northwest and began its rise into the mountains. "Park here! Now!" Charlie ordered after they had traveled about half a mile up the road. He jumped out and crawled to a high rock ledge beside the road to have a look back at the city. He didn't see any auto lights. *Are we too late? Did they take the other road*? He felt a growing concern.

Then, just as he was climbing off the ledge, he saw headlights. A vehicle was just leaving the city. *It's got to be them,* he decided, running down to the car. "Here they come," Charlie informed the others. "Bob, hide the car over there behind the rocks, then go with the sergeant," he said quickly in French. "Sarge, walk about twenty yards back and hide along the road in the tall grass. Let 'em pass." He was grabbing weapons and ammo as he spoke. "The major and I will stop them here, try to disarm them. But be ready for anything." To Major Hiroaka, he pointed to an outcropping along the road. "There! Behind the large rock." Everyone loaded their weapons and everyone but the Japanese major quickly moved to their positions.

"No, Major," Major Hiroaka said, confronting Charlie on the road. "It is my responsibility. I will halt them and arrest them. You take cover over there." He pointed to the same outcropping.

Charlie looked hard at the Japanese soldier for long seconds. "Okay, Major. It's your show." He headed for his hiding place.

Less than a minute later, the steady whine of a truck's engine announced the approach of their target. From his spot, Charlie saw the four-door Japanese Army command vehicle, shaped like a shoe box, pass Joe's position, moving at about twenty miles per hour. *Steady,* he told himself. His palms were clammy, and perspiration ran down his back. The driver of the vehicle downshifted to slow for the curve. Charlie, his weapon pointed at the windows, waited. He heard the engine shriek. *Where the hell is Hiroaka?*

The truck picked up speed. Finally, Major Hiroaka stepped out from the shadows into the middle of the road, pointing his Nambu directly at the truck's windshield. The light from the headlights shined brightly in his face. "Halt!" he yelled in Japanese.

The truck bore down on him. Twenty yards, fifteen...

"Halt!" Hiroaka yelled again. "In the name of the Emperor, I order you to surrender."

The vehicle kept coming directly at him.

The major opened up with four rapid shots, then dived for cover in a shallow ditch along the road, just in time. The truck roared by him. Gun flashes lit up the inside of the truck as its occupants fired in all directions through open windows. Lying facedown on the gravel, Charlie heard the snap of bullets overhead, striking the clay and gravel embankment and splattering dirt and rock.

The truck swerved, spinning out of control. The radiator hissed loudly. Steam and water splattered what remained of the shattered windshield. Major Hiroaka's well-placed bullets had done their job. Skidding sideways, then raising up on its right tires, the truck finally nosedived into the ditch. The left front side smashed into the embankment twenty feet from where Charlie lay.

Running toward the disabled truck, Joe opened fire on the rear panels. He hit the spare tire strapped to the back, luckily missing the gas tank by inches. There was a loud hiss.

Charlie came from around the large boulder on the opposite side of the road, clutching the M3. Two of the vehicle's passengers leaped out on his side just as he reached the top of the grade.

Joe stalked the rear of the vehicle, moving vigilantly around it. "Sarge, watch out!" Charlie yelled, seeing the two men. Joe had not seen them escaping from the passenger side.

The Smith and Wesson exploded from the far side of the road. Bob fired three fast rounds at the two Japanese just as they drew their pistols. "Jap!" Bob yelled at Charlie, pointing to a running figure.

Charlie turned just in time to see a figure charging him from across the road. He fired point-blank. The impact of the bullets immediately halted the soldier in his tracks, stood him erect, then threw him backward. The .45 caliber rounds killed the smaller man instantly. Charlie ejected the empty magazine, dropped it to the ground, and inserted another.

From the darkness of the ditch to his right, a Type 100 submachinegun opened fire, spraying a volley of bullets across the area. Major Hiroaka knew its sound too well. Splinters of rock and dirt jumped into the air around his head as the bullets hit the granite face of the mountain behind him.

"Get down!" Charlie yelled, again diving for the cover of the ditch.

At that moment, Joe stepped around the side of the truck. He saw the exchange of gunfire, pointed the grease gun into the shadows, and fired. The bullets danced across the lip of the ditch but missed their mark, streaking up and off into the darkness.

Reacting instantly, the Japanese soldier returned fire until he had expended his ammo. Discarding the weapon, he drew his pistol and aimed. He found his target. Three 8 mm rounds ripped into Joe's chest and midsection before he could find cover around the corner of the vehicle. He dropped the submachine gun as the bullets punched into him. He reached automatically for his chest. Blood swelled between his fingers. He staggered, and his legs collapsed under him as he fell to his knees.

"Stay down," Major Hiroaka called out and rushed toward him from the far side of the road. He fired his weapon as he ran. The Japanese soldier shot at Hiroaka's shadowy figure charging him from across the road, but his aim was wild.

Bullets raced overhead. Major Hiroaka calmly placed his automatic dead center on his target and opened up. The gun leaped in his hand. Squeezing the trigger again and again, he fired the remainder of the magazine's 8 mm rounds. The bullets pummeled the soldier, stitching him across his chest. He was thrown backward, dead.

The smell of powder, hot metal, and blood filled the night air.

"Two more," Charlie yelled to Hiroaka. Having seen Joe get hit, he ran to his sergeant's side. He quickly turned him over and tore open his fatigue jacket to get at the wounds. He pulled a compress from his cartridge belt and pressed it against Joe's blood-soaked midsection.

"Hold on, hold on. We'll get ya outta here," Charlie lied, trying to reassure him. He worked feverishly to stop the steady, dark flow.

"Right, Major," Joe said and coughed. Blood soaked his shirt. "Then home, eh?" he whispered, trying unsuccessfully to smile.

Charlie set Joe's head down on his folded jacket to make him more comfortable. "I'm sorry," he whispered, leaning over him. "I'm really sorry I got you into this, Sarge."

"I volunteered, remember?" Joe said, struggling to breath. He gasped for breath.

Charlie raised his head and held him in his arms. "You're a hero, Sergeant Catledge," he mumbled. "A real American hero." He kept pressing the dressing against Joe's blood-soaked chest. Pouring water from his canteen into the palm of his hand, he gave him a drink, allowing the water to flow into his mouth a few drops at a time.

"Major," Joe whispered. "Major. Stan-yak." He tried to speak but blood bubbled from his lips

Charlie moved closer to hear him.

"This ain't such a good job, is it?"

"No, it ain't," Charlie answered, wiping his own tears away. "And the pay's lousy. You'll make a fortune back home." He gently wiped Joe's lips with a handkerchief.

Joe made a rasping sound. With each breath, blood foamed on his lips and trickled down his chin. "Stanek, don't leave me alone out here. Not like Dixon."

"I'm not gonna leave you here. You're going home," Charlie told him, and he meant every word of it.

Joe gasped one last time, his body jerked slightly, and he was dead. His eyes stared up into the tropical night. Charlie reached down gently and closed them. Then he stood up and moved cautiously around the left rear corner of the truck. He still had a job to finish and tried to force the dead sergeant from his mind.

Major Hiroaka inserted another magazine and continued to fire at the truck. With no target visible, he placed a two-shot burst first into the front seat, then into the rear. He approached the vehicle from the right. The back door hung open, its window shattered.

"Don't shoot. I surrender," a voice screamed in Japanese from inside.

"The backseat," Major Hiroaka said to Charlie, pointing to the inside. Charlie understood. He leveled the grease gun at the back of the truck, careful not to offer himself as a target.

"Get out now. With your hands above your head," the Japanese major ordered, speaking in Japanese. He motioned for Charlie to step back.

A man in a pressed Japanese military uniform struggled from the floor of the backseat. He appeared to be shaken but unscathed. Charlie looked into the vehicle. He saw a Samurai sword in an ornate scabbard lying on the backseat.

"Where's the other one?" Charlie demanded to know. "One more man. Did he get away?" He leveled his submachine gun at the Japanese soldier's chest.

"Dead, I believe. You shot him," their prisoner replied calmly in English. "See for yourself."

"Captain Suzuki," Charlie said, recognizing him. "We've been looking for you." He reached in and grabbed the sword from the seat.

"I have him covered, sir," Major Hiroaka said, holding the automatic. "Go."

Charlie returned to Joe's body. He and Bob knelt down beside him. "Take care of him, will you?" he asked the Vietnamese.

"I will find something from the car to wrap him in," Bob replied, looking over at their single prisoner. Charlie saw the smaller man's eyes blaze in the darkness.

Charlie returned to where Major Hiroaka was holding the prisoner. He was barely able to control his anger. "I ought to kill you right here. Just like the two young men you left in the prison camp. And my sergeant. You bastard," he said slowly in English.

"Major, please, he is now my prisoner," Major Hiroaka said.

"Mr. Stanek, I know you would not do that," Suzuki said, sounding as if he were pleading more than stating a certainty. "These men, Japanese intelligence officers, they kidnapped me. They forced me to take them to where I hid the diamonds, or they would have killed me. Again, I am innocent, and an inquiry will establish this."

"Where diamonds?" Bob demanded angrily, using his few words of English. He had followed Charlie rather than take care of Joe's body.

"Give us the diamonds," Charlie said, holding Bob back. "I may not be able to hold him back much longer."

"Talk," the Vietnamese demanded from behind Charlie. He was pointing his revolver at Suzuki. "Shoot in leg. Talk. Talk or I shoot." he said in English again.

"Stop! Put the gun down," Major Hiroaka said.

"Do what I told you to do," Charlie snapped at Bob, but his eyes never left Suzuki.

"In the truck, in a wooden box," Suzuki said with a smile. "Look for yourself. They can make you all rich men, and your friends."

"Search their truck," Charlie, changing his mind, ordered Bob in French.

Bob climbed into the disabled vehicle. A few moments later, he returned, holding a twelve-inch wooden box carefully in his hands.

"Stand back," Charlie suddenly ordered, still barely controlling his anger. "I know the best way to deal with this murderer." He clicked the safety off the .45 and placed the barrel under Suzuki's chin. Looking into Suzuki's eyes, he smiled a cold unthinking rage. "This is the justice that you deserve for the men you've killed. This is for Sergeant Catledge."

Both Bob and Major Hiroaka were taken by surprise.

"I'm now a prisoner of war of the Americans," the Japanese soldier said shakily.

"Are you?" Charlie warned in a low guttural voice. "Who knows that, out here in the dark?"

"Major Stanek, he is my prisoner until he is turned over to the British. I must demand that you put your weapon down," Major Hiroaka ordered forcefully. He still held his weapon in his hand but he was careful not to raise it. For almost thirty seconds no one moved.

"You're right, Major," Charlie finally said, regaining control over his emotions. He lowered his weapon.

"Thank you, Major-san," Captain Suzuki said to Major Hiroaka in Japanese, bowing formally. His hands trembled.

"Shut up!" the major replied in their language. In English he accused, "You have disgraced the Emperor and the honor of Japan, Captain Suzuki."

"What honor?" Suzuki hissed. "There is no Japan. We are conquered and dishonored. The Emperor has surrendered. Now we are alone to survive as we must."

"Murdering and stealing. That is how you survive?" the major said contemptuously.

"It was war, Major-san."

"Silence, criminal!" Major Hiroaka ordered loudly.

"Here are the diamonds, Mr. Stanek," Bob said calmly in French, showing them to Charlie. "But I am ordered by Mr. Tran to take..."

"For what purpose?" Charlie snapped.

"They belong to Vietnam. My country," Bob said proudly and defiantly.

"Tie the prisoner up," Major Hiroaka ordered. Charlie translated the order into French for Bob. "We will talk about the diamonds later," he also said.

Bob nodded sullenly and, still holding the gems, marched their prisoner over to the car at gunpoint.

Charlie solemnly retrieved a blanket from the trunk of the Citroen and carefully wrapped up Joe's body. He tied it with a cord. "Will you help me?" he asked Major Hiroaka. "We'll put him on top of the car."

The Japanese nodded, and together they lifted the corpse to the roof of the sedan. Then Charlie tied it down tightly.

"Suzuki will get justice," Charlie vowed, watching Bob shove the prisoner into the backseat of the Citroen.

"Major Stanek, in war there is rarely justice, only survivors," the Japanese major said softly. "I am sorry."

Charlie understood.

They prepared to depart, packing weapons into the trunk. Charlie looked at each. "Mission Accomplished," he declared. The three and Captain Suzuki left the mountain, Sergeant Joe Catledge deep in Charlie's thoughts.

They drove slowly through Kontum and Pleiku and turned east toward QuyNhon. There they planned to hop a British ship for the Saigon trip. With few delays, they reached the coast quickly.Charlie and Major Hiroaka with their prisoner boarded the ship waiting for them, while Bob turned south, taking the coastal Route One to Saigon.

Aboard the *HMS Trigger*, a British destroyer operating off the coast of central Vietnam, Charlie stood at the railing of the ship's fantail, silently watching the wake foam and churn below him. The rendezvous with the destroyer had been planned in advance to return them to Saigon following their mission.

It's time to go home, he thought grimly. *I'm finished with all of it.*

Chapter 21

Behind them, the DC-3 roared to life. "Goodbye and good luck, Stanek," Major Blankston said, standing on the edge of the runway at Tan Son Nhut Airfield. He shook Charlie's hand.

"Thank you, Major," Charlie replied. "When we get to Pearl, I plan to bury Sergeant Catledge at the Honolulu National Cemetery, overlooking the Pacific. I think he would have liked that."

"Yes, good," Major Blankston said, looking down the runway. "Was your trip worth it, Major?" he asked quietly.

"I don't know. I really don't know," Charlie answered. Both men paused to watch six Gurkha soldiers carry the plain wood casket onto the plane.

"So, what'll you do when you return to civilian life?" Major Blankston asked.

"I'm still trying to figure that out," Charlie answered with a shrug. "But then, when you got nowhere to go, you're free to go anywhere."

"That's one way to look at it," Blankston replied with a smile.

Charlie saluted his fellow OSS officer and boarded the transport plane.

Truin heard the slow, steady drone of an aircraft overhead and wondered if it was him. She felt relieved that the American was finally safe and returning to his homeland. Dressed again in khakis, her hair pulled back tightly, she stood on the second-floor balcony outside Comrade Giau's office, looking east. The sky above her was darkening. The clouds were heavy with the monsoon rains.

Where will he go now? she wondered. Her cousin in the hotel had told her that Charlie had departed. He was gone, and she was weakened without him. *He was a hard man in many ways, and very brave*, she thought with tears in her eyes. *And I love him.* Truin felt an ache in her heart. But then, he only complicated her life. She knew that and could not allow her feelings for him to determine her destiny.

Truin had been overjoyed when she heard that Charlie had captured the Japanese murderer and returned to Saigon safely. Her faith in the American had been confirmed when Bob returned with the diamonds, telling her that Mr. Stanek had turned them over to him 'on behalf of the American people.'

"Comrade Truin!" Dinh called through the door. She sighed, resigned to her fate. She looked again to the darkening sky one last time, then turned and entered his office. Dinh stood passively beside Comrade Giau's desk. She felt the eyes of the two men on her as she entered the room.

Truin had planned to go at once to Charlie at the Intercontinental where the Americans were staying.

But Comrade Dinh had forbidden it. "You must not be seen with the American," he ordered. "The Russians say he is a spy." She had stayed in Vung Tau, but now she regretted having listened to him. *What does he know?* she thought, feeling overwhelmed with sadness.

The older man was seated behind his small desk, neatly dressed in a white shirt, dark trousers, and sandals. Papers were lined up carefully in front of him. He looked intently at her as she came to stand before him. "He was a good man, wasn't he?" he asked, mostly to soothe her feelings.

"Yes, comrade," she answered, appreciating his sympathy. She felt Dinh's glare on her.

"But it's for the best. You have a different destiny that must be fulfilled," Comrade Giau said.

"For the best?" Truin repeated, not understanding the old man's words.

"The Americans have great power. Yet they are a good people, and generous. They laugh often and treat other peoples as they treat their own. This I believe," he observed.

"Yes, comrade."

"But they have a great weakness, Comrade Truin. They have no past, and so they cannot read their own future. This means they cannot use their great power in ways that will benefit them most in the years ahead." He lit an American Camel cigarette, and slowly blew the smoke from his lungs. All the while he continued to watch Truin.

"They will support French interests here," he continued. "This I predict because, in their brief history, they have always supported peoples similar to their own. They cannot see beyond that. Their power will be used against us. Against our people and against our freedom. The Americans would help us back into slavery. Back under the terrible French yoke. That is something you could never live with."

"Charlie ... Mr. Stanek would not betray us, Comrade Giau," Truin replied quickly. "He returned the diamonds."

"A ruse! A simple trick," Dinh interjected. "The Americans care only about protecting their economic interests. That was why Mr. Stanek was in Saigon."

"Be silent, Comrade Dinh. Let Comrade Truin speak."

"Yes, comrade," he replied and bowed.

"He kept his faith with our people," Truin said, looking scornfully at Dinh.

"In his way and so far as he could, he was a friend," Comrade Giau agreed. "But Mr. Stanek is not all of America. You know well enough what I mean." He waited, studying her.

"I understand," she answered finally, staring out the window.

"Good. Good," he told her. "You and I are going to Hanoi tomorrow to meet with Comrade Ho Chi Minh and the Russian delegation. We will discuss their price for supplying arms and ammunition to us. It will be a heavy one."

Truin bowed.

Comrade Giau stood and walked to the balcony. "Ours will be a long struggle," he said, staring out through the double doors. "Perhaps neither of us will live to see its end. But that doesn't matter. We have dedicated our lives to it, and others, equally dedicated, will follow us."

"For an independent Vietnam," Dinh said, standing behind the older man. They both looked to Truin.

"I too remain dedicated, Comrade Giau," she said. *But I will hold Charlie in my heart forever*, she thought defiantly.

Outside, they heard the low, powerful murmur of distant thunder, rolling and rising over the land.

"A storm is coming from the sea," Comrade Giau commented. Truin looked up and wondered if she would survive to see her people's freedom.

Stepping off the DC-3 at Clark Airfield, north of Manila, Charlie was greeted by two MPs.

"Major Stanek," the shorter one, a sergeant, said, saluting. "We've been ordered to escort you to your quarters. Please come with us."

"By whose order?" Charlie asked, surprised.

"By order of the base commander, General Stevens. I am in charge of the security detail."

"I see. The general received the cable then?"

"Yes, sir."

The three men jumped in a jeep and sped off across the runway. They stopped at an old sun-bleached clapboard building. The Russian, Gregor Zerenowsky, was the first person Charlie saw upon entering.

"Welcome," Gregor said in Russian. "Come, I will show you where you will stay tonight. Then tomorrow we fly to America!"

"Who else knows you're here, Major?" Charlie asked, concerned. "Has there been any correspondence with Washington?"

"I think not, comrade. But you must talk with my host. Come."

"Wait," Charlie said. "Let's go back inside. We have some business to discuss." Gregor followed him. When they were well within Gregor's room and away from prying eyes, Charlie turned to face the Russian. In the next second, the larger man lay sprawled across the floor, felled by a solid right jab across his cheek from Charlie's fist.

"What? Why, my brother?" he mumbled, confused. He rubbed his cheek, checking instinctively to see if anything was broken.

"You lied to me. It seems you're always lying to me. And don't call me 'your brother,'" Charlie growled. "Now, I want the truth for a change."

"The truth?"

"The Vietnamese woman, Truin, told me that you gave the order to capture me. Why then help me escape? Tell me, or this is the end of the line for you, my Russian friend." Charlie pulled the automatic from inside his shirt and pointed it at the still prone man.

"I am defecting, escaping to America. I've had enough, Major. Russia is too dangerous to live in. I did everything for Stalin. Still he no longer trusts me and desires to dispose of me. Why?

Because I'm Ukrainian. The trains to Siberia never stop. My sister. They took her in May. The NKVD said she collaborated with the Nazis because she was not shot by them. My mother, as you know, was old. Her heart could not take it, and grew weak. She died one month ago." Gregor hung his head, weeping in a sentimental Russian way.

"That still does not explain why you had the Vietnamese kidnap me."

"I decided I must leave the Soviet Union," Gregor said, standing slowly and cautiously. "I am next on their list. Yes, I know this. One slip, and that's it for me. So I decide I must defect. I thought of my American comrade, Charles Stanek, often. I thought of his Wisconsin and its great forests like in my Ukraine."

"Keep going."

"I decide only the honorable Stanek can help me. I can trust no one else. And he owes me a favor, I think. Remember the trouble in the Ukrainian woods with the soldiers?"

"You said that evened things between us. I still believe you set the whole thing up, Zerenowsky," Charlie growled. "But go on."

"Spies in your capitol watch you, but I have special connection there and we develop plan," Gregor continued unperturbed by Charlie's accusation. "They learn of your trip to Vietnam, eh? So I arrange things so that the great American airplane pilot comes to Hanoi."

"That's a very elaborate and complicated ruse," Charlie replied.

"Yes, but it worked, I think."

"Major Stanek, when I received your letter, I was very suspicious. It's not every day I receive such a request as yours," General Charles Stevens began. "I checked you out to confirm you were who you said you were."

Charlie took stock of the general. Like him, Stevens was a tall man. But he was worn and weathered, thin with narrow shoulders and a small head. His khakis hung on him like a tired suit on an old hanger. He had piercing blue eyes, and at the moment they were focused intently on him.

"What did you find, General?" Charlie asked.

"I found that you are certainly who you said you were. My cable to Washington, it seems, was routed through the Pentagon and landed on a White House desk. They wasted no time in getting a response to me, well before our guest arrived."

"Good. That's good," Charlie said, feeling a sense of relief. "So we can get on with it then?" He easily read the older man, seeing that he had additional questions but evidently decided to withhold them.

"Yes, of course." The general glanced at the large darkening bruise on the Russian's face but said nothing.

"I appreciate your trust and your discretion," Charlie replied graciously.

"As you've probably gathered, Major Zerenowsky is an important Russian guest, and security is of the utmost importance."

"I thought as much," General Stevens said.

Later that evening, within the privacy of his room in the base's officers' quarters, Charlie sat quietly and watched as Gregor sipped his tea. He could hear the two MPs posted just outside the door, additional security he had insisted upon. They were talking about women, a not uncommon subject for soldiers. The sound of their voices floated through the windows, which were opened wide to allow in the sea air.

The room furnishings were a hodgepodge of old wood chairs, tables, some with broken legs, and mattresses hastily assembled from somewhere, probably from a ship. They had been provided to offer at least a rough equivalent of comfort.

The Americans, having retaken the base from the Japanese Army earlier in the year, had just completed its restoration. Japanese soldiers had inhabited it since early 1942.

"There were other ways, other people who could have gotten you out. Why me? Tell me again," Charlie finally said softly in Russian.

"Yes, there are many," Gregor said with a smile. "But I could trust only you. I knew you from the war and knew that you would never betray me. And you are such a clever man, able to do whatever it takes. Yes, I know this about you, my friend."

"Who told you I was traveling to Saigon?"

"This I told you already. Attila discovered that you would travel here."

"He acted pretty damn fast, since I didn't even know myself until hours before I left Washington."

"Yes, very fast."

"Then, you always seemed to know what we were doing … even in the Carpathians. Your spies watched us, and perhaps they did much more than spy on us, eh, Zerenowsky?"

"What do you mean?"

"It's never been clear to me who exactly in the NKVD betrayed us and almost got me killed. What do you know about this, Major Zerenowsky?" Charlie asked. "I have a right to know."

"Yes, my friend, you do have a right to know," he said with a sigh. "But it was not me. I could never do such a thing."

"Who then?"

"Stalin's Smersh detachment," he said. "Very bad, very dangerous. They are assigned to destroy spies, anyone who can threaten Comrade Stalin's power. And they are very good at their work."

"We weren't spying on the Soviet Union. Why did they go after us?"

"I didn't know their plans," Gregor replied defensively. "But I think they suspected you of being part of Rasputin's spy ring that everyone searches for..."

"I know that name."

"Rasputin heads a dangerous network of spies that we suspected American and British agents have been operating since 1943. Smersh agents are determined to eliminate them."

"And they thought I was one of Rasputin's agents. Is that it?"

"Yes, Major, they are still hunting Rasputin's agents. Many Russians have been shot or deported because we believed they were part of the spy ring."

"The NKVD colonel in Hanoi? He thought I was part of Rasputin's network?"

"Yes. Colonel Pavlov. He believed you were sent to Saigon to meet Rasputin."

"And you allowed him to believe that so you could use me to escape. Was that the plan?"

"Yes, that was the plan."

"You're a real bastard, Zerenowsky," Charlie said angrily. "A real son of a bitch."

"Yes," the Russian agreed.

"One more question."

"Yes?" Gregor said with a sigh.

"There in the Carpathians and in Hanoi... You were willing to have me killed if that was what it took to keep your cover, to further your plans. Am I right?"

"No, Comrade Stanek. I never wanted you killed. But I had to protect my own life, too. In war, we lose so much. You of all people must understand such things."

"Yes, I do. But you used me, deceived me. No, *tricked* me into serving your purposes."

"Such things happen, my friend. Didn't the Vietnamese woman use you to further her purposes? Knowing your feelings toward her, she still manipulated you. For artillery, eh? The

Czechs used you to assist them against the Nazis and to win back their independence. What did they care about rescuing captured American pilots? Don't be naïve, my American friend. I think we use each other. It is part of our daily lives. In war it is worse."

Charlie said nothing.

"But, I have brought good news for you."

Charlie stared at the Russian. "Good news? To ease your guilt?"

"I have information that is very important to you," Gregor said, ignoring the comment.

"I ought to just turn you over to the Russians when we get to Pearl."

"Will my torture and death bring you peace? I don't think so, and I don't think you believe that."

"Well, tell me, goddamn it."

Gregor smiled. "Your Czech woman. Yes, I knew about her and you."

"What about her?"

"You gave up your search for her too soon. She survived the camps, and she was alive when my agent last saw her."

"How? When?" Charlie said, shocked. His mind raced. Everything suddenly changed.

"In June, he saw her in Bratislava ... with an old man. Her father, I presume. The man you worked with."

"Maria ... alive," Charlie whispered. I can't believe it." *I'm free*, he thought, feeling a great weight lifted from his shoulders. *I no longer have to blame myself for her death.* He was overwhelmed with emotion and felt a great sense of relief rush over his body.

Charlie took a taxi to his meeting with General Donovan, who was still at his old headquarters on E Street Northwest. It was already late in the afternoon when he arrived. The day was chilly and overcast, in contrast to the humid warmth of Southeast Asia. Looking through the side windows of the sedan at pedestrians scurrying down the sidewalks in their jackets and overcoats, he decided he liked the tropical climate better.

He paid the driver, an older woman, and got out onto the sidewalk. He pulled the collar up on his overcoat and walked the last half block to 'Q.' He was dressed in civilian clothes.

Inside the building, a doorman instead of a soldier now sat silently behind the information desk. There was no check of identification. "Good afternoon, sir," the older man said, looking up. "How may I direct you?"

"I know my way," Charlie replied.

"Yes, sir," the man said, still watching him as he stepped into an elevator.

"Which floor, sir?" the elevator attendant asked, a look of boredom stamped on his face.

"Fourth floor, please."

The man gave him a quick look. "That floor is vacant, sir. Are you sure?"

"Yes."

The door was unlocked. Charlie entered without knocking. But this time, the room was nearly empty, with only a couple old wooden chairs that looked like they'd been borrowed from a discard pile. Standing at the window, his back toward Charlie, was General Donovan, now dressed in a civilian suit.

"Congratulations on the success of your mission, Major," General Donovan said. "I just finished reading your report and Major Blankston's." He turned to hold up the two documents. "A lot has happened this month." He saw Charlie still looking around the empty office. "I thought it would be much more private if we met here. And just like old times, wouldn't you say?"

"Yeah, General, just like old times," Charlie replied. The two men shook hands.

"Now Major, tell me everything."

Charlie looked hard at his commanding officer, and then sat down. "My mission, yes," he said softly. "It became very complicated, sir."

"So, it was the Annamese that killed Lieutenant Colonel Dixon. Do I have that right?" he asked, encouraging him.

"Yes, sir, maybe killed because he was mistaken for a European during the battle for control of Saigon. But it's very possible that Americans were targeted as well by the Viet Minh to…"

"Yes, Major? To what?" General Donovan asked, now interested. This point was not in either report.

"Sir, based on our conversation with the Viet Minh leader in the south, Tran Van Giau, Colonel Dixon may have been killed purposely. That is, his death could have been a message to the United States."

"A message?"

"Not to get involved in their war with the French. He claimed that we were arming the French Army against them, that we were violating our neutrality by supporting the French." Charlie watched the general's response. "Is that true?"

"I'm not aware of any change in US policy toward Indochina."

"Or…" Charlie began.

"Another possibility?"

"He was killed because of the diamonds. They knew he carried them, and they wanted them to fund their war effort," Charlie said. "A good motive for murder, I guess."

"A national treasure, I understand."

"Dixon's body was quickly disposed of by the Annamese. Probably in the Saigon River. I found the man who did that kind of work for them. But too late, I'm afraid. He had been killed just before we arrived."

"Killed? Murdered?"

"Yes, sir. Tortured and killed. By Japanese intelligence agents searching for diamonds. But this is all in my report, sir."

"Yes, I know it is, but I still want you to brief me."

"Yes, sir," he said. "I think the Japs believed that information on the whereabouts of the diamonds was still with Dixon when he was shot. When the old ferryman could tell them nothing – he knew nothing – they killed him."

"Major, according to your report, it was the Japs who had the diamonds."

"Sir, the war criminal Suzuki had them. My investigation suggests that men in their intelligence service knew the stolen diamonds were in Indochina somewhere, but they were not aware that Suzuki had them until they followed Dixon to Dalat. There they discovered Suzuki's secret. I think they suspected that Dixon and Suzuki made a deal," he explained slowly. "It seems that with the war over, there are other things to fight for. During the course of my investigation, I was forced to interview French witnesses and two British – a Major Clifton and a civilian by the name of Chatham-Brown. A Japanese soldier, Major Hiroaka, provided valuable assistance, but that's all in the report too. I would like you to commend both Hiroaka and Captain Joe Catledge for their assistance."

"Of course," General Donovan said, flipping through the reports. "How did Dixon discover Suzuki's treasure?"

"He knew of the diamond mines from radio intercepts he read in Manila. He discovered Suzuki had the diamonds from the transcripts of witness testimony taken from former prisoners of war by the Allied Control Commission. Remember, sir, that Dixon's job before he ever arrived in Saigon was tracking war criminals."

"I see. Please, continue."

"It seems Dixon devoted himself to tracking Suzuki down. He learned that he was in Dalat and made preparations to go there after him. The garrison commander had even placed him under house arrest at Dixon's request. But Suzuki reached another accommodation with Dixon, who then returned to

Saigon without him and, shall we say, seventy-five thousand dollars richer. But, unknown to Colonel Dixon, he returned to the city at the height of the battle between the Annamese and the British. He was killed before he could return to the hotel. The Vietnamese never openly admitted to killing him on purpose."

"I can't believe that Rolly Dixon was blackmailing war criminals for personal gain. I refuse to accept that. I've known him for years."

"General, it appears that about seventy-five thousand worth of diamonds was what it took to buy him off. I was told as much by Suzuki."

"I admire your, uh, commitment to catching the Jap. It appears you placed that above all else."

"Suzuki's a war criminal who has killed Americans in cold blood. But, in any event, he had to be caught. Like the rest of them, he must face the consequences of his actions." Charlie's voice grew louder. He felt a twinge of anger down deep in the pit of his stomach.

"Yes, well, don't get riled up."

"Sorry, sir," Charlie replied, feeling embarrassed by his outburst. He didn't know why he allowed the old man to get to him.

"I only meant that you placed the mission in jeopardy."

"The mission? That was the mission you sent me on." He looked hard at General Donovan. "But there was another mission, wasn't there? One you orchestrated from the very beginning, back in 1943, I think."

"You figured it out? They told you at Pearl?"

"No, General. No one told me anything," Charlie replied cautiously. He watched the old man for some indication of what he meant. "But I've learned enough to realize that Rolly Dixon's death wasn't the real reason you sent me to Vietnam."

General Donovan looked down and fidgeted with his fingers. "Shit," the old man mumbled to himself. "Yes, Major, there was another, far more important mission." He turned and strolled slowly to the windows again. His back toward Charlie, he stared out the dirty window. Seconds passed. "Would you believe it? The OSS is a part of the past. I'm an attorney again. But we made a great contribution."

"I've heard that the new office is called the Strategic Services Unit," Charlie said. "I was briefed yesterday on that."

"Yes, John Magruder will take over the SI and X-2 branches – your area," the general continued. "It's time I retired from the business anyway and turned the show over to younger men like yourself." With his back still to Charlie, he continued. "They need men like you, educated, experienced, and passionate about their work."

Charlie looked around the empty room and crossed his arms. He did not want to argue with his commanding officer ... or former commanding officer. He just wanted to leave. Get the hell out of this place, and get on with his life. He got up from the rickety old chair, preparing to leave.

The general turned suddenly to look at Charlie. He smiled proudly. "You've returned a different man, Major. Somehow more confident. A man who knows his future. I applaud you."

"I got a good education over there on a lot of things. A whole lot of things," Charlie replied. He tried to smile. "Anyway, the war is over for me. Remember what I told you?"

General Donovan looked steadily at Charlie, then sighed. "One war is over, all over, and we won, didn't we?"

"We did. Good has triumphed over evil, right General?"

"It did, Major Stanek, and don't ever believe otherwise," the general said, finding his opening. "But another war has already begun, and we're in it up to our necks, I fear. And it's up to young men like you to win it."

Charlie watched him without saying a word.

"Evil will never disappear. It just takes on a different shape, becomes a new threat. We have to be ever vigilant."

"What are you talking about?" Charlie finally asked, confused. "General, you're sounding like a politician now. We're soldiers who have to fight real men, not abstractions or ideologies. This thing you call evil. What the hell are you talking about?"

"The communists. That's what I mean. The war has just begun, and it's no abstraction."

"Yes, General, evil does exist, but it's not about ideas, dreams, or conflicting hopes. It's more about who we are as human beings and how we treat each other," he replied, displaying his hard-found knowledge and self-confidence. "And I can never accept the way you've treated me."

"The Soviet Union with its million soldiers in Eastern Europe is poised to strike at us. That's very real," General Donovan said, raising his voice. "And you're already a part of that war, whether you realize it or not. Hell, Major, we still need your intellect and, most importantly, your passion. It was your rage and your determination to survive that kept you alive." Donovan stepped closer and reached out to grab Charlie's shoulders. "I chose you for the job in Eastern Europe because I saw that passion, that mental toughness. I knew that would keep you alive."

Charlie stepped back. "The war you are speaking of is not my war. To hell with your grand strategy for winning it," he blurted out. "Tell me before I leave, and we never see each other again. I want to hear the details of the real mission you sent me on to Indochina, the one to rescue Major Zerenowsky." He lost control of his anger. "It's all about him, isn't it?"

The general stepped back. "He was your primary mission in Indochina."

"Evidently," Charlie said. "But you conveniently forgot to tell me about it!"

"I'm sorry that you were not briefed earlier, but I couldn't."

"I thought that was standard protocol before sending an agent out, General."

"Let me start at the beginning," General Donovan said, not able to look Charlie in the eyes. "Zerenowsky was our top agent in the Soviet Union. He has been supplying our operatives with vital information on Stalin and his bunch since about mid forty-three, through Stockholm. That's why you didn't know about his activities. No one did but me. I only briefed President Truman on his importance to us this summer."

"Are you sure we're talking about the same major? The Major Gregor Zerenowsky, Soviet Army, who was my official Soviet contact? Who you said I should never trust? I should commend you, I guess, for keeping his cover."

"I had to do it that way. I discovered that even our organization had too many leaks," he explained. "He contacted me in August to inform me that he was no longer safe. His family members were already being deported to Siberia because they were considered traitors. He believed it was just a matter of time before the latest purge got to him. So he decided to get out. We could not risk losing him and jeopardizing the network he's built within the Soviet Union."

"Rasputin," Charlie whispered, putting the last piece of the puzzle in place.

"Yes," General Donovan said softly. "Rasputin."

"Are you saying that Zerenowsky is the embedded spy that the Soviets had been hunting for?"

"Yes, that's exactly what I'm saying."

"He's not just another murdering Stalinist trying to escape his fate at the hands of the grand executioner?" Charlie hissed. The words lunged like a sword in the air.

"No, he's not," Donovan retorted sharply. "He's provided us with critical intelligence on Stalin's intentions in Eastern Europe and on other areas that I won't go into."

"Since we met with him in Tehran that November?"

"Before that, even."

"I think I understand," Charlie said. He felt used and betrayed by his commanding officer.

"No, I don't think you do," General Donovan replied. The clouds gradually parted, and sunlight streamed in through the window. "You know as well as most that war forces us to do many things we don't want to. You are a good example of that. How many men did you have to eliminate to complete your mission?"

"I don't believe it's the same, sir," Charlie replied defensively.

"I am not going to debate the morality of war with you, Major," Donovan said. "Zerenowsky was an important asset in the new war we are waging, easily justifying the sacrifices we've had to make to retrieve him. His assistance has been invaluable to the United States and our allies. I want you to personally debrief him. Get his sources and use them. I've already told General Magruder how important the Russian is to our intelligence efforts. He will give you his full support."

"He was worth sending me on a mission I knew nothing about? You were prepared to sacrifice my life to save his. Is that right?"

"Yes. President Truman himself made it the highest priority for our service to get Zerenowsky out safely and protect him and his sources," the general replied.

"I see," Charlie said, feeling tired, used, and more than ready to leave.

"I believe that your success in bringing him out is commendable. And, Major, it is recognized by the highest level of command. Who would have thought that we could retrieve a top agent from Moscow so easily through Southeast Asia?"

"Yeah, that was kind of a roundabout way to escape, wasn't it?"

"Ha! Yes, it was, except for one very important detail."

"Which is?" Charlie asked softly.

"You." He looked directly at Charlie.

"Me?"

"Yes, he trusted only you to rescue him. That was key to the success of this mission."

"Yet no one even had the courtesy to bring me in on the plan," Charlie repeated. "Just another expendable pawn in a new war. Is that it, General?"

"Please try and understand. We couldn't."

"You couldn't?"

"Major Zerenowsky believed he couldn't trust anyone, anywhere, including in the United States. You know how these Russians are. You worked closely with them," General Donovan said. "That is, no one except you could be entrusted with his life. It had to be you who got him out."

"Yeah, the bastard."

"When he discovered that Malinovsky was sending a delegation to Hanoi, he decided to act. He knew he could convince his commanders that there was a spy in the delegation meeting with the Control Commission, and that a top American agent would be sent to handle the exchange. The NKVD was already familiar with your work, and when they heard it was you, they responded as I predicted they would."

"That fit your plan perfectly, didn't it?"

"Perfectly."

"So they planned to capture me, break me, to reveal what?"

"The major convinced Colonel Pavlov that he had reliable information that you were traveling to Indochina, a very out-of-the-way place, to meet an important American agent. He said he had to go because he knew you and could get you to talk."

"Hmm, do I have this right? The plan you and he hatched was that, once I was in Hanoi, he would get me to help him escape?" Charlie said. "Was it also part of the plan that I would be kidnapped, imprisoned, and tortured?"

General Donovan looked at the floor. "I'm sorry, Major... And that's why we couldn't tell you in advance. We couldn't chance–"

"If they broke me, I wouldn't know anything. Is that it?"

"Yes, that's right," he answered softly. "Again, I must stress the importance of getting him out. You must try to understand. We had only limited control over the situation there in Hanoi. Zerenowsky planned everything himself. The message I received from him on September twenty-third said to send you to Indochina immediately and tell you nothing. It was his plan and classified for my eyes only. No one else saw it. That's how paranoid he was that his life was in danger."

"How did he expect me to get him out of Hanoi?"

"Major, you're such a talented man. He knew you were a good pilot. Don't you remember? He flew with you during the war. When we flew from Tehran to Moscow after the conference. You recall that flight, don't you?"

"General, we were damn lucky to get out of Hanoi alive."

"You're the only man who could have done it."

"So ... that was the real reason I was sent to Saigon?"

"Yes. Investigating Dixon's death was not your primary mission, only a cover."

"To fool everyone, including me." Charlie shook his head. He knew this whole mission seemed fishy from the beginning. And now he understood why.

"It was a very convenient cover. But if that one hadn't come along, we would have found you another."

"Everyone seemed to know that the investigation was a cover but me."

"That also was part of his plan."

"So you cleverly manipulated me into risking my life," Charlie said slowly and softly. "You sent me on a useless and unnecessary investigation."

"No, that's not true," the general replied. "As Major Blankston has stated in his report, your contribution to the mission of the American Embankment Team has been noted and greatly appreciated." He held up the report for Charlie to look at.

"I see." Charlie took the document and quickly scanned it.

"You'll get over it," General Donovan said. "Take some time. You must have twenty days of leave coming. Use it. Go fishing or something." He smiled, but Charlie wasn't having any of it.

"Goodbye, General," Charlie said dismissively. "And good luck with your new war." He prepared to leave.

"What do you mean?" the older man asked with a look of surprise.

"I've done my duty," Charlie said flatly. "My time's up. I'm finished. Find yourself another bagman."

"Where're you going? Back to Wisconsin to milk cows?" he asked caustically. "It doesn't suit you. You'll be bored in a couple of years."

"It's finally time I moved on," Charlie replied evenly. "Don't misunderstand me, sir. I see the importance of this new campaign against the communists. I just don't see myself as part of it. It's not the future I want."

"You're still tired from the long trip. Sleep on it. You'll change your mind."

"General, before the war, I was a young man with hopes, dreams. I had ideals. I had a bright future to look forward to," he said. "I need to find that man again."

"Major, you're a soldier in the United States Army, and your country still needs you," General Donovan replied directly.

"I'm getting out. I've made my decision, one I should have made long ago. In six months, I should be a free man. I'll gladly leave the war against this new evil to others."

"Don't underestimate the Bolsheviks, young man. They're hell-bent on destroying us."

"I don't think it's that simple. The time I spent in Eastern Europe and with the Vietnamese has taught me how complex people's motives and aspirations are."

"Complex? Nonsense," the general scoffed. "This Red plague is spreading across the world, and only we have the power to defeat it. I think that's simple enough to grasp."

"Not that simple. That's what I've learned," Charlie replied. "You may not believe this, but those people in Czechoslovakia and Vietnam believe they have rights too, and one of them is the right to be free and independent. They're willing to fight and die for that right. That has nothing to do with our fear of the Russians. It really has nothing to do with us."

"Yes, yes, Charlie, of course," the general said, now sounding conciliatory. "But the fact is, it's really a gray world out there that we must operate in. It's not all black and white, and I didn't mean to suggest it was. We are still engaged in a struggle with our enemies, and we are often called upon to do things that we wouldn't ordinarily do. The innocent can get in the way. Just like in the Carpathians, right?"

"Murder is not a gray area that I can accept," Charlie said sharply. "I learned a lot about myself working for you, sir, and I think we accomplished important things. But now I must place my own well-being before the good of the mission. I don't think the Army wants a man with that attitude."

"I understand. But never forget that what we're called upon to do, we do to preserve our way of life," General Donovan said, now standing only inches from Charlie. "We won the war because of the selfless actions of men like you, Charlie Stanek, and Joe Catledge, Jan Novotny, and millions of others. Don't ever forget that." He grasped Charlie's right arm and squeezed. "Your sacrifices were not in vain. Never!" he whispered.

Charlie thought he saw tears forming in the corners of the old man's eyes.

"I want to believe that. I really do," Charlie said softly, looking at the floor. "That's all I have to say, sir." He pulled his arm free and turned for the door.

"Where will you go? Do you have a job lined up?"

"Let's just say, General, that I have to follow my star," Charlie said, smiling broadly. He headed for the door before Donovan could say anything else, closing it softly behind him.

Chapter 22

Charlie was jerked awake again, his body thrown against the bulkhead of the freighter, *Oriental Princess*, by the tumbling sea. But he was relieved. He had been dreaming of his last days in the Carpathians again. Having departed Honolulu five days earlier, he was enjoying the cruise across mostly placid seas under a glorious Pacific sun despite sea sickness and boredom.

On the day he was released from the US Army in June, he had resolutely gone to Washington's Union Station and, without hesitating, bought a ticket on the next train leaving for Los Angeles. He headed west across the continent.

From California he promptly bought passage across the Pacific, to Australia from Long Beach. He had hoped to make a clean break, to see the world, and get a fresh start in life. *I'm free. No more deceit, no more lies,* he swore to himself. *I'll create a new life, and I will determine my own destiny. To find a little bit of paradise or, at the very least, a good escape for a couple of years. Maybe on a cattle or sheep station in the Outback.* He included the Outback into his plans when he had read about that country's need for immigrants. He smiled at the thought of running a ranch. The day-to-day chores, the honest hard work. No spies, no intrigue, no politics. Just the land, as harsh and unforgiving as it may be.

The last two years. Was it all just a horrible nightmare? Something that I dreamed? Charlie considered that. "A taste of hell," he managed to whisper. He raised his head to peer into the shadows of the cramped steel-walled room.

Lying on the thin, narrow mattress, Charlie stared up at the pipes that crisscrossed the steel ceiling in his small cabin. In the dim light reflected from a single hanging bulb, the small rectangular room reminded him of his prison cell in Hanoi. *No, this cabin is paradise compared to that place. Colonel Pavlov, you bastard. Were you a bad dream too?* He felt for the scar behind his ear and found it. *No, that was real.*

Finally, sitting up on the bunk, Charlie looked around slowly at his surroundings. His mind returned to his men – Jan Novotny and Joe Catledge. And he could never forget Gregor Zerenowsky, who had shadowed him from the first time they met in Tehran in 1943.

Charlie respected the Russian for his courage and for his selfless contributions to American security. He thought of his final meeting with Zerenowsky. Charlie had asked him why he was willing to risk his life to betray the Soviet Union, and Gregor had stated simply that he was Ukrainian. But what surprised him most of all was that General Donovan was able to keep Rasputin's secret even from his own staff. *That secrecy had probably guaranteed the success of the operation.* "Zerenowsky was Rasputin," he said slowly, still trying to grasp its meaning.

Charlie Stanek spent his many hours on board ship writing everything down. Not a memoir as much as for his own protection, and to give him something to do during the long days at sea. His pen scrolled swiftly, steadily across the notebook page as he composed:

I stood staring at the makeshift wood cross. Jan's name was already weathered away by the wind and rain. Slowly, I recited a couple of lines I remembered from Siegfried Sassoon's poem, 'To my brother.' I had learned it many years earlier, yet the words came to me easily...

"We are returning by the road we came.
Your lot is with the ghosts of soldiers dead,
And I am in the field where men must fight..."

I grabbed my pack and weapon, and then, for the last time, I turned and walked into the forest.

That concludes my story of war in the Carpathians, all that I remember or are willing to talk about.

Charlie set the pen down in the morning light, and closed the notebook, feeling surprisingly upbeat. He had taken the time to write down his war experiences in Eastern Europe, even including his love for Marie. He wrote little of his last mission that took him to Indochina. *There will still be more to write of Truin and the Vietnamese struggle for independence. I'm sure of that. I will write that story, too ... someday.*

They are all just memories now, ghosts that haunt my past. I will never be free of them. But I can live with them. He was learning to accept the past, and did not blame the Army and General Donovan for all that had happened. He knew Donovan had a job to do, an important job, and he had had to use his skills – skills at manipulating others – to get the job done.

Major Hiroaka may have been right, he decided, rubbing his left shoulder where he had banged it. *It is a world where justice hangs in the balance, decided by the latest victor in an endless struggle for power. Yesterday our enemies were the Germans and the Japanese. Today, according to many Americans anyway, the Russians are evil and must be vanquished. But I will not be part of that war.*

Charlie reached for a canteen of water beside the bunk. Slowly unscrewing the cap, he tipped it up and took a deep swallow. It tasted warm and brackish, but still it refreshed him. He smiled. For the first time in years, Charles Stanek, civilian, felt good about himself and the future he had chosen. Pouring water from the canteen gently into the palm of his cupped right hand, he splashed the droplets on his face, and then wiped his face with a towel he had tied to the bulkhead beside his bunk.

"Now, to a new beginning," he whispered.

A month later, a short notice appeared in the *Milwaukee Journal Sentinel*:

> Major Charles Stanek from the Milwaukee area was recently reported lost in a Pacific storm en route to Australia. Stanek, an Army Air Corps pilot, was a hero of World War II, having served with the Office of Strategic Services in both the European and Pacific theaters. His disappearance was reported by his former commanding officer, General William Donovan. Major Stanek is presumed dead.

If Charlie had known of his former commanding officer's efforts to protect his cover, he would have been forever grateful.

THE END

Epilogue

The victorious Allies brought more than five thousand Japanese citizens to trial for war crimes. During 1946-47, nine hundred of those tried by military tribunal, including Captain Isoruku Suzuki, Imperial Japanese Army, were executed. Captain Suzuki was convicted of having ordered the execution of six downed American flyers in addition to maltreatment of prisoners of war while assigned to the POW Camp at Plei Toan in French Indochina.

William Donovan was willing to use anyone, regardless of their backgrounds, to fight the Nazis. As a result, many communists joined the OSS. After the war, the Americans succeeded in breaking the Soviet cipher system, previously considered unbreakable. The code-breaking effort, known as Venona, clearly detailed how the OSS had been penetrated by Soviet agents during the war.

But perhaps for General Donovan, the most embarrassing revelation was provided by Soviet agent Elizabeth Bentley, who defected at the end of the war in 1945. She disclosed to the FBI that Donovan's executive assistant, Duncan Lee, was a Soviet agent code-named Koch. His interrogation revealed that he had been supplying the Soviets with OSS secrets since 1942.

Historians generally agree that throughout the war years, the NKVD knew far more about the OSS than the OSS ever knew about the NKVD. Soviet agents succeeded in breaching British and American security on many occasions, while the Western Allies were able to penetrate the Soviet veil of secrecy only with great difficulty.

On October 1, 1945, President Truman disbanded the OSS, but not before recognizing their sacrifices and distinguished service against the Axis Powers. Its branches would, in July 1947, be incorporated into a new, clandestine intelligence operation – the Central Intelligence Agency – designed to combat the new threat to American security. The espionage war against Soviet Communism had officially begun. Truly, an 'iron curtain' had descended, separating East from West, as Winston Churchill stated in his address of March 5, 1946, in Fulton, Missouri.

We hope you enjoyed reading Robert Tecklenburg's novel, *THE LAST MISSION*. If you have not had the opportunity to read his previous offering, *Prague, Darkness Descending*, it is available from BluewaterPress LLC online at bluewaterpress.com